THE

Nevada Badlands

by

Gary Jon Anderson

To my wife, Lorie, who encouraged, pushed and prodded me to get this book done. She is my best friend and greatest supporter for which I am so grateful. Without her standing by me, this book never would have happened!

My Story Publishing

CHAPTER ONE

Forty days.

Forty days he had been riding in the wilderness. Now Elijah Exeter rested under the shade of a spindly pine tree. It wasn't much, but it was a far cry better than being in the open, under the burning sun. He surveyed the buildings in the distance, wondering if this would be the place where he would settle. He had no reason to hurry and he would not ride into the town until he was satisfied with his surroundings. Impatiently, his pack mule side stepped, trying to shove his way into the shade as well.

Suddenly, the horse he was riding reared up, snorting in fright and twisting to the left. The mule jerked on the lead rope in an attempt to pull away. The rattling from the snake which had set the animals in motion immediately registered in the man's brain. In the same instant, his hand swept down to the gun at his side and the two shots sounded as one. The first bullet spattered sand all over the snake. The second one severed its head from its body and the reptile writhed and contorted in its death throes. The head lay where it landed, jaws wide, fangs exposed.

The man fought to control the frightened animals, hanging onto the lead rope of the mule with his left hand, while he spoke soothingly to his horse. With the gun still in his right hand, he held himself in the saddle by squeezing with his knees. The plunging mule nearly succeeded in yanking him out of the saddle. The horse shook his head and snorted, stamping his hooves in the sand, upset by the snake but not by the gunshots. The large gelding was used to guns being fired from his back, but there is only so much that he was willing to put up with and this animal drew the line at snakes.

Eli did not blame the horse, for he himself was not fond of the reptiles, but he tended to take an attitude of "Live and let live." Unfortunately, his mule nearly stepped on the sidewinder, creating quite a ruckus.

He holstered his gun as he patiently waited for his animals to calm down. When *they* had decided there was no more danger he leaned forward and gathered up the dropped reins, then nudged his heels into the flank of his horse and they moved forward. He would reload the spent chambers of the cap and ball pistol after he stopped for the night.

His salt and pepper beard was hot and itchy. It covered up a strong square jaw and a quick smile. His five foot nine inch frame appeared much taller simply because of his lean body.

"Boy," he scratched his chin as he spoke to the horse, "I think I'll lose this beard the first chance I get." Out on the trail, he had become accustomed to having conversations with the animal, to which he had never given a proper name. His mule, on the other hand, he called Absalom. It was named after the son of King David who was captured and killed when he got his hair caught in the branches of an oak tree while his mule ran off and left him. He figured this blamed critter would do the same thing if he ever got the chance.

Sweat stained the brim of the old beat up grey Stetson, which covered a mop of greying, brown hair. Too much time had passed since the last haircut and he had to tuck it up under the hat to keep it out of his blue eyes. Much more interesting was the revolver worn on his right hip. The Colt Dragoon pistol carried six .44 caliber rounds and the butt faced forward, giving the impression that he used his left hand and a cross draw. To the contrary, he would draw with his right hand, twisting the gun as it cleared the holster. It might be a tad bit slower than a standard draw, but he had practiced it since his childhood days. Had anyone witnessed the death of the snake, they would have notice that Eli was fast with a gun. Really fast. Not the lighting draw of the notorious gunfighters, but smooth and accurate with quick reflexes, all traits which had helped to keep him alive all these years. At 51, Elijah Exeter was an old man by the standards of the West.

Eli's father had died when he was 12 years old, leaving him the man of the family. While his mother had gone to work sewing and cleaning and doing whatever odd jobs she could find, Eli had the responsibility as the man of the family, to put meat on the table. His father had taught him to use a rifle from a young age and he knew how to hunt game and dress the meat. As a result, the family ate well. He had worshipped his dad, so when his father was trampled by a stampede, it had nearly ripped the heart and soul out of the boy. His mother was a woman with great strength and faith, and together, they learned to get by. His sister, Ruth, a year younger than him, took care of their baby brother and the house.

Elijah inherited a left handed holster and the Colt Dragoon pistol from his father. His dad had taught him how to use the cap and ball pistol when he was only eleven years old. The gun was large and difficult to wield for a youngster, but his pa was never one to coddle his children. He taught his son many lessons but one stood out. His father told him time and time again, "It's not the size of the hole that counts, it's where you put that hole."

It was a lesson Eli would never forget! He learned to make every shot count.

The gun was a bit heavy to use, but he practiced with it from the time he inherited it and that familiarity made him an expert with the weapon. He never did hear the story on how his father had acquired the gun, but he recognized it was a pistol his dad prized and so he treasured it too.

Because he was right-handed and his mother certainly could not afford to buy him a right hand draw holster on her meager earnings, he would put his dad's holster on, spin it halfway around his hips so the gun rested on his right hip, butt forward. He taught himself to draw with his right hand. He smiled as he thought about it. Later, when he became sheriff of his home town, this turned out to be a useful tool. People who did not know him assumed he was left handed, an illusion that he would encourage by holding his left hand in a ready position down low in front of his body, while his right hand rested a fraction of an inch from the gun butt.

This gave him the element of surprise, he mused, leaning forward in the saddle to squint into the distance. His opponent was not expecting him to draw with his right hand. He wore the holster slightly lower than a regular cowboy would have, which would have made for a difficult left hand cross draw, but was perfect for his own unique style. When he was older, he had a cross draw holster built for him by the local leather shop and boot maker. He practiced drawing the gun with both hands until he was proficient with either.

"Enough of this reminiscing," he muttered to himself. "I need to get into town." If he wasn't talking to his animals, he was talking to himself. He needed to find some human company soon.

Eli rode slowly into the town his eyes carefully moving from side to side, watching every door, every person, every animal, cataloging and then dismissing those that were of no threat. He saw the woman who just came out of the mercantile and reached up to tip his hat to her. She smiled sweetly before moving on. He noted the cowboy sitting in the chair in front of THE RIVER SALOON. He was dressed far too nice for a ranch hand and his dual rig was tied down. This one he would have to watch.

Eli nodded to the man, acknowledging him and moved on. He rode the horse and pack mule down main street. He counted three saloons and one church. Railroad tracks separated the saloon and business district from the houses and the single church.

With a chuckle he spoke to his horse. "I like the odds here" and in his heart, he knew he had found the place he had been looking for.

After making a survey of the town, Eli turned his horse around and rode to the saloon that had the appearance of being most unsuccessful. He had a crazy idea and he figured it would not work in a well-established place like The River Saloon, especially if there were saloon girls there. A newer saloon, where the owner was still trying to get things off the ground, now that might be the place that would give him a chance. The sign over the door was a plank that simply said, "SALOON," burned into the wood with some sort of branding iron.

Exeter tied his horse to the hitching post and the mule next to it. He pushed his way through the batwing doors and made his way to the bar, which was two heavy planks across several barrels. The shelving behind the bar was of similar construction, only there were crates between the shelves, holding the planks.

The hour was yet early in the afternoon, still a number of people had sought respite from the Nevada heat in the saloon. The air was still stuffy and hot, but at least they were out of the direct sun. At one table four cowboys were playing cards, each with a beer in front of them. There were two men standing at the bar, nursing their drinks.

Eli tossed a coin on the bar. "Beer please." The balding bartender wore a white apron with a multitude of stains on it. He nodded, wiped out a mug and filled it from the tap then slid it across the bar. Eli took a sip of the beer and then volunteered, "I'm new in town."

The bartender was the sort of man who enjoyed people, evidenced by his cheerful reply, "Welcome to Scorpion Wells. Where you from, stranger."

Eli was a little taken aback. That was a question not typically asked in the West. "I just came in from the east," he replied, evading a direct answer and then asked a question of his own, "What can you tell me about Scorpion Wells?"

The question was apparently the right one, for the information came flooding out. "The wells around here have been used for thousands of years by the Shoshone Indians. I don't rightly know when they were named Scorpion Wells, but this is a sort of a hub. People travel here, but then they have the choice of going north to Baker City in Oregon, to Idaho, Jackson Hole Wyoming or heading west into California. It has been highly favored by ranchers because there is water available for their herds and they thrive here. The Central Pacific Railroad came in here, ohhhh… in 69 or 70 and really put this place on the map. Now we have businesses and families living here and there's even a church in town. That there is something you don't always see here out west."

He paused and then asked, "So what's your business out here, if I may ask?"

Eli deflected the question, "I'm looking for the owner of this Saloon. I have a business proposition for him."

"The saloon is not for sale if you are thinking of buying," came the terse reply.

"Well I'm not buying, even if you were thinking of selling." Eli shot back. "Is it safe to assume that you are the owner?"

"I am. What were you considering, if you are not in the mood for buying?"

Eli paused for a moment, then asked, "How early do you open on Sundays."

"Sundays? I usually open around three, or four in the afternoon. It depends on how late we stay open Saturday night. I'm the only person working here." He paused, looking keenly into the cowboy's face. "Why do you ask?"

Eli replied, "I was hoping to become a part-time bartender here."

"Well, I don't have any money to pay a bartender, I barely make enough to keep myself afloat." For a moment his eyes sparked fire. "This ain't exactly Dodge City you know so the answer is NO!"

"Slow down and hear me out. I'm looking for a place to sleep and I noticed you have a little shed out alongside the building. I propose to work off my keep by cleaning up for you and serving some beers. In exchange, you let me sleep out back and let me use the place on Sunday mornings, when you're not open. You get an extra hand around here and I get to use the Saloon one morning a week."

It was obvious the man was intrigued by the offer. "I have the shed for storing overflow goods for the Saloon, though I haven't used it in a good many months. I could sure use the help around here though, sometimes it gets a little overwhelming for just one man." He glanced at the pistol on Eli's hip. "Do you know how to use that thing or is it just for show? On a Friday or Saturday night, you just may need it."

Eli saw the man was warming up to the idea, so he seized upon it. "I've been known to settle a problem or two in my day. I can handle trouble when it comes my way and I have never backed down from a fight. I will work to keep your place safe, though I don't cotton to the idea of shooting some cowboy just because he's had a little too much to drink."

The man reached out his hand and said, "Neither do I, it's not good for business. My name is Sam. I think we will try this out for a while, see how it works out."

Eli shook his hand. "My name is Elijah, but my friends call me Eli." he replied "When do you want me to start?"

"Why don't you get yourself situated and come around and see me tomorrow, say about noon? I think I'll have you sweep up and wash out the glasses. I've been wanting to cook and serve food around here and this may be the chance I was looking for."

Eli finished off the beer and set the mug down on the bar. "Very good. I'll see you tomorrow." He turned toward the door, but stopped when Sam called out to him.

"Eli, what do you want to use my Saloon for on Sundays?" The bartender asked.

"I'm going to start a church."

"A CHURCH?!!!"

Eli smiled. "Yes sir, don't you think the cowboys around here might be able to use some spiritual enlightenment?"

Sam shook his head and snorted. "I think you're crazy! That ain't going to work out here."

Out of the corner of his eye Eli could see that the cowboys in the room had turned to listen to the conversation. He took advantage, turning to the table and asked the foursome sitting there, "Do you feel like you are welcome in church over there across the tracks?"

One of the men drawled, "No sur, the town folk over there make sure our type stay on this side of the tracks." His voice was tinged with a note of bitterness. "We'uns ain't good enough to be seen with them there town folk."

Another volunteered, "They certainly don't want us near their daughters." This brought a chuckle from the rest of the room.

"If you could go to church here, would you?" Eli had seen this kind of discrimination before. The town's people liked the money that the herds and the cowboys brought in, but they viewed the cowboys almost like vermin. Definitely a lower class of people, at least in their eyes.

"I don't know," the man responded, "I ain't got nothing agin' church. I just ain't sure I could come into a saloon without having a cold beer."

"Of course there will be beer" came the retort. "As the newest bartender, I will serve the drinks before I start the preaching."

The cowboy smiled, "I might haf to come jess fer thet" he said, "I ain't been in church since I was knee high to a jackass. My momma used to take me, but I never could sit still to listen to the parson drone on and on. I jess couldn't get my mind wrapped around all them there "thee's and thou's and wherefores."

Eli grinned right back at him. "Neither could I," he replied, "I promise you that I will not bore you with all the "thee's and thou's" if you come Sunday. I also promise the bar will not close longer than 15 minutes for the sermon. Does that tickle your fancy?"

"What time you figgerin'?" asked the cowboy.

"We'll open at 11:00 Sunday morning." Eli spoke off the cuff, making it up as he went along.

"I ain't got no Sunday go to meetin' clothes." The statement was made as if the cowboy just remembered that fact.

"You come as you are" Eli responded "Although I'm sure everyone would appreciate it if you took a bath."

This comment caused a laugh from the others in the room and even the cowboy smiled. "Once a week, whether I need it or not," he shot back.

One of the other cowboys at the table countered. "Oh you need it, that's for shore." The rest of the men hooted.

"Then I will see you men on Sunday!" Eli walked to the door and turned to face the room. "And don't you all forget. Let your friends know as well."

He stepped out the door and whispered a prayer, "Thank you, Jesus." He walked down the boardwalk, humming a tune to himself.

Eli brought his horse and mule around to the back of the Saloon and removed his saddle bags from the horse and then took two trunks off of the mule. He set them down about six feet apart, then rooted around the back of the shed amidst some old lumber until he located several planks of similar length. He laid them across the trunks and tested them. Once he was assured they would hold his weight, he retrieved his bedroll from behind his saddle. He rolled the blankets onto the planks and made sure his bed was ready. Several candles from his gear were set upon shelves for later and a spare blanket over the door-less entryway offered him a level of privacy. Once he was finished, he surveyed the room and decided for the time being it would do.

Then he walked his animals to the stable. The hostler came out to meet him, mopping the sweat off his forehead with a dirty red handkerchief. "What can I do for you?" His red face nearly matched the color of his handkerchief. His stocky build spoke to his hard work and good eating.

"How much to put up my horse and my mule?" Eli asked.

"How long you planning to stay?" Came the reply.

"A good long while."

"Five dollars a month per animal and that includes a bait of corn each day."

The price was fair and Eli valued his animals. His horse had cost him a hundred dollars at a time in which a mustang could be bought for ten. He knew the importance of a good, strong animal with stamina, especially in his former line of work. "Is there a place to store the saddles as well?" he asked.

"Of course, it's included in the price."

Eli shook his hand. "You've got a deal."

He fished out the ten dollars and handed it over. Together they walked into the stable and he removed the saddle from the horse and the packsaddle from the mule. They were placed into the storage bin and then he handed over another coin. "Would you see that they get a good rub down?"

The man bit down on the coin. When he was satisfied it was real, he replied, "Of course, sir, whatever you wish."

Eli started to walk out, then turned back toward the man. "By the way, I'm the new preacher in town. If you're not going to the other church, why don't you come on over to mine."

"I don't believe in God." The hostility in the man's gruff voice was immediately apparent.

Eli did not let any emotion show. "That's alright. I just wanted you to know that you're welcome." He paused and then continued, "Should you decide to change your mind, we are meeting at the Saloon at eleven on Sunday."

The man nearly snarled, "What makes you think I'm going to change my mind?"

Eli continued softly. "I have noticed many people who don't believe in God, are people whom have been taught God is up there," he pointed to the sky. "Just waiting for them to make a mistake so he can bring the hammer down on them. Well that's not the God the Bible tells us about. I would love to clear up that misconception, if you'll give me a chance."

The man's tone softened slightly. "I'm really not interested," he paused, "but thanks."

Eli walked out of the barn, on the boardwalk toward the Sheriff's office. His knock on the door was acknowledged and he stepped inside.

"How can I help you?" The sheriff stood tall and slender, about twenty five years old. He wore a single gun, right hand draw and looked to be competent, although Eli knew that looks could be deceiving.

"Sir, I am Elijah Exeter and I'm new to town."

The sheriff looked up with interest at the mention of the name. "Eli Exeter from Utah?"

Eli nodded.

"You're the one who cleaned up the Bigelow gang a few years back." It was a statement, not a question.

Eli replied, "I did, but don't think that I did it all myself, there were a number of men from the town that helped me out."

"Well, if you're looking for my job, the election was just held and there won't be another one for three years." The Sheriff had a look of amusement on his face.

"I'm not after your job" Eli said, "I am a preacher now."

"A preacher! Well I'll be go to Hell" came the shocked reply. When he realized he had just cussed in front of a preacher, he added, "Sorry 'bout that."

Eli smiled and shook his head, "You're going to have to do a lot better than that to offend me."

"A preacher," he repeated. Pointing to a chair, indicating Eli was to sit down, he introduced himself. "My name is Matt Wheaton. So what made you decide to become a preacher?"

Eli took the offered chair and pondered his answer for a moment, wanting to keep it short. Finally, he responded, "I spent thirty years, keeping peace in that town and over the years, I realized I was dealing with many of the same people, over and over again. They didn't change, they just got harder and more cunning in their commission of crimes. For the longest time I realized that jail just wasn't working and something had to change.

He leaned forward. "They needed to change and that change needed to start on the inside. I knew I already had the answer inside of me. I have been a Christian most my life and I recognize what I would be if I did not have Jesus in my life."

He continued, "Our son grew up and went back east to college and when my wife died last year..." Tears choked his throat and he paused for a moment to calm his emotions. "There was nothing left to hold me there. I asked myself what I could do to make this a better world. I began to read my Bible more and more, just for the comfort of it. As I healed from my sorrow, I knew God was calling me to take that healing to others. I sold my place in Utah and here I am."

"Well I'll be go to Hell." This time he did not apologize. "Where are you going to open your church?"

"The Saloon."

"*Well I'll be go to Hell.*"

Eli raised an eyebrow. "That's the third time you've said that," he commented. "It is my goal to get you heading in the other direction. Why don't you join us on Sunday? The service starts at eleven."

"No, no, I go to the church across town" he said "My wife wouldn't let me go to a church held in a Saloon. Not by any means." He smiled at the thought. "Nope that will never happen....But surely you did not come in here to invite me to church, did you?"

"No, you're right. I came in because as I rode into town today I noticed a cowboy, dressed all fancy with two guns tied down. He was sitting in front of THE RIVER SALOON. I'm pretty sure that it was Rob Handy and if you look in your wanted posters, I guarantee you'll find him there. When I left Utah, he had a poster out for murder."

The sheriff looked Exeter straight in the eyes. "Yeah, that's Handy, but I don't dare try to take him alone. The thirty bucks a month I get for this job isn't enough to make my wife a widow." He looked up at Eli. "Now if you want to help me?" He left the idea hanging in the air

Eli sighed. "I gave up being a lawman to become a minister. I have no intentions of getting back into that line of work."

"Yeah, well everyone else around here doesn't want to get involved either. Seems they feel as long as he keeps his nose clean while he's in this town, they don't have a dog in the fight. They're not going to risk their necks to bring him in." Matt continued, "I wired the territorial Marshall and never heard back from him. If he ain't interested, I figure why should I be?"

Eli knew what it was like to have the town folks who were willing to look the other way, because they were afraid for their own lives. They probably all knew Handy had bragged he would never go to jail, and they also knew that in a shootout Rob would not be the only one to die, he would take more than one with him and nobody wanted to be dead. The right man, the right leader, could make it happen, but the young man sitting in front of him was not that man, not yet anyhow. Give him a few more years of being Sheriff under his belt and he might be ready for the job. He felt sorry for the Sheriff and he simply nodded.

There was an awkward silence and finally Eli stood up. "Sheriff, thanks for your time."

As Eli walked down the street he pondered the conversation he'd just had with the Sheriff. He was not quite sure where he wanted to go at this point, maybe just walk around and get to know the people of the town. Out of the corner of his left eye he saw someone change direction and start walking toward him. Mentally he chastised himself for letting his guard down but at the same time he silently thanked God that he had noticed the man. *Rob Handy was coming straight toward him.*

Eli secretly flipped the thong from around the hammer of his pistol with a movement he hoped could not be seen by the gunman, then left his right hand hanging casually near the butt of the gun. Handy stopped a mere three feet in front of Eli, blocking his path. Eli stopped and calmly looked the man over. He was dressed in black pants with tooled black leather cowboy boot, no spurs. Eli's eyes narrowed. That right there was a tell. Most working cowboys wore some sort of spurs.

A gunman would not want anything rattling to give away his location. It allowed him some stealth.

Carefully, Eli noted more details. Handy's shirt was a lavender color, made of an expensive looking material, possibly silk. He had a black silk bandana around his neck, not for keeping the dust out his mouth and nose while on the trail, but just as an accoutrement to his outfit. Everything about the man screamed "Dandy" except for those two guns, tied low on his thighs. It was the kind of outfit which would make the average cowhand figure they were dealing with a tenderfoot. It seemed as if he was waiting for someone to insult him with a laugh, giving him an excuse to kill.

"I see you were over visiting the Sheriff," Rob Handy said with an ever so slight sneer. The statement was fraught with a hinted insult—this man was ready for a fight. The look in Handy's eyes let Eli know there was something not quite right in this man's mind. He recognized that even though he was not afraid to die for his faith, as a martyr for Jesus, there was another part of him which wasn't willing to die just because of this man's blood lust. He knew he had to proceed carefully, or the next few moments could be his last. Though he was confident he could kill Handy, he knew at this distance he would also die. In his heart, Eli believed Handy just didn't care and that in itself made him an extremely dangerous man.

He spoke quietly so Rob had to lean forward to hear. "Yeah, I invited him to church."

"Church?" The gunman was incredulous.

Still speaking softly, so Handy had to lean in closer to catch all the words, Eli responded, "Yes, I'm the new pastor in town. Would you like to join us on Sunday? We are meeting at The SALOON at eleven."

Handy's eyes narrowed. "You're a preacher? Why are you wearing a gun? I've never seen a preacher carry a gun before."

"There are snakes out there that need killing. I have no desire to be bit by a rattler." The double meaning was totally lost on Rob.

"What kind of preacher has church in a saloon?" He asked, clearly thrown off guard.

"One that doesn't have a church building or a tent to meet in. It doesn't matter where a church meets, what matters is that the good news of Jesus' love is spread! That it is spread to all of the world, to all men."

The gunman shook his head obviously confused over the direction the conversation had gone. "Jesus doesn't love men like me."

"On the contrary, Jesus loves everyone. He loves the whole world. In fact he died for men *just like you*."

"What's that supposed to mean?" Rob demanded.

Eli moved a bit closer and his voice took on a hard edge. "You're Rob Handy, hired gunman. You're wanted in at least three states for different crimes including murder. Rob, *Jesus loves you*. A long time ago, when the church was just beginning, Jesus saved Saul, who was also a murderer, killing Christians, or least having them killed. Jesus saved him, changed his name to Paul who became one of the greatest evangelists ever known. Paul was a missionary, God's Missionary and he ended up writing most of the New Testament in the Bible. That's the kind of God I serve, one who is willing to forgive any sin. *EVEN YOUR SINS*. I'll see you in church on Sunday."

With that, he stepped around the gunman and walked away, half expecting a bullet in the back but praying at the same time it wouldn't happen. He did not know what came over him, to speak so boldly, so dangerously. Then he suddenly knew those words were given to him by the Holy Ghost and he was being used the way he prayed every day that God would use him.

He continued to walk away, praising Jesus, leaving the utterly confused man behind.

CHAPTER TWO

Rob Handy stood in the street. He was shaken to the core. He knew he should be angry, but he wasn't. That preacher just called him out and he, Rob Handy, had let him. He did not understand why he didn't kill him right then. He just couldn't do it. Instead the man's words kept repeating themselves in his head, "EVEN YOUR SINS." No one had ever talked to him like that, at least not since he was fourteen and killed his first man.

His thoughts suddenly took him into the past.

The man had been drinking and was probably pretty drunk when he called Rob's mother a whore. Before he had time to realize that Rob's gun was coming out of its holster, the back of his head was missing, blown out by the .45 slug that entered through his left eye. Rob knew he would never forget how the man's body looked as it slumped to the ground like a sack of flour. Even the men standing in front of the General Store were stunned by the speed of his draw and not one of the man's friends was willing to attempt to avenge his death.

Murderous anger burned deep in Rob's soul. He didn't even feel remorse for killing the man, not even a twinge. If the gunman had a conscience, it was hidden so deep in his soul it might never surface. In a small, small town where there was no law, the fastest man with a gun became the law. No one was willing to call him out for what he'd done, so he went unpunished. The man he had murdered had no family to pursue the issue and the incident died with the drunken cowboy.

Rob's natural skill with a handgun was supplemented by hour after hour of practice. He found a rocky canyon a half hour ride from his house where he worked on drawing his gun and shooting rocks until the larger rocks became small rocks and the small rocks, pebbles. He learned to draw and fire from the hip with deadly accuracy. He practiced daily until he could palm the hammer so quickly that two shots sounded like one and two rocks, ten feet apart, exploded into fragments. He practiced with both his left and right hands till he was comparable with either.

Buying ammunition to practice got expensive so Rob learned to supplement his income with cattle rustling. It started out small at first, grabbing young unbranded calves off the range. He would herd one or two into one of the neighboring towns and sell them off. Pretty soon he quit working doing odd jobs for different people in town and settled into a life of crime. Petty theft and rustling became a way of life and he was doing fine until a rancher confronted him.

He had made a dry camp with seven head of unbranded young cattle in a rope corral he'd thrown up. When he heard the horses coming, he moved away from the small fire that he had his coffee pot on and hid himself behind a tree. He was so arrogant of his skill that he did not even bother to draw his pistols out of their holsters, he just waited. When one of the cowhands kicked his coffee pot over, he stepped out from behind his cover.

"Hey you," bellowed a large man on a black horse. "You're stealing my cattle. You're going to hang for it."

Some people like to talk and bluster, working up their courage to act. But Rob wasn't one for words. He drew and shot the man out of the saddle. Horses began to rear and plunge and several of the other men were creased by Rob's bullets but in the melee, not one of them got off a shot. Instead, they put spurs to their mounts and raced away, leaving their dead boss behind.

Rob threw a saddle on his horse and rode out of there like someone had lit his tail on fire, for he knew the cowboys would be back with reinforcements and he wanted as many miles behind him as possible. He recognized some of the men and they knew him.

He left the country a wanted man. He also left behind the life of petty crime and began to hire out his guns. He could earn more in a week than an average cowboy could earn in a year. He owned the most expensive horse and wore the most expensive clothes. He was able to buy all the women he wanted. The one thing he never touched was liquor, not even a beer. He didn't want to lose his edge. It was the one thing he could not afford if he wanted to stay alive. Anything else he desired, he had the money to buy it.

As his skill and reputation with a gun became known, his price went up. If a rancher wanted to win a range war, he hired Rob Handy. The man with the most money to spend was the man who would win. More than once, a rancher who was not willing to let go of his hard earned money, ended up losing it all to the one who was free with his purse strings. Out in the west, strength was power and Rob Handy felt powerful.

One day though, he began to realize that all these years he had worked hard for other men to strengthen their position in the community. But where had it gotten him? He had money, but he was a vagabond, a wanderer. What if he took over some of those lush grass lands? What if he put his power to use for himself? He could take over some range and he would become a man with strong position in the community. People had short memories; if he put on a veil of respectability, changed his name and hung up the gun belts, he could stop running. He just needed one more score, one ranch that he could take over, where no one would question his methods. Far enough out from town that folks wouldn't talk. He rode into Scorpion Wells looking for that final conquest and now he had been called out! Called out by a preacher!

* * *

Steven Bosco woke up in the thick brush behind the stable. He typically slept in the loft. But last night some generous cowboys bought him lots of whiskey and it seemed he never made it back to the stables. Apparently he'd had enough presence of mind to get headed in the right direction, he just never made it there. Judging by the sun, which stood high in the morning sky, he knew he had passed out and slept a good part of the morning away. As he rolled over, he realized two things. His head was pounding from the rotten liquor and he had urinated all over himself in the night.

He wrestled himself to a sitting position with his elbows on his knees. He held his head gingerly in his hands and moaned, "Oh I need a drink."

Steven had not started out to be the town drunk. He had been a top hand, a wrangler for one of the local ranches. He would sweep the desert and round up wild horses, bringing them into the ranch, where he would spend his days breaking them for the ranch hands to use. He was so successful that his boss was able to sell off horses to neighboring ranches, which made Steven a valuable asset.

He loved being a wrangler, but he also loved Friday and Saturday nights, going into town, drinking and dancing and womanizing. After a while, it was not just the weekends, but he would buy bottles to take back to the ranch with him so he did not have to go a day without his whiskey. He soon found himself in a daily alcoholic haze. He began to forget about the girls and the dancing. All he wanted was the amber liquid that would burn down his throat to quench his desire, at least for the moment.

He groaned as thoughts of the past pestered his burning brain. His boss had put up with his drinking far longer than he probably should have. He finally fired Steven when he failed to show up to work for more than ten days because he had been on a binge. No one would hire him after that, so he was left with the task of scrounging for money and begging for booze.

No one in town would have ever thought Steven Bosco would end up mucking horse stalls for his keep, he thought. But the hostler was kind enough to let him sleep in the loft in return for a couple hours of clean up. He was generally able to stay sober long enough to complete that and then it was off to get drunk again.

Some days he scored with the cowboys who felt sorry for him and bought his drinks. Other times he would get nothing and spent miserable nights, sick and shaking from the withdrawals, praying for morning so he could resume his search the liquor he needed so badly, but could not afford to buy. Gritting his teeth, he bent his body into a crouch. As of yet, his pride, his upbringing would not allow him to stoop to stealing, but he did not know how long he could hold out. His need for liquor was about ready to overcome any morals he had left.

He staggered to his feet after several attempts. He still had enough sense to hope that no one noticed the dark stain on the front of his pants. He stumbled down to the river and after he laid on his stomach and drank his fill, he rolled over until his lower body was in the water because he did not think he could stand up again. He washed away the evidence of last night's shame and relieved himself in the flowing water. There he lay in the river's edge until he was thoroughly chilled.

The cold water woke him up some. Steven was able to crawl onto a large flat rock along the riverbank, in the sun where he dried himself and spent the next half hour getting the cobwebs out of his head. As the hot sun dried his clothes, a song his mother used to sing in church kept going through his head. He remembered the tune, but for the life of him, he could not remember the words. Something about being washed, washed in the water, or washed in the blood. He just could not get his mind to focus, to recall.

"It was such a long time ago. What has happened to me? To my life?" He shook his head as if to remove the reverie. Too much introspection was not good for him. It made him miss what he could never have back again.

When his clothes had sufficiently dried, he carefully got up from the rock and made his way slowly back to town. He realized it was closest thing to a bath that he'd had in weeks and recognized he needed to wash his clothes and scrub himself down as well. His nose wrinkled in disgust at his own odor. He'd better wash them soon too, or no one would let him come near to them.

Once he had mucked out the stables enough to satisfy his landlord, he headed toward the saloon district, hoping to score an early drink. It suddenly dawned on him there was a new man sweeping off the boardwalk in front of THE SALOON. Steven removed his hat and ran his fingers through his hair, hoping it helped to give him an appearance of respectability. He shoved the battered old hat back on his head and advanced toward the man.

* * *

Eli had washed the glasses and cleaned the bar first thing. He'd put some beans into a pot and set it on the wood stove. He'd diced up some ham and threw it into the pot and then put in some seasonings. The beans had been cooking for a while and the aroma filled the air. Next he swept the floor and mopped it; then stepped outside to sweep the boardwalk in front of the saloon.

A man approached, wearing clothes that seemed to be damp from the waist down. His hesitant, stumbling gait caught Eli's attention. The man paused and took off his grubby hat, ran his fingers through a mop of unkempt hair and replaced the hat. Eli continued to sweep while watching the raggedy man out of the corner of his eye. When the man had advanced close enough, Eli stopped his sweeping and turned his attention to him, leaning on the handle of the broom.

At first glance, the unshaven man appeared to be his age or older, but upon closer inspection Eli realized that he was looking at a reasonably young man. His gaunt face and whiskers along with his ill-fitting, stained clothes gave the illusion of age. Years of experience as a town sheriff caused him to realize that he was looking at one of the local drunks.

"Sir," the words were slightly slurred, "If you are open for business, I would like a drink." The incongruity between his looks and his formality caused Eli to smile.

"Of course," he replied "how would you like to pay for that drink."

"Put it on my tab," came the response.

"Well sir," Eli said, "I am new here and I have no knowledge of who has a tab and who doesn't, I will have to refer you to the proprietor of the establishment." The man's expression fell and Eli felt sorry for him. "I cannot give you any liquor, for that would mean my job, but I have a pot of ham and beans on the stove and some coffee. I would be happy to share lunch with you." He stepped down and held out his hand. "My name is Eli."

The man returned the hand shake, "Sir, my name is Steven. Steven Bosco. I'm pleased to make your acquaintance."

"Come in and sit down. I'll finish up out here real quick and be right in." He swept the last few feet of boardwalk and then proceeded through the batwing doors. Steven had already taken two chairs down from atop a table and set them on the floor. Eli went to the stove where the ham and beans simmered and served up two bowls. He cut a couple thick slices of bread from the loaf on the sideboard, slathered them with butter and brought the food to the table.

It was obvious it had been a long time since Steven had eaten anything of substance. It seemed as though the aroma of the beans was nearly making him drool. Eli recognized the state he was in and did not prolong his agony by making him sit through a prayer. Instead he pointed to the bowl and said, "Dig in." He grabbed the coffee pot and poured up two cups of the steaming brew and brought them back to the table.

Eating was a serious business and no words were shared until the bowls were empty. The two men sopped up the last of the beans using the bread. When Eli was finished, he sat back in the chair. Steven was looking at his bowl with a wistful expression on his face.

"There's more in the pot" Eli offered.

"Thank you sir, you are so kind." Steven pushed the bowl across the table toward him. Eli picked it up and walked to the stove.

"How long has it been since you've eaten," he asked, as he spooned the last of the thick beans into the empty bowl.

Steven finally dropped the formality, "I honestly don't remember, two days, maybe three."

Eli glanced into the now empty pot and ruefully thought of the dinner that was no longer an option. Then with the glint of a smile, he turned away to set the bowl of beans and buttered bread down in front of Steven. "I can't give you any liquor, but if you need food, you are welcome here. I will never turn anyone away from my table hungry."

Through bites of beans and ham, Steven expressed his thanks. When the bowl was empty, he mopped its sides once more with the bread, getting every last drop. He finished up and then leaned back in the chair with a cup of coffee. "I can't tell you how much I appreciate this," he began. "You make good coffee, but it would taste better with a little pinch of something in it." He leaned forward hopefully, but Eli ignored the implication. He cleared the bowls off the table and then sat down across from him.

"Sunday morning, I am going to have a church service here at the saloon. Why don't you come early and we'll have breakfast together." He noticed the puzzled expression on Steven's face and continued in way of explanation, "I'm the new preacher in town."

"But you're working in a saloon," Steven blurted out.

"I need to eat just like you do," he replied with a smile, "Besides, where else can I find so many sinners?"

"I can't argue with you there." Steven was feeling the need to find some whiskey and he needed to find it fast. His last night drunk was wearing off. "I don't know that I can make it. I'm busy you know."

"Well, if you can we start at eleven. Remember to come early for breakfast."

The man stumbled to his feet and swung out the saloon doors. As Eli watched him go a verse whispered into his thoughts, "A*nd whosoever shall give to drink unto one of these little ones a cup of cold water only in the name of a disciple, verily I say unto you, he shall in no wise lose his reward*."

Eli chuckled, "Lord, I hope a cup of coffee will do."

* * *

After Steven had mumbled his thanks, he hurried away as fast as his wobbly legs would let him. That talk about church made him feel uncomfortable, but at the same time he was struck by the genuine kindness of the man. Most of the town folk wouldn't even give him the time of day, much less a meal. Yet, here was a preacher who fed him and invited him back for more. He pondered why a man would do that, even as he began to figure out where to get more whiskey.

* * *

The week flew by for Eli as he worked the saloon and got ready for Sunday morning. Between the two, he hardly had time for anything else. He continued to wear the gun, as there was no safe place to store it in his open little shed. It was one of two things that he had left to remind him of his father; that pistol and a worn Bible.

He had developed a nice schedule with Sam that was of great help for the Saloon owner. He got up early and swept and mopped the floor, while he heated water for the dishes. Next he would wash and dry all of the shot glasses, beer mugs and any dishes that were used the night before and piled in the wash tub.

Sam, true to his word, had begun cooking and as a result, Eli had more dishes to wash, but he didn't mind. When the Saloon was cleaned up and the dishes dried and put away, Eli used a pitcher to tossed the dirty water out front and settle the dust. Since the Saloon did not open till noon, he found a pumice stone and would work on a section of the bar for a little while each day, sanding it smooth.

Word got around fast that not only was the SALOON opening early for chow, it turned out Sam was a pretty good cook in his own right. Eli became the early bartender, then after dinner he hung up his apron and Sam took over. The pair got along well and it was apparent Sam noticed Eli not only worked hard, but he did not have to worry about the cash box coming up short. Eli recognized Sam watched him like a hawk, and it did not escape his notice that not once did he try to pocket any of the money he handled. This seemed to puzzle Sam who had been quite vocal about preachers who 'always had their hands out for money.' Eli worked harder than Sam, but he did not complain about their arrangement. He sensed this did not escape Sam's ever-watchful eye.

Saturday night, Eli took off his apron and hung it on the hook. His pocket watch told him it was seven o'clock, a little later than normal. Eli walked over to where Sam was serving customers. "I'll be back in the morning," he yawned. "I'm thoroughly tuckered out."

Sam reached into his pocket and pulled out four dollars. "I know it's not much," he apologized, "But it's all I could spare for now." He handed the money to Eli. "You've worked hard. Way harder than I expected." He gestured toward the now smooth planks that made up the bar.

"Thank you." Eli was touched by Sam's generosity.

"You've earned it. I did not expect you to work this many hours each day. I may have to actually start paying you a regular wage if you keep this up."

Eli pocketed the money and slipped out the back door to his shed. He sat down in an old broken chair he had repaired and placed out back. He read his Bible in the waning light of evening. He contemplated the Scripture he had just read for a while and took time to pray for the town, for Sam, for Steven and even for Rob. He asked nothing for himself, except that he would be faithful to God's word when he spoke tomorrow and that the words would be authored by the Holy Ghost Himself. When he had finished his time with the Lord, he turned in. He had an early day tomorrow.

Morning broke and a rooster crowed off in the distance. Eli got up out of bed and went out to the pump, where he splashed water on his face and head. The cold water woke him quickly and he shook off the remnants of sleep. He ran his fingers through his hair, wishing for a haircut and sighed knowing it would have to wait.

He went into the saloon and began his morning ritual; putting up each chair, praying that whoever occupied that chair this morning would receive God's word into their heart. He swept and mopped and finished the dishes in record time, settled the dust out front and then rearranged the tables and chairs in a semi-circle. No one must have their back to the bar.

At ten o'clock, he set Sam's left overs on the stove and began to heat them up, adding a little water to the stew and brewing a fresh pot of coffee. He was hopeful that Steven would come in for an early lunch but as the hour of eleven approached, there was no sign of him. *Probably sleeping off last night's bender*, Eli speculated with a sigh. *How many people have I seen destroy their lives with liquor*? He understood, on one hand, how many preachers had come to rail on the evils of alcohol, but then again, he himself did not want to put his words into God's mouth. He wanted to speak God's truth.

At a quarter to eleven, he put on his apron and went out front where he hung the wooden "OPEN" sign.

At eleven fifteen, he glanced at his watch for the umpteenth time, afraid that his venture was a total failure. At eleven eighteen, the doors swung open and the four cowboys who had been in the bar that first day came walking in.

"Sorry we're late," volunteered the one he had spoken to five days ago "Hank here couldn't get his sorry ass...I mean *behind,* out of bed." He seemed embarrassed at the slip of the tongue.

Eli pretended he didn't notice and slipped behind the bar. "What'll you have?" he asked.

He served the drinks and a few more cowhands wandered in. At eleven forty five, there were seven cowboys seated with their drinks in front of them. Eli took off his apron and laid it across the bar and then walked around to the front. He was not dressed up fancy like most preachers would be, in fact he looked no different than the cowboys in front of him.

"Boys, the bar will be closed for the next fifteen minutes," he began as a good natured groan came from the small crowd. He turned to the cowboy with whom he had interacted with on Tuesday. "Like I promised, I am not going to bore you with the "Thee's and Thou's" and I also promised I would not close the bar for more than fifteen minutes." He pulled out his pocket watch and noted the time. "So here we go."

"I want to clear up some misconceptions that y'all may have about the Bible."

"Miscon' what?" came the query from one of the cowboys.

"Misconceptions," Eli answered "wrong ideas people get about what the Bible says. I want to get the truth out to you." Then he asked them, "How many of you have heard whisky referred to as the "devils drink?" There were a number of "yups" and nods of affirmation from the group, acknowledging the statement.

"Well I am here to tell you that nowhere in the Bible can you find that statement. Let me tell you what the Bible says about alcohol." He did not pick up the Bible but simply started reciting from memory.

"In John chapter 2, the first recorded miracle Jesus performed was the changing of water into wine. Not only did he make it into wine, the Bible tells us it was very good wine, the best." He continued on, "And in 1 Timothy 5, Paul tells Timothy to drink a little wine for stomach medicine."

Interest grew in the eyes of the grizzled cowboys as they listened.

"So, why do people preach against liquor?" He asked rhetorically and then answered his own question. "In Genesis we read the story of Noah. After the flood waters had receded, he planted a vineyard. One day he got drunk and was lying around, naked. His one son saw what he had done and gossiped to his two brothers. The two brothers, out of respect for their father, took a covering, placed it on their shoulders and walked backward to cover up his shame." A couple of cowboy just shook their heads.

"And you know about Sodom and Gomorrah?" This time all the men's heads bobbed up and down. "Lot's wife turned to a pillar of salt when she looked back. His daughter's hatched a plan to get their father drunk so that they could get pregnant by him."

"What?" exploded from one of the cowboys, "That's disgusting."

Eli smiled at the interruption. "Yes it is, but one thing you'll never see is the Bible sugar coating the truth. It tells the story, a lot of good and a lot of bad and yes, the disgusting. Lot's daughters thought the entire world had ended when Sodom and Gomorrah had been destroyed and they believed there was no other man left on earth. Their solution to repopulate the earth was to get pregnant by their own father. They got him drunk to make that happen. The point is that getting drunk can create a lot of problems. Let me ask you this, do you think Lot would have had relations with his daughters if he'd been sober?"

Eyes wide and brows furled into their hairlines, the men shook their heads. "Neither do I," said Eli. "But because of the alcohol, Lot allowed himself to be used in a way that I don't think he would have approved of."

"The Bible never tells us not to drink, but what it does say is that we have to use good judgment in the use of all things, including liquor. We are told in Ephesians not to be drunk with wine. "

"So why do we hear preachers talk about drinking like it is so wrong?" Eli continued. "I can only guess. Some of it may have to do with their own experience with liquor. Maybe they are preaching against their own demons. Maybe it's because they have seen others who have destroyed their lives with liquor. I know there will be those out there who will say I am wrong for teaching the Bible in a Saloon because it is a place where liquor is sold.

Eli grinned. "And that is why I chose this topic for my first Sunday, because I want you to know that I am not going to stand and point a finger at any of you and tell you how bad you are. I have made my mistakes, plenty of them. What you need to know about me is that I am a sinner, saved by grace and I want each and every one of you to experience that same grace."

"Let me finish by pointing out that Jesus was accused by the religious leaders of his day of being a glutton and a drunkard. Was he? No! Jesus did not sin. He was accused simply because he hung out with gluttons and drunkards. He was accused because he did not associate with many religious people, he associated with those who were sinners, the people who recognized they needed help."

"So are yer sayin' Jesus didn't drink, he jest hung out with them that did?" The question came from Hank.

Eli shook his head. "On the contrary, at the last supper, Jesus was in the upper room with his disciples and he held up a glass of wine as a representation of his blood. He drank that wine and ate the bread with His disciples. He knew that soon, he was going to the cross. He was going to die and his blood was going to wash away the sins of the world. The wine and the bread were representative of his blood and his body. The only way for his blood to wash us clean, was if he was without sin. If Jesus drank wine, then the act of drinking is not a sin. The Bible tells us it is drunkenness that is the sin."

"What you need to understand is that what you do, or don't do, won't save you from your sins. If each and every one of you quit drinking liquor today and never had another drink in your life... ***that would not get you any closer to heaven***."

Quiet filled the room, then a burst of sound. "What do you mean preacher!"

Eli scanned the room, looking each man in the eye. "Men, there is only one way to heaven. Jesus said the way to real life is narrow, but the path to destruction is wide. That one way, the narrow path is to have faith in Jesus Christ. When you recognize you are a sinner and accept the forgiveness Jesus offered by dying in our place and being raised from the dead, then you will make it to heaven. That is the only way. You cannot work your way to heaven."

Eli glanced at his pocket watch and realized he had reached his time limit. He really wanted to give an altar call, but he also recognized he had to be true to his word, or he would lose all credibility. "The bar is open once again" he finished, "But if you have any questions or want to know more, you all know where to find me."

He walked back around the bar and put his apron on. One of the cowboys came up, his partner trailing along. "I have to admit, I only came today because you told us you were going to serve beer in church. The truth is, I ain't never hear'ed a preacher talk like you did today." He held out his hand, "My name is Frank, but everyone calls me Slim. This here's Lefty."

Eli shook both their hands. "Have you ever trusted Jesus as your Savior?"

Slim held up his hand and said, "You know, I ain't ready to give up the Friday night drunks and the women jest yet, but I certainly will think on it later."

Eli looked at him, "What if later never comes? What if some drunken cowboy shoots you in the street, or you get caught in a stampede, or your horse throws you? There's no guarantee any of us will see tomorrow, Slim. I hope you will think about it sooner than later."

"I ain't plannin' on dyin' today" came the reply, "but like I said, I'll think on it."

Eli desperately wanted to tell them about the young boy he had held in his arms as he died after falling out of a tree. He wanted to tell them of the numerous young men he had helped bury, victims of disease or accident, but he sensed that he better not push. "Well I hope to see you back here next week."

"I reckon I will," Slim replied.

"Yeah, I'll probably come too" offered Lefty. They went back and sat at the table.

As the afternoon wore on, Eli tended the bar. He noticed that the conversations centered around the day's Bible lesson. Even the ones who came in later were drawn into the discussion by the ones who had been there. When Sam finally came in to take over for him, Eli was ecstatic and at the same time emotionally drained. He decided to slip off to the river and do a little fishing, a past time that he had not enjoyed for quite a while.

The afternoon was sunny and hot. A good stiff breeze had kicked up and it had the feeling of a hot furnace blasting on him. Eli pushed his hat down onto his head to shade his eyes and walked to the river with his fishing line, bobber and hook. He would look for a good branch down at the river bank to use as a pole.

As he walked along the bank, searching for the right branch, he noticed a shady grove of trees ahead. As he approached he heard giggling from behind the trees. He decided to go in another direction, not wanting to interrupt the privacy of the people ahead. As he turned his back, a female voice called out, "You don't have to leave on our account, mister."

Thankful for the cool of the trees, Eli discovered three ladies enjoying the shade. Two were seated on a blanket and the third sat on a fallen log. He removed his hat, "I'm sorry to disturb you ladies, I'm just looking for a fishing pole." The women were in their twenties he guessed. They were plainly dressed and none of them were overly pretty, yet neither were they ugly. They all looked like the "girl next door."

The dishwater blond on the log spoke up, "Why? Did you lose your pole, cause we ain't seen it." The other two snickered as Eli noticed the empty bottle of wine on the corner of the blanket.

"No ma'am, I never had it, at least not yet." He replied.

One of the women on the blanket commented, "I haven't seen you before, are you new in town?"

"Yes ma'am, been here about a week."

The third one spoke up. "You got a name mister?"

"Eli....Elijah." He answered.

"I heard about you. You're the one who wants to start a church in a saloon, ain't you?"

Eli leaned against one of the trees in the grove and folded his arms. "Not 'wants to', I did. We had our first service this morning." He paused for a moment and then commented, "I'm surprised you've heard of me already, I didn't think I've done anything to merit notice."

"Mr. Elijah, anytime anyone decides to start a church in a saloon, that merit's notice."

"Well now, you know my name, but I did not get any of yours."

The blond was obviously the unofficial leader of the group. Brushing a strand of her hair out of her eyes, she replied, "My name is Peggy, the one with the turned up nose and auburn hair is Susan and the brunette over there is Mary." Each of the other girls bobbed their head as their name was mentioned. "We all work over at THE RIVER SALOON," she added."

Without their makeup and saloon dresses, Eli would have never pegged any of them as "working girls" if he'd seen them just walking down the street.

If the woman were expecting any reaction at the announcement, they were to be disappointed for Eli had an excellent poker face and he used it now.

"Well ladies, I shall not bother you any longer." He replaced his hat and turned to go.

Mary called out, "Wait a minute! You haven't found your fishing pole."

"No I haven't, but I don't really see what I need around here."

Peggy chimed in, "are you scared to talk to us? Afraid that being around us might cause you to go to hell?"

Eli flashed a big smile at them, "Aren't you afraid I might talk you into Heaven?"

This time it was Peggy's turn. "Mister, God's not interested in the likes of us."

"I would disagree with you on that. You are exactly the type of people God is interested in." He moved to sit on a stump so he faced all three girls. "In fact, may I tell you a true story?"

"Sure." He had their attention now.

"Nearly two thousand years ago, Jesus had been invited into the house of a leading religious man for dinner. While he was seated at the table, a woman had heard he was eating there, and came into the house bringing a jar of perfume. She began to wash his feet with the perfume and her tears and dried them with her hair. The religious man was thinking to himself, because he knew that this woman was a sinner, 'If this man was really a prophet, he would know what kind of a woman is washing his feet.'"

Eli paused, looking in to their troubled faces. "You see, this woman was probably a prostitute and the religious man knew it. Do you know what Jesus did?"

The women leaned toward him, their faces a study in curiosity, "No, what?"

"Jesus told the religious man a story--something He called a parable. He said to the man, 'A money lender had two men who owed him money. One owed him 500 days wages and the other owed him 50 days wages. When neither man was able to pay him back, he forgave both of them the debt they owed.' He then asked the religious man, 'which one of the debtors will love him more'? The religious man answered, 'I suppose the one who was forgiven the most.'" Eli paused for effect. "Do you want to know what happened next?"

All three of the woman answered as one. "Yes!"

"Jesus told the religious man, 'You are absolutely right. I came into your house and you did not offer me any water to wash my feet, yet she has wet them with her tears and wiped them with her hair. You gave me no kiss, but since I have been here she has not stopped kissing my feet. You did not anoint my head with oil, but she anointed my feet with perfume. So I am telling you that her sins, which are many, are forgiven, for she has loved much. He who is forgiven little, loves little."

Susan queried, "I kind of get it, but what about the washing feet and the kissing and the oil? That all seems kind of strange to me."

Eli explained, "In Israel, it was very dusty and people wore sandals, kind of like Indian moccasin's except there was just leather straps around the feet and ankles. When a person came to someone's home the custom was to wash the dust off their feet. A kiss on the cheek was also a customary greeting at that time and anointing with oil would have shown that the host was paying respect to an honored guest."

"In this case, the religious man did none of these things which indicated that he did not believe that Jesus was an honored guest. I'm sure he thought he himself was very important and that Jesus should feel honored to eat with him."

"On the other side of the coin, the prostitute wept because she knew that she was a sinner in the presence of greatness. She knew she was in the presence of God himself. Jesus forgave her sins because she realized she needed to be forgiven."

The women nodded as Eli continued. "Jesus will forgive you in the same way. All you must do is acknowledge you are a sinner and ask Him to forgive you. The Bible tells us 'For by grace you have been saved, through faith, it is a gift of God, not of works, lest any man should boast.'"

"Do you really think God would forgive all the things I've done?" Mary asked, tears brimming in her eyes, "There are so many things..." Her voice trailed off.

"I know that he will. He promised! All you have to do is accept that gift. You don't need to change a thing about yourself to come to God. He wants you just as you are."

Peggy stood up suddenly and faced her friends, "You're not buying into this drivel, are you?" With a flip of her shoulders and a mincing twist she said, "Next thing you know, he'll have you carrying Bibles around and preaching on the street corners. God doesn't care about women like us." Susan and Mary began to blush as Peggy made fun of them. Eli watched as Mary slipped a finger to her cheek to brush away her tears.

He turned to Peggy. "Why are you so concerned if these two want to make changes in their lives? Are you afraid your friends here might make something out of themselves? Become better than you? What are you afraid of?

It was Peggy's turn to have the color rise in her face. "I think you have over stayed your welcome." She turned her back on him in dismissal.

Eli stood as well. "Ladies, if you have any questions, or just want to know more, I am staying at THE SALOON. Church services are at eleven on Sunday and you are all welcome." He tipped his hat to the women and walked away, all thoughts of fishing were now far from his mind.'

* * *

Monday morning dawned another sunny day. Eli Exeter started the day as he always did. A cup of steaming coffee in hand, reading a couple of passages from the Bible, one in the Old Testament and then one in the New Testament. He made it a point to think over what each of the passages meant and how they might apply specifically to his life.

The highlight of his morning was prayer. He prayed for each of the cowboys who had shown up in church yesterday. He prayed for the three woman he met at the river. He prayed for the sheriff, for Steven Bosco, for Sam and even for Rob Handy. He prayed for the people of the town and those who he would have contact with today. He prayed for his son and his son's wife. And then, he prayed that today, God would give him the opportunity to speak truth into someone's life.

An hour had passed and he was on his third cup of coffee. The bright blue skies above promised the day would be a scorcher. He downed the coffee, then filled his canteen with cool water from the pump. He ran his fingers through his hair and promised himself a haircut today.

He made himself a quick breakfast of scrambled eggs and toast and let the stove burn out so it would not be too hot inside.

He swept and mopped and began his day at the saloon. Mid-morning, the door swung open and there stood Steven, with a crumpled smile, swaying on his feet. "I come for breakfast and the church meetin."

Eli thought Steven might be joking, but he quickly realized he was not. Somewhere along the way, the disheveled man had lost a day.

"Come on in and take a load off." Eli pulled down a chair and set it on the floor. He walked over to the stove and poured a cup of coffee and brought it over, setting it in front of Steven. "Will bacon and eggs do for breakfast?"

"That'd be mighty fine." Steven slurped the hot coffee.

Eli stirred the coals into flames with a few pieces of fresh kindling. He went into the back room, sliced a couple pieces of bacon from the meat hanging there and grabbed two eggs. He returned to the kitchen area which was open to the bar and asked Steven, "How would you like your eggs."

"Fried." He said simply.

Eli fried the bacon and then set it aside using the bacon grease to fry the eggs in the cast iron skillet. When it was done, he put them on a plate and set it in front of his guest. Steven dug into the food and while he was eating, Eli refilled his cup with the last of the coffee. He set the pot down on the corner of the stove and then pulled a chair down for himself. He sat down across the table from Steven.

"Today is Monday."

"It is?" The surprise in his voice was genuine.

"Yes sir, it is."

Steven shifted uncomfortably in his chair, "Well, I shore am sorry about that."

Eli shrugged his shoulders, "Don't worry about it. There's always next week."

Steven tried to explain, "I'm not very good with the days of the week."

"Where do you stay?" Eli asked. "I can wake you up on Sunday mornings."

"I sleep in the stables, in the loft." Came the reply.

"Good. Come Sunday morning, I'll go roust you. It will let you have a chance to get up and get an early start on the day. Then you can come over for breakfast."

"I do appreciate that," Steven said "I promise I'll be at the meetin' this Sunday if'n y'all will do that."

"Consider it done" came the reply.

Eli's thoughts were in turmoil. As Steven left the saloon with his wandering gait, he found himself wondering; should he have told Steven he'd come on the wrong day? The poor man—he didn't want to embarrass him. He just wanted to make him feel accepted.

"I'll leave it in your hands, Lord," he murmured. "You have asked me to trust you. So I'm asking you for your guidance as I do your work among these people."

* * *

Once again, Steven walked away in amazement. Not only did the preacher feed him again, he did not make him feel guilty for getting the day mixed up. Seemed like all the preachers he'd known had just made him feel guilty. This one made him feel...welcome. That's it, he made him feel welcome. Steven didn't understand it, but he sure liked the feeling.

CHAPTER THREE

Eli finished getting the bar ready for opening and still had time to spare. True to the promise he'd made to himself, he shut things up at The Saloon and walked to the barber shop. He came out feeling like a new man. A fresh shave and haircut made him feel so good, he decided that the bucket baths he'd been taking every day weren't sufficient. Across the street and down a ways was a bath house and Eli decided to treat himself.

He glanced up and down the dusty road and there was no horse traffic, so he angled across the street. He'd made it most the way, when behind him, he heard a woman scream. At the same time a man yelled. Several gunshots were followed by the pounding of horse's hooves. Eli sprinted the last couple steps to the covered sidewalk, grabbed a support pole with his left hand and used it to pivot himself around the pole.

Three men on horseback rode toward him at a full gallop down the street, bandanas over their faces, guns in hand shooting randomly behind them. A woman who had not found shelter screamed as she became the victim of one of the shots. As she slumped to the ground, Eli felt the recoil of the Colt in his hand, over and over again. The lead rider was the first to slump across his saddle, two bullets to the chest. The rider closest to Eli took one in the throat and fell from his horse, only to be dragged down the street, one foot hooked in the stirrup.

The final bandit turned his gun toward the new threat and fired, but Eli had already moved. The bullet struck the wall directly behind where Eli had been a moment prior. He had stepped to the left, dropping to one knee as he fired two shots into the gunman's side as he rode past and another shot towards his back. At the same time the bandit's gun hand swung back toward Eli.

Eli's bullet entered into the man's hand, travelled up his forearm and exited out the elbow, shattering the bone. His gun dropped to the ground and he struggled to stay on the horse, but the life blood was draining out of him and it was a lost battle. He fell from the horse less than a hundred feet down the road, his body crumpled and hit the dirt, the last of his blood soaking into the dust.

Eli slid the gun back into the holster with a much practiced maneuver, hoping no one had seen him draw. He hated to put away an empty gun before he advanced to the closest man, but he was left with no choice. It was obvious the outlaw had died the moment the bullet hit. It had gone in through the throat, but had broken the man's neck as it exited.

He looked down the street at the other man lying in the road. He knew by the way the man was laying he would never get up again. The first outlaw he had shot was gone. The man had taken the bullets, slumped over the saddle horn, but had somehow remained seated.

Now that the shooting had stopped, people began streaming out of the buildings into the streets. Eli hurried to the woman that he had seen go down. She appeared to be about thirty, maybe a bit older, but very pretty, or at least she had been. A bullet had creased her upper cheek, leaving a large flesh wound on her face.

Eli lifted her in his arms, moving to the nearest door as it opened. A young lady ushered him inside and he laid the injured woman on the table. To his great relief, he could see she was breathing.

He turned to the young woman, "Can I get a cloth and clean water?" She hurried from the room and returned shortly with the requested items. Eli bathed the wound and held a clean dressing over it to stanch the bleeding.

"Is there a doctor in this town?" he asked.

"Yes, I'll get him," came the reply as she hurried out the door. While he waited, Eli fixed the dressing firmly in place and washed the blood from the woman's hair, then stood by with her until the doctor arrived.

"I washed and bandaged it." He said as the plump little man bustled through the doorway.

"Yeah, I see that," the doctor said. "Now could you ask that young lady to come in and assist me?" As the doctor turned his attention toward his patient Eli did as he was asked then slipped out the door.

A posse was just returning with the bodies of all of the outlaws, riding in with the men tied across their saddles. The Sheriff stopped his horse in front of Eli. "I want to see you in my office." He ordered. Without waiting for a reply, he reined his horse around and rode away. After giving instructions to the posse in regards to the bodies, he rode the horse over to his office and got off, going inside.

Eli, a little put out by the Sheriff's demeanor, pushed aside his feelings, walked over to the Sheriff's Office and followed him inside. Sheriff Wheaton motioned to a chair as he sat down at his desk but instead of speaking, he began shuffling through papers. Eli sat patiently. He understood the technique because he had used it himself and he decided he did not like being on the other side of the desk. Regardless, he was not going to be the first to speak. He waited for several minutes before Wheaton finally pulled a paper out of the pile.

"I thought I recognized them. Those were the Baker brothers. Here's a poster on all three of them." He finally looked up at Eli. "Several citizens told me what happened out there. A rather interesting story I got from them. I thought you weren't interested in my job."

"I'm not. You have nothing to worry about. I wouldn't take it if it were handed to me on a silver platter."

"Good, because I like what I do. Still, I have half a mind to throw you in jail."

"And what would your justification be?" Eli kept his voice even, though he felt irritation mounting up inside him.

"Shooting up the town, acting like a sheriff, I don't know, but I'm sure I could think of something." The sheriff leaned back in his chair.

"Perhaps you might check with the woman they shot before you do that."

The chair crashed down to the floor with a thud, "What!" he demanded.

"They shot a woman in the face." Eli replied. His voice took on a harder edge than he intended. "That's when I started shooting, not before. Before you threaten to arrest me, you might want to get all the facts."

"Who got shot?" the sheriff demanded.

"Don't know her name, she was out cold when I went to help her. The doc is with her now."

Matt was calmer at this point, "I'm sorry I over reacted like that." He paused. "Can you tell me what the woman looks like?"

"She's about thirty or thirty five, five foot two with black hair pulled back into a bun. She has an olive complexion and she *was* very pretty."

"Was?"

"The bullet cut across her cheek and it's fairly deep. She'll carry a scar for the rest of her life."

Wheaton shook his head and sighed, "Poor woman, she just can't catch a break."

"You know who she is then?"

"Judging from your description, I'm sure it's the widow Franco." Eli waited for the rest of the story and after a moment Matt continued, "She lost two children when they were just young'uns, then last year her husband died of a fever. Strong as an ox one day and the next, we're putting him in the ground. She has been working hard, trying to adjust and to get by, but it has been a tough year for her. Now this. "

Eli digested this information and made a mental note to check up on the woman, see if there was any way he could help out.

"It looks like you are owed three hundred dollars for those three." The sheriff held up a wanted poster. "I'll wire them for you."

"Thanks." Eli stood up to leave. "By the way, what were those three doing in town today?"

"They were trying to rob the bank. They shot the teller when he followed after them, winged him in the arm. He'll be braggin' on that for a while, telling us what a hero he is. I don't know how we're going to live with him after this."

Matt changed the subject. "Before you go, I have a question for you. If you're really a preacher, how come you still carry a gun?"

"I live in the shed behind the saloon. There's no door, just a blanket. I have no way of securing my gun and it is one of the only things I have left from my father. I'm not going to lose it to some light fingered thief."

"Not very trusting for a preacher, are you?"

"Remember, I used to be in your position. I know how wicked ***all*** men can be."

"Does that include you?"

"Especially me. I know what I was like without Jesus in my life, I know how I can be when I am not following Him the way I should. *I know what I am now because of Him."*

"Don't let Brother Smith hear you say that."

"Brother Smith?"

"The other preacher in town. He doesn't want to let anyone know he has ever sinned."

"Matt, any preacher worth his salt has to realize how much he's been forgiven, before he can preach to others about their sins."

"Well, that logic makes sense to me, but I don't think Brother Smith would agree."

Eli grinned and walked from the office, pausing before stepping out the door so he could survey the street. Old habits die hard he thought to himself as he realized what he was doing. Everything had calmed down and people were going about their business as if nothing had happened. He stepped onto the boardwalk and was headed toward the SALOON when he saw Rob Handy. Rob saw him at the same time and walked over to greet him.

"That was quite a show out there," he said. There was respect in his eyes as he spoke, "Especially considering that old hog leg you carry."

Eli dodged the issue and redirected. "I didn't see you at church yesterday."

"You really didn't expect me to show up did you?"

"Of course I did. Why don't you come next Sunday? I'll buy you a beer, I promise."

"You're startin' to nag like an old woman," Rob said as he walked off.

Eli just smiled. Rob hadn't said no.

Sunday rolled around and true to his word, Eli went over to the Livery Stable and rousted Steven out of the hay. He splashed water in his face to wake him and prodded him until he followed Eli out of the stable. After a breakfast of ham, eggs and coffee, there was still more than an hour left before the saloon was to open. Steven sat back in his chair with his coffee and looked at the floor.

"I ain't got no money for whiskey and you can't give me any. I know I told you I would come to church but I'm not sure I can sit here and listen to you while everyone's drinkin."

Eli was startled. It was a dilemma he had not even considered, yet Steven was right. It would not only be difficult for him, but also unfair. The last thing Eli wanted to do was to cause more temptation for the man who was already in way over his head. He pondered it for a moment and then was struck with an idea.

"Steven, I never got a chance to practice my sermon last night, so how about I practice on you now? Then you don't have to be here when there is temptation."

Steven thought for a moment then replied, "I think that's mighty fair, since you fed me already."

"Alright then." Eli went to the stove, got the coffee pot and refilled their cups.

"So let me start out by asking you, 'how do you think God sees you right now? What kind of feelings do you believe God feels toward you?"

Steven thought hard for a while, then looked at Eli. "I think He's really mad at me right now."

"Why do you think that?"

"Well, when I was a youngster, my dad caught me sneakin' some of his liquor and he took me out to the wood shed and tanned my hide somethin' fierce. I figure God probably wants to do the same thing to me right now."

"So you view God in comparison to your dad?"

"I 'spose so."

Steven didn't sound like he enjoyed answering all his questions. "What if I could show you that God is not mad at you? Would that interest you?"

Steven gave a little laugh, "Yeah, it would be nice to know God ain't goin' to wup me up'side the head anytime soon."

"It is not unusual that you would compare God to your dad. Throughout the Bible we are told about God's character and in numerous parts of the Bible, He is referred to as our Heavenly Father. Your dad here on earth was not perfect, because no one is perfect. He made mistakes at times, even if he was the best dad ever."

"He wasn't," Steven interrupted. "He beat me black and blue when I was a kid."

"I'm not saying your Dad was. What I'm trying to say is even the best dad in the world is not perfect and therefore makes mistakes. God, our Heavenly Father, is perfect. He doesn't make mistakes and he doesn't strike at us in anger."

Eli placed a gentle hand on the man's shoulder. "John 3:16 says 'For God so loved the world', not the planet that we live on, but the people on the planet, 'that He gave his only begotten Son', that would be Jesus 'that whosoever believeth in him should not perish but have everlasting life.' Steven, he goes on to say, 'For God sent not His Son into the world to condemn the world, but that the world through him might be saved.' Eli left his hand on the shoulder and leaned toward him, "Steven, do you think that sounds like a God who is mad at you, ready to wup you up'side the head?"

Steven twisted his shoulder away. "No. But why? Why would God do that?"

"Because God loves the people of this world. He created us and he wants to have a relationship with us. He could have forced us into a relationship, but that would have made us His slaves. Instead He wants

us to choose Him. If we choose to follow Him, that makes us, you and me, His sons. It is a choice. We can choose to follow Jesus. In Romans..."

"Wait, what's Romans?" Steven asked, cradling the cup of coffee in his fingers.

"Romans? It's another book in the Bible. I should tell you the Bible is made up of multiple smaller books, written by many different men God used to tell His story."

"Oh." Steven stared thoughtfully into his cup.

Leaning his elbows on the table, Eli continued. "In Romans we are told, "All men have sinned and fall short of the Glory of God". Steven's grizzled face showed confusion and Eli tried to explain. "That means since God is perfect and we as men are sinners, we can't meet Gods standards. The book of Romans also teaches '...the wages of sin is death, but the gift of God is eternal life'. That refers to spiritual death, separation from God. It is what we have earned with our sin."

Steven's forehead furrowed, as he seemed to struggle to understand.

Eli quickly continued, "But the gift, the gift is forgiveness of our sins and eternity in heaven, in the presence of God. You see, because of our sin we were supposed to die, but Jesus who was perfect, took our punishment. When He died on the cross He took the sins of the entire world upon himself. He was buried, Steven, but then He rose up from the dead, leaving our sins buried. You are already forgiven for every bad thing you've ever done, or will ever do, all you have to do is to accept that forgiveness. That is the free gift."

"He did that for us?"

"Yes, He did. Steven, would you like to have that relationship with God? All you need to do is to accept the forgiveness that God offers. I know right now, all you want is another drink, because liquor is the love of your life. But it's killing you. God offers a better way. Once you receive His gift, believing He died on the cross for you, and give yourself totally over to him, He can change you. He will change you. He did that for me."

"I don't know. It all sounds too good to be true." He placed the coffee cup onto the table and leaned away, his calloused hands clenched into fists.

Steven was obviously having a hard time accepting what Eli knew he had never experienced in his life. From Steven's story, his own father had never really cared for him, especially the way God did. Eli realized the man wanted to believe he could be free, but was struggling with his disbelief.

"Steven, when I asked Jesus to forgive my sin, He sent his Spirit to live inside of me so I could live a full life, pleasing to God. I was adopted into the family of God and now I call him my Father. He can be your Father, too-- You can have an abundant life, instead of the life you're living now."

Steven pushed back from the table, suddenly, almost violently. "No. ***No!*** Maybe that works for you, but it ain't for me." He jammed his crusty hat onto his head and rushed out the door.

Eli hung his head, wondering if he had pushed too hard, yet he knew it was the message Steven needed to hear. He bowed his head right where he sat and prayed for Steven.

The doors opened at eleven and to Eli's surprise there was a posse of men already waiting to come in. Toward the rear of the crowd, he saw Susan and Mary follow the men into the saloon. Eli began to wonder what had happened to cause the crowd to triple from last week.

It did not take long to find out.

* * *

Matt Wheaton pushed back from the table, "Becky that was a wonderful breakfast. Thank you." His wife, like many frontier women, had learned to cook early and at twenty-two, she was an old hand at making delicious food, often from limited means. Since he'd been elected Sheriff, they'd had a steady income and he was eating well. They had been married for four years. He was still deeply in love with her and he knew she was pleased he still acknowledged her efforts.

"I won't be able to make it to church this morning," Matt continued, "I have some business to attend to."

"Your business is taking you away from church far too much." Becky complained. She smiled hesitantly, a crease of concern wrinkling the smooth skin above her eyes.

"Don't worry about me. Me and the Good Lord have a good understanding." Matt sighed. She had confronted him about his looking for excuses to get out of going to church. But thinking about it, could she really blame him? Brother Smith was the only reverend in town and he was one of those "Hell Fire and Brimstone" type preachers, always harping on what you shouldn't be doing as a good Christian. Often times, he wished the preacher would tell them what they should be doing, or talk about God's grace and mercy, the things his wife had shared with him from her morning devotions.

He knew she didn't blame him for how he felt, but she did worry about him. She worried about his safety as a lawman. She worried about the type of people he had to be around, but mostly she worried about his walk with God. He had placed his trust in Jesus many years ago. But admittedly, it seemed lately he was letting the distractions of life interfere with that relationship.

"I've hooked up the buggy already," he ventured. "I'll drop you off at church on my way to the office"

The twenty minute ride was enjoyable as they trundled along in the early morning sun. Matt thought about the woman sitting at his side. He knew he was a lucky man to have her, yet he also recognized he often took her for granted. He felt guilty about not going to church with her, but on the other hand, the thought of sitting through one more of Brother Smith's sermons was enough to make him want to put his gun into his mouth and pull the trigger. He hated being made to feel guilty about stuff he wasn't even doing.

He reached over and pinched the part of Becky's butt he could reach.

"Matt!" She looked around to make sure no one could see what he had just done, as if there were someone lurking in the scrub brush lining the road. "That was not appropriate!" She chastised him, but he saw she hid a little smile. He knew secretly she was pleased that he still liked to flirt with her.

They had a happy life together, but it bothered him to know she was heartbroken. She blamed herself because she had not been able to provide him with children yet.

He loved her dearly and would do anything for her that he could. He just wanted her to be happy.

Shaking his sad thoughts away, he smiled and put his arm around her trim waist. He held her close until they got closer to town where people might see. He drove the buggy to the church and stopped the horses in the shade of an ancient Pondarosa tree. He jumped out and walked around the buggy and as he helped his wife down, he gave her a peck on the cheek, "I will see you this afternoon. If I get done with my business, maybe we can have lunch at Maggie's."

She smiled and nodded, then walked into the church. Matt mounted his horse, which had been tied to the back of the buggy and rode across town to the Sheriff's Office. He made sure the horse had shade and water, then went into the building to retrieve an envelope from the locked desk drawer. He stuffed it into the inside pocket of his vest and walked out, locking the door behind him.

It was a short walk to the SALOON. He pushed his way through the door, to find a crowded room.

* * *

"Hey preacher, I hear you gunned down the Baker Boys."

So that was it, people were here to meet the pistol packing preacher.

"I wouldn't exactly say I gunned them down," Eli replied, "They were doing a fair amount of the shooting themselves."

"If you're a preacher how come you're carrying a gun?" It was obvious Eli was not matching up to people's expectations for a preacher. He was upsetting the status quo.

"You never know when there might be a bank robbery." Laughter rippled through the room.

Eli made sure everyone was set up with drinks, then poured himself a cup of coffee and once again stationed himself in front of the bar. He had just launched into his message when he looked up and saw Sheriff Wheaton standing by the door. A big smile spread across his face as the Sheriff quietly took a seat in the back.

Eli explained about the gift of salvation which Jesus offered and gave an altar call, but no one responded. When the service was over, people came forward, but it was to buy more drinks. He glimpsed the two women hurry out, as though they had places to go.

During a lull in the action the Sheriff walked up to the bar. He pulled an envelope from his pocket and handed it to Eli. "This came in on yesterdays train for you. Take it over to the bank and you can get your money." He said.

Eli opened the envelope. Inside was a bank draft for three hundred dollars. He looked up at the sheriff with a smile. "Thank you Sheriff."

Matt turned to go, but before he reached the door he heard Eli called out to him. Turning around, he walked back to the bar and Eli handed the envelope back. "Would you make sure this gets to the Widow Franco? Just don't let her know where it came from, please?"

Matt grinned. "Yeah, I can do that." There was a lengthy pause and Eli waited. "What you said here today, about God wanting us to have a relationship with Him, that he loves us. I never heard it put quite like that. I liked what you had to say. It reminded me a little of what my mother used to teach me about God and the Bible."

It was Eli's turn to smile. "I am so glad you came this morning, Matt. I hope to see you here again next Sunday."

"Yeah, I'm not sure how to work it out with my wife..."

After the short church service, Matt returned to the office and waded through paperwork for another hour, or so. He glanced at his pocket watch and realized it was time to pick his wife up from church. He stepped to the door and opened it slightly and when he had cleared the portion of the street he could see, he opened it wide to make a sweeping survey of the street before stepping out of the shadows into daylight. After locking the door behind him, he mounted his horse and rode to the church, arriving just as the rush of people emerged from the building. He dismounted by the carriage and tied his horse to the back.

Becky stepped out of the church and as she walked toward him, he noticed Brother Smith cast a disapproving look in his direction. Ignoring the preacher, he helped his wife onto the buggy and sat beside her. As they drove away he could see out of the corner of his eye that Brother Smith watched them go. He could not help but wonder if the man's interest was in his lack of attendance, or if he was paying attention to the pretty woman at Matt's side.

They rode to the diner and once they were seated inside and had placed their order, Matt turned his full attention to Becky. "How was church today?"

She gave him a half-hearted smile, "It was alright."

"That doesn't sound very convincing. What's the issue?"

She grimaced. "Brother Smith's sermon was mostly about how bad it is to have a new preacher in town."

"Eli?" Matt was incredulous. "I don't see Brother Smith going out of his way to minister to those cowboys, so what's his beef?"

"He claimed only a heretic would preach in a saloon."

Matt pondered for a second then looked over at Becky. "My work took me to the SALOON today and I got to hear Eli preach. Let me tell you, he spoke simply and clearly. His message was short and sweet, but I learned more in twenty minutes of listening to him than I have in all of the shouting and ranting I have heard from Brother Smith."

"Well," she replied. "Brother Smith wants to run Mr. Exeter out of town. He was trying to gather support from the men in the congregation to do it."

Matt smiled at the thought. "He might find he has bit off more than he can chew. I don't think Eli is a man that will be easy to run off.

"You speak like you know him." Becky observed.

"More like what I know about him. He was a sheriff in Utah and he made quite a name for himself. The story is that a gang of outlaws came in and began to terrorize the town. Eli organized the town's men to confront them and when it was all said and done, the entire gang was wiped out. Then just the other day, he took out those bank robbers."

"So why is a preacher carrying a gun? I've never seen an armed preacher before."

Matt told her the reason Eli had given him.

"Still, I think he needs to decide on whether he wants to be a preacher or a gunman," she said, clasping her small hands together in her lap.

"You know if it hadn't been for his quick action, innocent people could have been killed," he reproached her gently. "The widow Franco was injured by the robbers." He had not given Becky all of the details when he related the incident earlier, because he knew that she would worry about such things and he had wanted to spare her. But now, he felt the direction of the conversation warranted the dissemination of information.

Becky gasped in horror, her hands flew to cover her mouth. "She was? What happened?"

"A bullet cut open her face, opened it up pretty good. Doc says she is going to be alright, though there will likely be a severe scar."

"You should have told me sooner," she scolded him. "I could have helped her, been there for her. I wondered why she was not in church today."

"I have an errand to run out there anyhow. Did you want to ride out with me this afternoon?"

Their food arrived and when they had been served, Becky gave her answer. "Yes, I think that would be nice."

When lunch was finished they rode out to the Franco spread, a few miles out of town on the opposite side from their own house. Mrs. Franco greeted them with a large bandage still on her face. Becky jumped down before Matt could give her a hand and rushed to the older woman. "Oh, Elizabeth," she exclaimed. "Are you alright? I'm so sorry! I just now heard about what happened." She gave her a big hug.

Elizabeth Franco reached up and patted the younger woman's cheek. "I'm fine, it's just a scratch." She smiled and asked, "What brings you folks out this way?"

Becky answered as Matt walked over. "I didn't see you in church and then Matt told me about the shooting. We wanted to see how you were doing."

Matt interjected, "I also brought something out for you." He reached inside his vest and pulled out the envelope and handed it to her.

"What is this?" Elizabeth asked. She opened it and pulled out the bank draft. When she saw what it was, her eyes grew wide. "But, but...why, what is this?" she stammered.

Matt replied, "It's the reward for those three outlaws. The money came on the train yesterday. The town decided it belongs to you."

Tears welled up in her eyes and spilled down her cheeks. Matt began to feel uncomfortable and was suddenly glad he had brought Becky with him. Becky enveloped her with another big hug and let the woman weep on her shoulder.

After a moment Elizabeth pulled back, wiping the tears away with the back of her hand. "I don't know how to thank you...how to thank the town. This is as much as I could make in two years!"

Becky asked, "Elizabeth, what are you going to do now?"

"Please, I've forgotten my manners, come on in. I have some coffee on the stove." She bustled them in and served the coffee before answering Becky's question.

"I've been thinking long and hard about that. Franklin, my late husband, he loved my baking. I would make him bread and rolls and pie and every once in a while, I would save up enough for a little sugar and make him a cake. Oh he loved my chocolate cake! I have wanted to open a bakery in town, but never had the money to make a go of it." She turned to Matt and asked, "Is there any place in town available for me to open up a bakery?"

Matt pondered the question, going over in his mind all of the places in town he thought might work. "There is a building which was a small leather shop," he confided. "The owner pulled up stakes and headed up to Oregon. Said our weather is too hot for him. If we tell the men folk you want to put in a bakery, I'm sure we can get enough volunteers to get it together for you. You fry up a couple dozen doughnuts and you'll have cowboys fighting to help out." Matt was really speaking out of turn, but felt confident he was right. Some of those men hadn't had a tasty treat since they'd come out West and they would just about kill to get one.

Elizabeth was catching the excitement. She laughed, "Oh Sheriff, do you really think so? Do you think I can make this dream a reality?"

They discussed the prospect until the coffee was gone and Matt and Becky took their leave.

The air was clear and the afternoon was bright as they rode in the buggy back toward town, Becky chatted excitedly about the Bakery while Matt relaxed alongside of her, enjoying the sound of her voice as she continued to make plans about decorating. The ride to town took no time at all and as they headed down Main Street, Matt saw Eli riding toward them.

He stopped the carriage and waited for the preacher to ride up to them. "Eli, I would like you to meet my wife, Becky Wheaton. Becky this is Elijah Exeter."

She inclined her head in acknowledgement of the introduction, while Eli removed his hat. "Ma'am, pleased to meet you," he drawled.

"Pleased to meet you, sir." Becky gave Eli an appraising glance. He had a fresh haircut which was slightly mussed from removing the hat. Eli might not be what she would call good looking, but there was something about him...ruggedly handsome. Yes, she would consider him ruggedly handsome. There were several small scars on his face, showing white against the sun weathered skin. He had a good face. There were laugh lines permanently furrowed along the side of his eyes, giving the impression he smiled a lot. His blue eyes had a sparkle to them and she felt immediately comfortable in his presence.

Matt spoke up. "I delivered that envelope to the Widow Franco." He said. "She is very excited and wants to use the money to open a Bakery."

"That sounds wonderful. I haven't had anything to satisfy my sweet tooth in a long time." Eli smiled at the prospect.

Becky saw the laugh lines deepen as he smiled and she decided she was right. He was a man who smiled a lot.

"Yeah, it seems she already has some great plans." He said.

Eli smiled again at Becky. "It was a pleasure to meet you ma'am." He replaced the hat and rode off down the street.

"I wish you could hear him preach," Matt mused. He turned back toward Becky. "But it just ain't proper for a decent lady to go into the SALOON."

"I would love to have a chance to hear another preacher," Becky admitted. "Do you think he will start a church? I mean, actually have a church building?"

"I don't know. The way I understand it, he wants to reach out to folks everyone else has ignored up until now. To do that, he has to go where they are. Maybe someday he will move his church into another building. I don't know," he repeated.

* * *

Eli took a ride out into the hills. He needed to exercise his horse, who was getting fat and lazy, and he needed some alone time with the Lord. As he surveyed the country side around him, he prayed for the men and women who had showed up for the service. He thanked the Lord for the beauty around him, all the while keeping an eye out, scanning the country side. He stopped his horse when he saw the mountain goat on the hillside. He lifted the rifle which had been resting across his lap, steadied his aim and squeezed off the shot, dropping the animal in its tracks. He continued to pray as he rode over to skin the animal. *"Thank you Lord, for all you are doing, and for providing me with this meat."*

The following Sunday was an amazing event. As he had done before, Eli served the men drinks. After he had drawn the last beer and poured himself a cup of coffee, he removed his apron and walked around to the front of the bar and opened his Bible. He looked up in time to see the silhouette of a man's head appear over the batwing doors. It took him a moment to recognize who it was.

"Rob," he called out to the gunman. "It's good to see you, come on in. Welcome."

Handy entered cautiously, his left hand pushing open the door, his right hand hanging casually near his gun. It was obvious he had not intended to come in. He had just wanted to take a look. As he came through the door, it was as though an unseen force had gently pushed him into the room. He seemed surprised to find himself there.

"Can I get you a beer?" Eli offered. Rob shook his head. "How about some coffee then? Have a seat." Eli walked around the bar and poured the coffee and came back around, handing it to the gunman, who took it in his left hand. Eli walked back to the Bible he'd set on the bar and turned to his "congregation." But before he could speak, one of the cowboys on the other side of the room stood up and walked toward the door.

"Hank, where are you going?" Eli's question stopped the man and he turned to face the preacher.

"I ain't sittin' in church with him," he growled.

Eli turned to face Rob and saw the gunman stiffen. "Rob," he said sharply, "There will be no gun play in here."

Rob never said a word but he visibly relaxed. It was obvious the man remembered Eli's handy work when the men robbed the bank. His eyes narrowed, evidencing that even though he thought he could beat him, he realized he would catch at least one bullet. His posture softened. "There's no problem here, preacher," he conceded. "I ain't goin' against the two of you and I don't want to get shot." But Hank's body remained tensed and his hand still lingered near his gun.

"Hank, sit down and shut up!" Eli did not raise his voice, but spoke with the authority which comes with having carried a badge and many years of experience. With a venomous look in the gunman's direction, Hank complied, but he was muttering to himself.

Eli shut the Bible up and set it down on the bar, then addressed the people in front of him.

"I want one thing made straight here... Everyone is welcome at this church!" He paused to look into the eyes of each individual, ending with Rob. "How many of you would feel welcome going into the church across town?" He answered his own question, "Not too many of you. In fact, not a single one of you!" He turned his attention to Hank, "Do you want to be like those high-browed folks over there, turning your nose up to snub others, just like they turn their noses up at you? Is that really the way you want to be?"

"Jesus," he pointed out, "chose to be with anyone who would follow him. Tax collectors, fisherman, thieves, prostitutes and even some religious folks. He didn't care what their background was or what they had done. He came to save the lost and to heal the sick and He even raised the dead. But He never, ever turned anyone away who was willing to follow Him. That is the way this church will be run!"

Eli turned back to Hank, "Now, if you want to leave you can, I will hold no man here against his will."

Hank remained in his seat, red in the face like a young boy who had just got spanked by the school master, but he did not stand up. "No sir. I'll stay." There was a long pause as the cowboy looked like he had more to say. Eli was just about to speak up again when Hank continued. His eyes were serious as he looked across the room at Rob, "I'm sorry. I was wrong."

Rob gave a nod, "It's all right."

With the apology, the tension in the room, which had been so thick it felt like one could cut it with a knife, just vanished.

Eli hurried to finish his message in the time frame he had allotted himself. When the service ended, the gunman hurried out of the bar before Eli had a chance to talk to him.

* * *

The next few weeks were brutally busy for Eli. He did his work at the saloon and it became a daily routine to go into town to find Steven. He was burdened for the man and had a great desire to help him.

He knew if things went on the way they were going, Steven would eventually drink himself to death. He grimaced in frustration. *If only the man would listen.* Eli knew the message of eternal life could deliver Steven from the addictions which controlled his life. He longed for his friend to find hope, so he pursued him. He provided him food and water and in Steven's rare moments of clarity, Eli would share with him the power of Jesus.

He made it a habit to swing into the saddle and ride out to the different ranches in the area, meeting new men and inviting them to come out to the church service on Sunday. He was left with no time for himself and the days flew by as he reached out to the many.

Early every Sunday morning, Eli would wake Steven, who would then stumble into the saloon where he ate breakfast and, somewhat grudgingly, heard a preview of the morning's sermon. The words of hope Eli gave, at times, appeared to touch him deeply. Steven was always grateful for the meal, but then seemed to distance himself from the message. Still, Eli was encouraged. From comments made, Eli knew that Steven appreciated the fact that he reached out to him.

Eli knew the love of Jesus, a love which did not judge, but met a man where he lived, was beginning to break down Steven's defenses.

Every week the small congregation heard about God's grace. In a series of three sermons Eli spoke on God's mercy. The next week he spoke of God's love, explaining the various Greek words for love. The word for erotic love brought a few laughs from the crowd and a couple of good natured jabs at each other. He explained phileo as brotherly love, a love which says, "I care for you because you delight me to no end." Then finally Agape Love, a love totally given over to another no matter what a person has done. He explained how Jesus' decision to go to the cross to pay for sin was the ultimate example of Agape love.

To his disappointment, Rob did not return to church. He prayed for the gunman, having sensed the great need within the man.

After each message, Eli gave an altar call, an opportunity for people to come forward and accept Jesus as their savior, but there were no takers.

During the time he worked the bar, his mind was busy praying over the men he served. As he wiped the bar down with a washrag or poured the beer into fresh mugs, he lifted his new friends to Jesus. Their needy lives burdened his heart and he would not give up on them.

CHAPTER FOUR

It was after the sixth Sunday service Brother Smith appeared outside of the SALOON. He had a small group of men with him from his church, including one woman.

He set a wooden crate upside down out on the sidewalk and stood on it. His face drew itself into a self-righteous snarl. "This is a den of iniquity," he shouted, drawing the attention of the people who were walking along the street. "The men and women who abide here are going to Hell," He continued at the top of his voice.

A small crowd began to gather as his tirade continued. He puffed out his chest and gestured toward the saloon with a weighty hand. "These types of people are the problem with this town. They all bring us down with their drunkenness and debauchery. Because of them, crime is rampant in our streets. Our woman and children are not safe to be out in public!"

Eli heard the shouting as he tended the bar after the service. Almost immediately he recognized it for what it was and felt an intense annoyance wash over him. His first reaction was to walk out and plant a fist into the man's teeth. He quickly quashed that feeling and sent up a prayer for wisdom. During his time as a lawman he had many opportunities to deal with this type of situation, but this was the first time he'd seen it, since he himself had been called as a minister of the gospel. Now the rants were directed at him and made him shudder. He gritted his teeth and his jaw hardened. He wanted to represent his Lord properly.

Listening to the man, Eli knew no one had been a victim of crime as a result of the cowboys in the SALOON. Obviously Brother Smith cared little about truth. But the crowd was growing. And from the man's words, he realized Brother Smith was on a rampage to kick the new preacher out of town. His rant grew louder and more accusing as the growing crowd congregated around him.

One of the cowboys sitting at the bar stood up and drew his pistol. "I'll take care of that loud mouthed Son of a...." He started for the door.

Eli held out his hand and stopped him. "Put that thing away," he interjected. "I'll talk to him."

Eli removed his apron and draped it on the bar. As he walked out the door, he was instinctually aware of the small group of men inside the bar who followed behind.

"Mr. Smith," Eli relaxed and smiled. "It appears you are lost. I believe your church is on the other side of the tracks."

Brother Smith turned toward the voice. He seemed ready to argue him into the ground. One could see the preacher was upset over Eli's apparent lack of respect.

"I am a preacher, and I have every right to be here to speak to this evil. " His annoyance showed on his face and Eli knew that he had the upper hand.

"Look at him," Brother Smith continued in a loud voice, "He doesn't even dress like a preacher. He looks like a cowboy. Who could possibly trust what he says?"

"What is a preacher supposed to dress like?" Eli protested, speaking just loud enough to be heard. "If you are going to use the Bible as your standard, where are *your* robes and breast plate? Doesn't the Old Testament teach that those are the garments of the Israelite Priests?"

"Where does the Bible tell you to dress like that?" gesturing to the black broadcloth suit and stiff white shirt, in which Smith was clad.

Brother Smith sputtered for a moment and then gathering himself, launched back into his attack. "What kind of a preacher holds church in a Saloon? It is a den of iniquity. You yourself are probably a drunken sot."

Eli smiled and turned to the crowd. "I recall a few times that Jesus went into the temple to teach, but mostly he met people where they were at. He went to them, he met their needs and then he showed them The Way. The religious leaders of the day even referred to Jesus as a glutton and a drunkard. Our Lord came to heal the broken people of this world."

Brother Smith seized upon that, "So now, you are comparing yourself to Jesus!" He seemed to believe he had Eli now and was gloating over the turn of events. The group became restless and murmured their disapproval.

Eli turned once again to the crowd. "I am a follower of Jesus which means I would like to be like Him in any way I can." He turned to Smith, "The truth is, I would compare you to the Pharisees, men of religion whom Jesus called 'White washed tombs.' They're pretty on the outside, but dead as a doornail on the inside. You and people like you are a brood of vipers with poison on your tongues and on your lips." He declared into the silence, "Where is the Love of Jesus within you?"

The mood of the crowd suddenly changed. Someone yelled, "You preach it, Brother! I like what you are sayin'". In a turn of events, many in the assemblage began to shout their support for Eli.

The frowning men standing behind Brother Smith, the ones who had come with him, took a step away, distancing themselves from him. Eli smiled as the man's supporters faded into the crowd.

Then his jaw tightened but he spoke with a deadly calm, "You spew out your words of hate, but how many times have you come to this side of town to tell these men and women about the Salvation God offers through the sacrifice of His Son? How many times have you shown real, Godly love and kindness to them?"

To Eli's amusement, as the crowd continued to grow, the men who had come to support Smith were trying to sneak away without anyone noticing.

"Yeah," came the shout from one of the men in the crowd. "You never even bothered to give us the time of day. He needs to git outta here."

"Yeah, let's run his carcass out of town," the crowd jeered.

Eli spoke with authority. "Men don't lower yourselves to this man's level." It took him several minutes to calm the crowd. "Let him go. Please men, let him go back to where he came."

Brother Smith sneered as Eli stepped closer, emphasizing his words as he placed one booted foot onto the soapbox. His eyes narrowed as he said, "You'd better get back to your side of town before they change their minds, Mr. Smith."

He paused a moment then added, "If that's your real name." It was a comment made out of the blue. When he saw Smith visibly flinch he realized he might be onto something. Eli made a mental note to look into that some more.

It was then Smith seemed to realize his support had left him alone with the crowd. He looked around him with alarm. Then he and his remaining follower, a woman, slunk off around the edge of the crowd, leaving his soapbox behind.

* * *

Brother Smith was fuming inside. His followers had left him, just like the disciples had left Jesus in the garden. They would pay for leaving him in the lurch. He made an excuse to the woman who had stayed with him to the end, and separated himself from her.

He stomped along the board walk toward the only church building in town. He needed to think. He couldn't just let that man ride in here and talk to him like that!

"'Vengeance is Mine' saith the Lord" he muttered. His mind roiled with fury. It seemed to him the Lord could use his help on this one. "I'm going to squash that preacher like a bug," he said under his breath.

"Who you talking to?"

Smith had been so angry he did not even see the two cowboys on the boardwalk near him. He stopped, opened his mouth and was about to make up another excuse, when he realized these two had not been a part of the crowd back there. From their dusty attire, he judged them to be a couple of drifting cowhands who had probably just rode into town.

He quickly made up his mind. "I'm sorry gentlemen," he began with an apologetic grin. "I have a lot on my mind. For sure and for certain, I should not be talking to myself out loud. Are you fellas new in town?"

"Yep, we just rode in and we're looking for some work right now. Do you know if any of the ranches are hiring?"

Smith lowered his voice, "I might have a need for a couple of men in a few days. The job will pay fifty dollars." He was talking even as the idea blossomed in his mind. He could get the money out of the church coffers. He was doing the work of the Lord, after all.

"Fifty dollars each? Cash money?"

Smith hesitated only for a moment. It wasn't really his money. "Yes, fifty dollars each, cash," he replied.

"Mister, I'd kill for that kind of money. I haven't seen cash in over a month and a half."

His friend interjected, "Yeah, we've been chewing on boot leather seems like. Ain't had a good meal since I don't know when."

"No, no, nothing like that," Smith explained. "The truth is, I want you to remove a dangerous man from this location. Can you men be discreet? The good people of this town would be mighty thankful to you."

"I don't know what that means mister. But I can be anything you want me to be for fifty dollars."

"I don't want people knowing what happened," Brother Smith pointed out. "I need you to be tight lipped about what I ask you to do."

"Mister, for that much money, we will ride off and you'll never see us again."

Smith surreptitiously glanced around him. He did not want to be seen talking to these men. "Meet me behind the church, over there, in a half hour and don't let anyone see you. Do you understand?"

The men nodded and drifted off down the boardwalk. Smith glanced around again. Anyone who might have seen them would just assume it was a cordial exchange of pleasantries and would have no reason to suspect him of duplicity. He hurried off toward the church to get ready for their meeting.

* * *

Matt Wheaton was puzzled. He had seen Brother Smith walking, and even from across the street where he stood in the deep shadows, he could make out the man's angry face. His body language was unmistakable.

As he watched, Brother Smith turned it off in a moment. As soon as he began talking to the two strangers, his attitude changed like the flame of a candle blown out in a hurry. Matt, in his short tenure as sheriff had become a student of people and he was a quick learner.

His eyes narrowed with suspicion. What he'd just seen was out of the ordinary. The two men had seemed to wander off aimlessly, but Brother Smith had walked away with a purpose.

Matt thoughtfully headed back toward the sheriff's office, and filed the incident away in his memory.

* * *

Eli was tired! The day had been full and his confrontation with Brother Smith had sapped his energy. He grabbed a piece of scrap lumber discarded against the side of the shed to use as a desk, then sat down in the chair, armed with a piece of paper and his pen.

He missed his son. It seemed like it had been a lifetime since he'd seen Ben. It always helped when he was discouraged, to write his feelings down and it had been a long time since he'd written to his son. His pen moved across the page as he poured out his heart in a letter.

Dear Ben,

I cannot even begin to express how much I miss you and Naomi. I so wish you were here with me. As I wrote previously, I have moved to Nevada. You will be surprised to know I have since started a church for the cowboys around here. Son, I wish that I could tell you it is going great, but that would be a lie.

I don't know if you remember, but when you were a young boy, we travelled through some badlands. Nothing grew there to speak of. Our wagon had to be loaded with everything we would possibly need on that trip.

Well son, I believe I have located the badlands of Nevada. I would describe it as a spiritual badlands, where people are going to hell, they know that they are going to hell, and they just don't care. I have poured myself into these men and women and have received absolutely no response. I am discouraged. I feel like I made more progress in the lives of men when I arrested them than I have here.

There is another church here in town and I am not impressed with the pastor nor the church members. They tried to run me out of town today, though they did not have any success. Still, if that is the caliber of Christians in this town, maybe I need to find someplace else.

Please pray for me and the ministry here. I felt I was called here by God—but I need to hear from Him. I don't know if I should stay here or find some other place. At times I feel as if I am the only one who even believes in God. But even as I write that, I think on some of the people I have met here and I know some of them have a relationship with Jesus.

I hope I will find others who love Him like I love Him. Everyone is so busy with their lives it seems like they don't have time to nurture their walk, other than to show up at church on Sundays. And their lives show their lack.

Please tell Naomi hello and give her a kiss from me. I love you both so much. I really do miss you.

Affectionately, Dad

* * *

In the half hour prescribed, Brother Smith met with the two strangers in the shadows behind the church where it was unlikely anyone would see them.

He explained the plan to the men, discussing a few details. As the clandestine meeting was about to split up, Brother Smith reached inside his jacket and pulled out an envelope. "There is $25 in here. I will give you the rest, once the job is finished."

One of the men grinned a nasty smile and reached a grubby hand for the money.

But Brother Smith pulled the envelope back, "Wait a minute," he snarled, "I want your word you will get this done right away."

"Mister, we will get it done before the money runs out, but we need to make sure we don't get caught. It may take some doing to get it done."

The man grabbed the envelope out of Smith's hands. "But don't you worry, Preacher. When we take money for a job, the job always gets done." He stared at Smith until the preacher averted his eyes. "We'll be back for the rest of our money."

Brother Smith felt anger welling up inside him. He had been stared down and had looked away. A pathetic cowpoke had made him feel inferior. *That snot nosed hireling*! He could feel the heat creeping up his neck to his face.

He took a deep breath and gritted his teeth in repressed anger. He had to get a hold of himself. These men were going to take care of a prickly problem for him and he needed them. He could deal with a little insolence if they were able to get the job done! Slowly he calmed down, then walked back inside the church, unseen.

* * *

Eli had begun to fall into a daily routine, something he had never allowed himself to do when he was sheriff. Back in those days, there were too many people out there who might want to hurt or kill him, but now, he was a bartender and a preacher, so he allowed his caution to dwindle.

He had decided to walk a spell that Wednesday evening. He loved hiking in the desert just before he readied himself for sleep. The desert cooled down quickly once the sun disappeared and it cleared his head to walk in the cool of the night, spending time in prayer as he got some exercise.

He liked the night time. His many years as a sheriff, making night rounds had taught him the darkness hid him as well as the bad guys! Many a times, he had snuck up on someone in the middle of a nighttime crime and made an arrest. He smiled. There was a supernatural aspect to his lack of fear. He knew as long as he had the Light of the World inside him, he need not fear the dark.

It was a cool Monday night and Eli walked the streets, illuminated only by the light coming from an occasional window. It was a moonless starry night and he enjoyed the bright beauty of the heavens above.

Suddenly a figure rushed out of an alleyway. The female was vaguely familiar as she cried for help and then darted back where she came from. Eli drew his gun as he raced after her. He saw her outline as she knelt down in the center of the alley over the form of a prostrate man. He slowed down his pace to take in the scene. Then, there was a sickening thud on the back of his head and everything went black.

* * *

Steven Bosco struggled out of a drunken stupor as unusual sounds in the stable disturbed him enough to cause him to awaken. He sat up, discarding the thin blanket in which he had wrapped himself for the night. He had sense enough to keep quiet, for he did not want someone to steal his half-finished bottle. Two men were saddling their horses, sharing swigs from their own bottle.

"Let's get the rest of our money and skedaddle out of this town."

The other replied, "Shore thing. Beats all though, you ever hear of a bartender preacher before?"

Steven suddenly sobered at the mention of his only friend.

"Yeah, well, he won't be doing either in this town anymore. By the time he's discovered, that train will be far from here."

The other man laughed, "Yeah, did you see him fold up when I hit him? He went to the ground like a sack of flour."

"Yeah, but it didn't make it easy loading him into that train car. That much dead weight is hard to sling around."

"Hurry up and get that saddle on. I want to get out of here."

They each pulled another drink off the bottle and mounted up. "Here's to Scorpion Wells," said the one, lifting the bottle as he swayed in the saddle. Together they rode out of the stable.

Steven got to his feet, still unsteady from the previous night's drunk, but suddenly sobered by what he'd heard. He carefully brushed hay from his pants then went behind the building to relieve himself.

Once that was done, he went to the watering trough to splash some water on his face to help clear his mind. He had to do something, but he wasn't sure what at this point. He needed to focus on the problem, but his brain was foggy from the liquor. He sat down and tried to think. He needed to come up with a plan, but what?

To get moving would be the first thing to do. He got up and walked toward the saloon. It was still night and the saloon was in full swing as he pushed his way through the batwing doors. He staggered up to the bar and waited to get Sam's attention.

"You have money on you?" Sam asked.

Steven shook his head. "I don't want a bottle, I need some coffee. I need to sober up."

Sam raised an eyebrow in surprise. Steven had never asked for coffee and he certainly never wanted to be sober. He went back to the stove, wiped out a mug with his apron and filled it with the coffee he'd made hours earlier that night. He placed it in front of Steven.

"Are you all right?" he asked.

"I don't know. I got to think," was Steven's slurred reply.

Sam moved on to his other customers and Steven sipped on the hot, burnt-tasting coffee. It wasn't really helping, but he finished the cup and made his way toward the door.

Sam called out, "Steven, is there anything I can help you with?"

Steven was surprised at the man's concern. Maybe Eli was rubbing off on him, too.

Steven turned unsteadily, still feeling the fog of the liquor, "I don't know. Have you seen Eli?"

Sam shook his head, "No, not since last evening."

"Thanks." Steven still didn't know if the events in the stable were a dream or real and he wanted to be sure, so he didn't make a fool of himself.

He walked back out to the water pump, drank deeply of it, and ran more cold water over his head, determined to beat the fog of drink.

Suddenly he was reminded of something Eli had told him about the woman at the well. Jesus told her, "Everyone who drinks of this water shall thirst again; but whoever drinks of the water that I shall give shall never thirst; but the water that I shall give him shall become in him a well of water springing up to eternal life." He shook the water from his face.

Steven drank more water, then sat down on the boardwalk. He kept trying to clear his mind, to focus, but it was hard to do. "God help me," he prayed, remembering how Eli had taught that God cared and would be listening.

He began to drift into sleep, when suddenly he was jolted awake with a thought. He swayed to his feet and stumbled toward the rear of the saloon. He spoke up outside Eli's sleeping quarters, calling his name.

When he did not receive an answer, he pulled the curtain aside. Steven could see in the dim light Eli was not there and the bed was neatly made up.

He staggered back out onto the street, unsure what to do. Making his unsteady way back to the stable, he sat down on a storage locker. Despite his best attempts to draft a plan, he drifted off to sleep.

* * *

A knock on the door of the church office, where he often slept, startled Brother Smith out of a deep satisfied sleep. He lit a lantern and cautiously opened the door. The two drifters were standing there, one held a gun belt and a gun. With a grand gesture he offered it to the preacher.

"The job is done," he bragged. "Here is his gun and gun belt for proof."

Brother Smith took the proffered item and examined the old gun. Eli's name was etched on the handle.

"That was made long before the war," one of the men commented, "Don't know why anyone would carry one of them anymore."

"What did you do with him?" Smith demanded.

"We put him on a train headin' out of town," came the answer from one of the men.

The other laughed and sneered, "Yeah, and he won't be in any shape to get back on the returning train either. He's close to bein' dead."

"You wait here," Brother Smith commanded. He shut the door and hurried across the room to his desk. As he retrieved the rest of the money from the drawer, he thought about short-changing them, but decided against it. Doing such a thing would likely work against him in the long run.

He opened the door and held the money out to the men. The one who took it counted it carefully, holding each of the bills to the dim light of the lantern until he was satisfied that all the money was there and that it was good.

Brother Smith was suddenly glad he had opted to pay in full. "You men are going to ride out pronto, correct?" he queried.

"Well we sure ain't a' gonna stick around after what we done." One of them pointed out. "It wouldn't be healthy for us if'n we were found out."

The man's evil smile made Smith feel sick to his stomach.

"No, it would never do if we were found out," the man mused.

The two men pocketed the money, then mounted their horses saluted, with an insolent gesture and rode away.

Once they were out of sight, Smith made sure to lock the door behind him. He removed Eli's pistol from its holster and examined the gun in the dim light of the lantern.

He double checked to make sure the name was not newly etched into the wood handle then he shoved it back into the holster and wrapped the belt around it. He walked to the wardrobe and pushed the rig under his spare blanket. Once that was done, he returned to his bed and blew out the light. It didn't take long for him to fall to sleep. Feelings of guilt or shame over what he had just orchestrated and paid for, never even entered his mind or his dreams. His was the comfortable sleep of man whose work was well-done. After all—he'd been helping God do what was right.

* * *

Dawn brought a shaft of light into the livery stable, stabbing Steven in the face. He awoke and this time, he was sober enough to recall the events of the previous night with clarity. He quickly completed his chores and then hurried to Eli's room in the shed. The bed had *not* been slept in! Anxiety shook him into action. So last night was not a dream.

He tried the saloon, but it was locked. He pounded on the door, but he knew Sam was a heavy sleeper. When he did not get an answer, he sat down on the boardwalk to ponder his situation. He listed in his mind all the men who might be able to help, but they were working out in the range.

He finally decided whatever needed to be done, he was going to have to do himself. Once he reached that conclusion, he was galvanized to action. The idea of going to the sheriff never entered his mind.

He ran to the stable and located Eli's horse and mule. He retrieved Eli's saddle and gear from the locker and got the animals ready. Next he went to the shed and collected supplies he would need.

As he worked, he accidentally knocked over Eli's Bible. A stack of money spilled onto the floor. There were still supplies he needed to purchase. He reasoned that Eli would understand.

Making his way to the general store, Steven purchased what he needed for his impromptu trip. Finally, he walked over to the River Saloon which was now open, where he bought four bottles of whiskey.

'I don't know how long it will take to find Eli, I'll have to learn to ration my liquor while I'm gone.' He thought to himself.

Once he was had packed all the supplies—he allowed himself to sit a moment. Eli's Bible was in his hands and he knew his friend would want it. Standing unsteadily to his feet, he went to the stable and located his half bottle of whiskey.

Steven pulled himself into the saddle and began his lonesome ride toward the railroad depot. He had traveled on trains before. He knew that the Bull, the railroad detective, would not allow anyone to ride for long on a train without a ticket.

His fear was that Eli, likely wounded and beaten, would be tossed off the train and he would never find him.

He reached the Depot and called out to the station clerk, who stuck his head out the door.

"Which way did the train get out of here last night?" he asked.

"East," came the reply.

Steven waved his thanks and rode east, following the tracks. He had to find Eli. ***He had to***.

CHAPTER FIVE

Eli woke to the rumbling of the train and a throbbing headache. When he opened his eyes it brought a piercing pain that sliced through his head and he shut them again, quickly. His body ached everywhere. He was sure he had some cracked ribs. Someone had worked him over pretty good and he mentally kicked himself for being a fool.

A voice cut into his distracted and disjointed thoughts. "You drunken bum, get up." The toe of a boot nudged him none too gently.

Eli tried to say something in his defense, but all he could manage was a groan and a croaking noise.

"So you're not going to do this on your own, eh? Well then let me give you a hand." The sarcasm was thick as the man grabbed him by the nape of his shirt and his belt.

"No. Please…" The words escaped, as Eli felt himself being lifted and then the weightlessness of flying. His body hit hard against the ground and he rolled into the sand with the momentum of the moving train. Darkness washed over him and he knew nothing more.

* * *

Sam woke late in the morning and stretched. He had gotten used to the comfort of Eli opening the saloon for him. He laid in his bed and listened for a while.

Suddenly it dawned on him that it was very quiet downstairs, too quiet. He slipped into his pants and brought the suspenders up over his shoulders, then hurried down the stairs. To his surprise, Eli was not there and the saloon was a mess from the night before.

Angrily, he hustled out to Eli's room. But his anger turned to concern when he realized the room had been looted and the man he had begun to consider a friend, was nowhere to be found. He noted Eli's bedroll was gone and wondered if he had pulled up stakes and left during the night.

But that would not be like the man he had come to know. Sam noticed the trunks which made up the base of the bed. He removed the planks from top of them, and opened the trunks up. Inside was a large supply of Bibles and hymn books. The other was full of personal items, things a man would never leave behind.

He clenched his jaw and frowned. Now he was worried, really worried. The truth was, in the short time he had known Eli, this was way out of character for him.

* * *

Sam was almost at a run when he burst through the door at the Sheriff's office. Matt looked up to see Sam partially dressed in his red Union Suit under garment, pants, suspenders and stocking feet. It didn't take a trained investigator to perceive that something was wrong.

"What is it, Sam?"

He was out of breath. "Eli's gone missing."

"What do you mean, 'gone missing'?" Matt puzzled.

"Just what it sounds like." Sam was obviously irritated. "He didn't show up for work this morning. His room has been looted and he left a mess of personal things behind."

Matt pushed away from the desk so violently that the chair went over backward. He grabbed his hat as he ran out the door and shoved it down on his head. Sam huffed as he hurried after the sheriff.

"Have you noticed anything strange happening in town lately?" Matt asked as they arrived at the shed.

Sam thought a moment, trying to catch his breath. "As a matter of fact, Steven Bosco came in last night and asked for coffee to sober up."

Matt's face registered a look of surprise as Sam continued, "That's how I felt too. Boy was I surprised. But the funny thing is, when I asked him if he needed help, he just asked if I had seen Eli."

Matt pulled aside the blanket to let the sunlight flood in. A quick search of the room confirmed what Sam had already told him. He did a more thorough search, looking for clues, but did not find anything which would help.

Matt left Sam and headed toward the stable in search of Steven. Not only did he not find Steven, Eli's horse and pack mule were missing. He located the hostler.

"Do you know where Steven is?" he asked.

"Naw, ain't see'd him today." Came the reply.

"Do you know if Eli Exeter came and got his animals?"

"Nope, ain't see'd him either."

Matt sighed and then thanked the man. Deep in thought he walked past the general store.

"How you doing, Sheriff?" The grocer was tossing some dirty water into the street and his inquiry brought Matt out of his reverie.

"I'm puzzled," he replied, "I'm looking for Eli Exeter and Steven Bosco and I can't find either one of 'em.

"You know, it's funny you should say that. Steven came in this morning with cash money and bought a bunch of supplies."

"What kind of supplies? And where did Steven get cash?" Matt was all ears now.

"A few medical supplies, you know, bandages and the likes and a mess of canned food." The grocer answered. "I have no idea where he got the money."

"Do you know where he went when he left here?"

"Yep, he headed right over t' the River Saloon."

"Thank you, you've been a great help."

"Best of luck to you Sheriff, I hope you find 'em."

Matt spun on his heel and hurried to the River Saloon. He pushed his way through the batwing doors and caught the bartender's eye. He met him down at the empty end of the bar.

"Did Steven Bosco come in here?"

"Yeah he did. He paid cash for four bottles of whiskey," he answered. "I wondered where he got the money, but figured it weren't any of my business."

"Thank you." Matt did not bother to answer him as to where the money came from. He had a pretty good idea where the source was, but didn't want to jump to conclusions "Did you see where he went from here?"

"Nope. Why? Is he in some kind of trouble?"

"I don't know. I really don't want to say at this point, but thank you for your help."

Matt strode back outside and looked around for a moment, then he removed his hat and scratched the itch on top of his head. It was time to do some old fashioned detective work.

He began to canvas door to door, seeking information on either Eli or Steven. At last he hit pay dirt at one of the little shops on Main Street. The little old lady who did mending for a living told him she'd seen Steven riding toward the train depot with a mule behind him.

Next Matt went to the train depot and woke the clerk from a nap. "Did you see Steven Bosco this morning?" He inquired.

"Yes sir," came the reply, "He asked me which way the train went last night. I told him it went east and he rode down the tracks in that direction."

"Was he leading a pack mule?"

"Yes sir, he was."

"What time was that?" Matt queried.

The man pulled out his pocket watch and checked the time. "No more'n five, or six hours ago."

Matt thanked him. Then he walked back to his office and poured a cup of coffee. He did not like what he was finding out. Something just did not add up. Steven was a drunk, not a horse thief and a burglar. He took a swig of coffee and grimaced at the bitter taste. It had been on the stove way too long. He opened the door, tossed what remained in the cup out on the ground and then walked to the stove and removed the pot.

It was lunch time anyway, so he went to the café and ordered some stew. While he waited for the young lady to bring his lunch, he pondered over what he'd learned.

Sam poked his head in the door, and when he saw the Sheriff he made a beeline for his table. Matt motioned for him to take a chair.

"Have you found out anything yet?"

Matt weighed his words before answering. "Right now, it appears Steven Bosco may have robbed Eli." He spoke quietly so the other patrons could not overhear their conversation. He did not want any rumors to get started.

Sam registered his surprise. "Steven? I can't believe it. He's never stolen anything in his life."

"I know, but I have witnesses who saw him riding out of town on a horse and leading a pack mule. Eli's horse and mule are missing from the stable. His room has been ransacked and Steven used cash to purchase supplies and liquor."

He stopped talking as the girl brought his food to the table. Once she was out of earshot he declared, "I just can't figure out what happened to Eli. I don't want to believe Steven could have hurt him, but I can't think of another explanation. How else would he get a hold of Eli's things?"

Sam shook his head, "I don't believe it! Besides, Steven was the one looking for Eli last night."

Matt nodded. "True enough. Well, until I see proof otherwise, that is the theory I am working on." He had learned not to let his own prejudice influence an investigation, rather to let the facts speak for themselves. In spite of that, he did not want to believe that Steven could do anything so evil. The one thing was that no bodies had surfaced and in a town this size if Eli were dead, someone would have located his body by now. He found the whole thing baffling and suddenly Matt found himself praying for Eli's safety.

The Sheriff finished his lunch. He saddled his horse and rode east out of town. He easily picked up the trail of the horse and pack mule. He did not know how long he could follow the trail. Steven had at least a six-hour head start.

Besides, he had an obligation to the town and duties he felt he needed to be on top of—he struggled with himself—he could not be out on the trail for a long time, especially if it was a wild goose chase.

Still, he considered Eli a friend and so he rode on.

* * *

Eli woke to a blazing sun. His head was pounding, every inch of his body ached and his throat burned with thirst, but there was no water.

Twenty feet from where he lay, he saw a tree... shade! He tried to stand up, only to crumple into a heap. The pain pounded him into the ground.

Lifesaving shade was only steps away and he could not even stand! He clawed his way into the sand. But as he tried to pull himself toward the shade, a wave of pain washed over his entire body, then everything went black again.

* * *

Steven rode past lunchtime. The sun was high in the sky when he stopped to pull a biscuit and some jerky from the saddlebag. He rested the animals in the shade of a single oak tree, giving them water and then wetting down a handkerchief, he washed the dust from their noses. "There you go. This'll help you."

Even when bleary from drinking, he had not forgotten how to care for an animal. Out here in the desert, failing to do so could mean the difference between life and death. For them and for him.

Once he had cared for the animal's needs, he took a long drink of water from the canteen. He'd drank more water over the course of the morning than he had in the last week.

He desperately wanted a swig of whiskey, but the need to find his friend overrode his desire for the stuff.

Still, the more he tried to ignore his desire for the liquor, the more his thoughts kept turning to the bottles in his bag. He kept telling himself he needed to stay sober for Eli's sake.

He could almost hear the amber liquid calling his name. He could feel the burn of that first drink sliding down his throat.

He shook himself, "No," he shouted to empty desert, "I have to find Eli!"

But the whiskey. It was there, only an arm's length away. Steven was in a quandary. He had not voluntarily gone without drinking for this long in many a year and his body was revolting against the sudden drought. His hands! They were shaking so bad. Sweat poured down his face, not only from the hot sun, but from his desire – his body's need for the liquor. Alcohol had been his only friend, his solace for too many years and now...

Steven did something he had not done since he was a child. He prayed.

"God. Jesus...If you're there, I need you. I can't do this by myself. Help me, please. Oh God, please." Unbidden tears began to flow from his eyes.

He didn't know what else to pray. He only knew if he were left to his own devices, he would fail. Yet the desire for the whiskey remained. He tried to fight it back, but it felt impossible. *God didn't care about Eli. He obviously didn't care about Steven. God couldn't even answer a simple prayer*!

Steven reached into the bag and grabbed the partial bottle he had not finished the night before. He lifted it towards heaven and screamed, "Here's to you, God."

The whiskey burned as he took a long swallow from the bottle, but as soon as it hit his stomach, it came right back up. He retched and the liquor spewed out onto the ground. He was stunned. He had not thrown up from drinking since he was a young man, and that was after a binge! Yet here he had just vomited after one drink! Incredulous, he tried to swallow another gulp *with the same result*. His amazement didn't end there. As he replaced the cork in the bottle, he realized his hands were no longer shaking.

He put the bottle back into his saddlebag and looked again up into the sky. With tears now streaming down his face, he cried, "Oh my God. I'm sorry. I'm sorry I got so angry with you. I'm so sorry God. You *do* care."

* * *

Eli drifted back into consciousness. His eyes were nearly swollen shut and his lips were peeling. As recognition of his situation returned to him, he knew that it was imperative that he get out of the sun.

This time, he dug the toes of his boots into the sand and with his good hand, he began to inch forward toward the tree. The pain nearly overwhelmed him, but he was determined not to die.

"God help me," he prayed, "Let me make it to the shade. Please." He pushed on by prayer and shear will power. Each time his eyes began to blur, he thought of the men and women back in town who were dying in their sin. God had called him to Scorpion Wells and he could not believe it was the will of God that he die here.

His work... God's work through him was not done yet. So he pushed on, inching his way across the scorching desert sand. The heat reflected back against his hot face. His bare hands were burned by the hot sand, yet he pressed on.

It took him nearly thirty minutes to push himself to the shade, but he made it! His energy was depleted. With a whispered thanks, he passed out once again.

* * *

Matt rode until mid-afternoon. He realized the folly of his pursuit. It was a burning hot day in the desert, and he didn't have proper supplies with him. No one knew where he was. And Becky would be worried. He wanted to find Steven, and Eli for that matter, but he also recognized he couldn't even figure a crime had been committed until he had a victim.

For all he knew, Eli had lent his animals to Steven. He knew Eli had befriended Steven and had taken him under his wing. Maybe there was nothing to this whole situation at all. Matt paused under a shade tree and watered the horse using his hat as a bowl. Next he took a drink of water from his canteen, then mounted the animal and regretfully turned his horse back toward town.

* * *

Steven stayed in the saddle until darkness made it impossible to see. There was only a sliver of the moon visible and it did not cast enough light to help out at all. He realized in the dark, he could ride right past Eli and not even know it unless the horse stepped on him.

Frustrated, because he knew that stopping could mean life or death for Eli, he recognized there was nothing he could do until morning.

He was still marveling at the miracle that had happened to him. He had gone nearly nineteen hours without a drink of liquor and he was still not suffering any side effects. Now he prayed he would find Eli before it was too late. *God had answered one prayer today, so why not try for a second one?*

Up ahead in the post dusk he could see the outline of some trees. They were not really more than large bushes, but he decided to make camp there. He would bed down and start out again at the crack of dawn to resume his search.

He tied the horse and the mule and began removing their saddles. He then hobbled both animals to keep them from wandering off during the night and removed the horses bridle. When he had cared for the animals, he then set about laying down his bedroll. He laid Eli's rifle alongside the bedroll on top of the ground cover to protect it from the sand, *you never know what kind of danger that you might face in the night.*

He crunched through the undergrowth looking for sticks for a fire. He was not worried about pursuit from the two men from the stable—they had no idea anyone knew what they had done and he knew a small fire would help keep the animals away.

He had gathered a bundle of wood, when he heard a small rustling noise on the other side. The rifle lay behind him ten feet away and he carefully began to inch back toward it, being as quiet as he could. He strained with his ears, but did not hear anything more as he bent to pick up the Winchester from his bedroll.

He swung the gun muzzle toward the direction of the sound and jacked the lever, chambering a round. At that moment he heard a muffled groan.

"You better have your hands in the air when you come out," he said fiercely in the direction of the tree.

There was another groan, but no other noise. He waited a moment then decided to risk lighting a match. He carefully made his way to the other side of the tree where he struck the match on the rough cloth of his pant. As the flame flared up, he saw a large cloth covered bundle. He cautiously approached, keeping the rifle in his right hand and the match in his left. The match was quickly burning out, so he snuffed it out in the sand and lit a second one. The bundle groaned for a third time and Steven realized that he was looking at the battered face of his one and only friend!

He dropped to his knees. "Eli! You hang in there, I'm here to help you."

Eli opened his swollen eyes and then closed them again.

Within a few short minutes, which actually seemed like eternity, Steven had a fire going and was boiling water in the coffee pot. In the flickering light of the fire, he examined Eli's wounds. The injured man was in bad shape.

Eli had somehow situated himself under the tree in a way which was bearable and Steven opted not to move him. He took the heated water and began to gently bath the sores and the wounds on Eli's face and hands. He retrieved salve from the saddlebags and tended to Eli's sunburned skin. Then he got out the whiskey and poured it over unconscious man's cuts to keep them from getting infected. Eli moaned in pain, but did not awaken.

Once Steven had done all he could for the injured man, he covered him with a blanket to ward off the chill of a desert night and then settled himself in for the night. Throughout the night, he woke to check on his patient, doing all he could to make the preacher comfortable.

When daylight broke, Steven rolled out of his bed and stoked the fire. He got the coffee going and went over to check on his sleeping friend.

As he tended his wounds, he realized Eli was burning up! He found cold water and began sponging him off, working to bring his temperature down. Steven was not a doctor, but he had tended to a number of injured cowboys in his days as a horse wrangler, so he had a good idea what was needed. He used most of the remaining water in the canteen to cool the fevered man's skin, bathing his face and chest over and over. He managed to get some water past the parched lips without choking Eli. Judging from the flinching and moaning of the unconscious man when he put even the slightest pressure on the ribcage, he surmised that some of the ribs were broken.

It was mid-morning before the fever broke. When Steven was sure the danger was past, he turned his attention to the water situation. Without water, both of them would quickly die out here. He stood beside his friend—shading his eyes as he intently gazed into the distance.

He was not unfamiliar with this area, having hunted horses here many years back, although it seemed like a lifetime ago. He moved to higher ground and began looking for familiar landmarks.

Yes! Now he remembered. There was a waterhole not far from here, he figured an hour to get there and back. He saddled the horse and checked on Eli one more time. Satisfied there was nothing more he could do, he mounted the animal and began his search for water.

He made the trip in record time, filling all the canteens and every vessel that he had, including the five whiskey bottles. He even dumped the liquor to refill the bottles with water! He never thought he'd see the day that would happen. Trying to bring back as much water as possible, he filled a cooking pot and held the lid in place to retain the water on the ride back. Half way back to the camp, he let the horse drink from the pot. Once the horse had his fill, Steven drank the rest and tied the pot on behind the saddle.

He rode back into camp to find Eli laying quietly, with his bruised and puffed up eyes barely slit open.

"I've often wondered what angels look like, but I never thought they'd look like you." Eli's voice came out as a croak.

"You shut up and let me take a look at you."

Steven helped ease Eli into a semi-reclined position, then gave him a swallow of water. When Eli tried to drink more quickly, he held him off. "Not too much too fast or you'll get sick. If you start heaving with those broken ribs, you'll be in a world of hurt."

Eli listened, sipping the water, slowly increasing the amount he took in. He dozed, waking only to drink more water. Steven kept a close eye on his friend as he worked to make the camp more comfortable. He gathered wood throughout the day and as the sun moved across the sky, he helped Eli shift his position to remain in the shade. He removed stones from the ground and pushed the soft sand up under his friend to ease the pain of his broken ribs. He cooked up some broth, boiling some diced up jerky in water and fed the stuff to Eli, who could barely speak to express his thanks.

Steven realized though their position was not bad, eventually, they would need to do something about water. For now, he could ride back and forth between the waterhole and their camp. He knew it would be much better for his friend if they were nearer to the water hole.

It was late evening before Eli was up for conversation.

"What are you doing here?" he asked Steven. His voice was raspy, evidence of the trauma he'd been through.

"I overheard two men at the stable talking about hitting you over the head and throwing you on the train. I figured the railroad detective would throw you off the train when they found you, so I came a'lookin."

"Thank you. You saved my life." Eli drifted back to sleep, the small conversation having taken its toll.

Steven covered his friend with the blankets, banked the fire and rolled into his bedroll. He was fast asleep in moments.

* * *

Matt looked up from the wanted posters that had arrived in the mail, just as the livery stable keeper came in, a perplexed look creasing his face.

"Hi, Adam, what can I help you with today?"

"I've been looking for Steven all day and I didn't know where else to go. He never showed up at the stable last night, nor this morning'. I was wonderin' if you knew anything."

Matt scratched his cheek. "He rode out of here yesterday." He replied.

"But he ain't got a horse."

Matt nodded, "Yeah he was riding Elijah Exeter's horse as far as I can tell."

Adam exploded, "You mean he *stole* one of my customer's horses?"

"Slow down," Matt protested. "We don't know yet if anything like that happened. In fact, Eli seems to be missing too. No one I've talked to has a clue as to what happened. It's like he vanished into thin air."

Adam calmed down somewhat, "Two men missin'. Not what you'd expect around here." He paused for a moment, ran his fingers through his hair and then continued, "Well if you see Steven tell him to git down to the stable, will ya?"

"Of course."

Adam left his office and Matt had no more answers than he'd had the day before. He had talked it over with Becky and she agreed he needed to ride out and find out what had happened to the two men. He had made arrangements with one of the local men to keep an eye on the town while he was gone. Becky had packed him provisions and he was saddled up and ready to go.

He needed to wrap up a few things at the office, then he would be on his way. He knew where he'd left the trail yesterday, so the first part of the ride would go by fast. After that he'd have to track Steven, though he didn't think it would slow him down much, because Steven had not been trying to hide his tracks.

That gave him pause. He hadn't thought about that yesterday. He muttered to himself, "If Steven had stolen all of Eli's worldly goods, wouldn't he be trying to cover his trail?"

Of course if the man was drunk, he might not be thinking of someone tracking him. But on the other hand, the horse he had followed yesterday had not wandered aimlessly. It seemed the trail he'd left was one with purpose. Matt shook his head. More questions and still no more answers.

He removed the reins from the hitching post where he'd tied the horse, and mounted up. One of his neighbors would check up on Becky while he was gone. He turned his horse eastward and kicked him into a ground eating trot.

* * *

Morning came and Steven rolled out of bed. He stirred up the fire and pushed the coffee pot onto the coals.

"Good morning," Eli spoke from his bedroll.

Steven thought Eli already sounded way better. "How are you feeling?"

"Like I've been trampled by a herd of buffalo," came the reply.

"Yeah, you used to be prettier you know. Are you up for some breakfast?" Steven got the frying pan out, even as he asked.

"I think I might be able to eat something." Eli's voice was feeble. He moved slowly to a better sitting position, leaning against the tree. "I noticed you're not drinking."

"There's a funny story that goes along with that," Steven disclosed. As he made up the meat and beans, he told Eli what had happened on his trip. "I struggled because I bought four bottles of whiskey with your money. It was calling to me. But I knew if I drank it, I wouldn't be able to live with myself. I didn't want to fail—I had to find you. I knew you would die if I didn't. Then God answered my prayer—I am a sober man." He glanced over at Eli, not sure what to expect. "I will never drink the stuff again. It upsets my stomach to no end."

Eli gave him a weak grin. "God is so good and He is a God of miracles. Steven, *you* are one of His miracles."

"I want to know more. I want to know Jesus like you know Him. I want to be like you."

"First, you need to know that it is not enough to just believe in God." Eli began.

Steven flipped bacon into the frying pan to sizzle with the potatoes. "What do you mean?"

"The Bible tells us even the demons believe in God and they tremble because of it."

"So then what do I need to do?" Steven stirred the food in the pan.

"Steven, the Bible teaches us every man on earth in both past and present have sinned. We are born sinners."

Steven gave him a lopsided grin and handed him a cup of steaming coffee, "I certainly can't argue with that."

"Good, because God is perfect, He is sinless and man is not. Because of that there's a separation between a sinless God and sinful man. The price required to pay for our sins is death, spiritual death." Eli sipped the brew in his cup. "Good coffee," he said, taking another swallow.

"Thanks. It'll make the hair on your chest curl." Steven's face grew still as he attended to their breakfast. "So, if I am spiritually dead—how do I get close to God?" He sat listening for the answer with rapt attention.

"Well, here is the problem. The sacrifice for our sin had to be perfect. Had to be sinless. No human could accomplish that, so God sent his only Son, Jesus, to take our place. He took our sins upon Himself and died on a cross. He took our punishment. He was buried and our sins were buried with Him.

Steven was confused. "But if He is dead, how can He help us now?"

Eli smiled. "Here is the beauty of it, Steven. Jesus didn't stay dead. He rose from the grave. He is alive." He shifted his position and let out a groan as he did so. He was tired and wanted to rest, but this was too important.

Birds in the distance had begun their cheerful song and the aroma of the food was making his mouth water. "The Bible tells us if we accept the forgiveness from sin that Jesus offers, we will be saved. Saved from that spiritual separation, spiritual death. We are given eternal life--once this life on earth is over, we will live in the presence of God forever."

Steven thoughtfully stirred their breakfast. Now he pulled the pan from the fire and gave Eli his full attention, "Can I do that now, accept his forgiveness?"

"Yes you can. Let me lead you in a prayer and you just repeat the words after me."

Steven bowed his head as he had seen Eli do in the past, repeating the prayer as Eli spoke the words out loud. "Jesus, I admit that I am a sinner. I need you to forgive me for the things I've done. I want you to come into my heart. Amen." He looked up at Eli, "Is that it?"

"For now it is. If you meant those word you prayed, you are now a child of God."

Steven repeated the words with wonder, "A child of God!"

"When I'm feeling better, I will explain to you what it means to live your life for God." Eli was exhausted after their exchange. His eyes started to close.

"Wait a minute, don't you fall asleep on me yet," Steven said, "I can't eat all this by myself."

"I'm still with you," Eli replied, suddenly realizing he was famished. "I'm ready to eat whenever you are."

Steven dished up two plates and then asked, "What d'ya say when you pray over a meal?"

"Well, it's kind of like talking to you. I just thank God for the food and I tell him how I appreciate him providing for me."

"Can I pray?"

"Of course!" Eli sounded like he could not have been more pleased.

Steven bowed his head again. "God, thank you for this food." There was a long pause then he continued, "Thank you for letting me find my friend in the dark. Amen."

The two men ate their breakfast in silence.

* * *

Matt's horse stumbled and then began to limp. Matt got down to check him out and discovered the right front fetlock was starting to swell. He probed around the injured leg with his fingers and when he was finished, he was satisfied the horse did not have a broken leg. He smacked his thigh in frustration. He was two hours out of town and nowhere near where he had left off the trail yesterday.

He stowed his saddle under a tree and then slung the saddle bags and canteen over his shoulder. He noted the landmarks, so he could locate the saddle when he came back that way. It was going to be a long walk back to town. He sighed. He was thankful the gelding had not broken its leg. He really liked this horse, they worked well together.

His heart filled with worry for the two missing men as he turned back and began to lead his limping horse back to town.

* * *

By evening, Eli was now able to stand, with help. It was painful, but Steven had wrapped his cracked ribs, so it was manageable. His cuts were healing, but the bruising was now in its full glory. He ruefully fingered the purple, blue and green spots on his face. He knew he had to get up and moving in order to heal. Besides, he was never one to lay around anyway, so he got up in spite of the pain. He took a couple of steps then sat down on a rock, thoroughly winded.

Steven looked closely at his friend. "I will need to go for water tomorrow, are you going to be okay here alone?"

Eli nodded his head, too tired to speak for the moment. A wave of nausea washed over him and when it had passed, he addressed his friend. "You do what you need to do and don't worry about me."

"You're still in no shape to be riding," he reasoned. "I probably should ride back to town and get some help. That would mean being gone for two days."

"I've been doing some thinking on that and I don't think it's a good idea."

Steven shot him a puzzled look.

Eli continued, "Whoever did this to me thinks I'm long gone and while I'm still busted up it's better that way. You are doing a great job of taking care of me and if you don't mind toughing it out awhile longer, I would be grateful. I already owe you my life."

Steven was embarrassed by the praise, "But you need a doctor."

"What is a doctor going to do that you haven't already done for me except give me some laudanum," he exclaimed. "If I don't move too quickly, the pain is bearable, so...I just won't move too quickly."

Steven nodded his assent. He then switched subjects. "I found a Bible in your room when I was putting things together back in town. I almost left it behind, but didn't. I was wondering if I could read it some while we are out here."

Eli laughed but then grimaced with pain. "Of course you can, in fact, would you mind reading it out loud?"

"I don't know, I ain't read out loud since grammar school and I wasn't very good at it then."

Eli smiled, "It's just you and me and the prairie dog and I promise I won't laugh at you. Besides, you'll never get better unless you practice and this is the best place to do it."

Steven eagerly retrieved the book from his saddlebag. "Where should I start?"

"Why don't you begin reading from First John, chapter three? It's toward the back of the Bible."

Steven began flipping through the book and volunteered, "I found First Timothy."

"Keep going. After that is Second Timothy, Titus, Philemon, Hebrews, James, First Peter, Second Peter and then First John."

"Got it." Steven read haltingly, then interrupted himself, "There it is, God loves us so much that he made us his children. I am a child of God." His eyes shown with excitement.

Eli gave a lopsided smile from the side of his face that was not so bruised, "Now you know why I love this book so much."

Steven continued on and his reading was just short of atrocious. True to his word, Eli did not laugh. Instead, he answered the questions Steven had, how to purify himself by setting himself apart for service to God and what it meant to abide in God.

Steven couldn't seem to get enough of reading the Bible. "If the world hates you, keep in mind that it hated me first." Steven observed, "I already know what that feels like," he said, "People look down on me now like I'm a piece of trash. Oh some of them feel pity, but I can see in their eyes what most of them are thinking."

"That was the old you," Eli responded, "God has made you a new creation and in Him you will be hated, but not because you are a drunk, but because you will shine God's light and in doing so you will reveal the evil deeds done in the dark. It had been this way since the day Jesus rose from the dead. People will either accept the message, or reject it. When they reject it they hate the messenger. Regardless, God loves you so it doesn't matter what folks think of you."

Steven nodded and continued his reading. He was hungry for the words that he was reading and when he had finished the chapter, he went back to the beginning of First John and read until daylight waned and he could no longer see the print. Eli answered his questions as they came and when his reading time came to an end, Steven was silent.

"Is everything alright?" Eli queried.

"I'm just wondering how I am going to understand all this when you are not here to explain it."

"The Holy Ghost will be there to help you to understand. Just ask for wisdom."

"The Holy Ghost?" Steven questioned.

"After Jesus rose from the dead, He promised His followers that He would send a helper. He sent the Holy Ghost, the Spirit of God. He lives inside of us. Everyone who accepts Jesus as their Savior also receives the Holy Ghost." Eli smiled. "Steven, you have the Holy Ghost living inside of you." With that sentence, he felt totally worn out and laid back, closing his eyes.

Steven picked up their tin plates, scrubbing them off with sand to clean them and settled them on a flat rock at the edge of the fire. He did the same with the frying pan. Then he banked the fire and the two men bedded down for the night.

* * *

Daylight broke and Steven was on his way back to the water hole. He had left food and the last of the water with Eli and carried all of the empty water vessels.

He was back to camp before the heat of the day settled in. It was a lazy day of reading and discussion and Steven drank it all in, deliberately saturating his mind with God's word the way he had once saturated his body with alcohol.

CHAPTER SIX

Matt was up early, getting ready for one more trip into the desert in an attempt to find Eli and Steven. He had just cinched down his bedroll and supplies when gunshots rang out west of the office. Throwing his leg over his spare horse, he galloped toward the sound. He found several people milling about in front of the Wells Fargo Office. Quickly dismounting, he didn't have a chance to ask what happened, as he was inundated by onlookers.

"Marshal, they robbed the stage office!"

Matt ignored the improper title and motioned for people to calm down. "Is anyone hurt?"

The bearded clerk was obviously shaken. "I went for the shotgun under the counter and they fired a couple shots at me. I don't think I was hit." He laughed shakily, "Got a few splinters in the face though."

"Do you have a description? What did they get and which way did they go?" Matt was all business at this point.

"Eighteen dollars! They almost killed me for eighteen dollars! There were three of them and they went that way." He pointed down the street toward the west.

Matt began to organize a posse, specifically picking one man he knew was a good tracker. The rest of the men quickly gathered their gear and soon the hunt was on. Unfortunately, they were heading in the opposite direction of where Matt really wanted to be.

* * *

After breakfast, Steven looked up at the darkening sky with a worried expression. "I don't like the looks of that," he commented.

Eli followed his gaze, "Yeah, it looks rather ominous" he replied.

"If the wind kicks up, we won't have much protection. I noticed an outcropping of rocks nearer the water hole which would give us a whole lot more cover than here. Are you up for a ride?"

"You get me into the saddle and I'll make it," came the reply.

Steven quickly broke down camp and loaded the pack mule. He helped Eli onto the horse, but felt concern when he saw how much pain he was in. His face was grey. "Are you sure you can make it?"

Eli gave him a sickly smile, "The hardest part is done. Let's ride."

Steven took the halter in hand and began walking, praying for his friend as he went. He was worried, he did not want them to be caught in the open if the sky opened up. The spot he was thinking of had an overhang of rock to provide shelter. He had a tarp strapped on the mule. He was pretty sure it was a cover for one of the old Conestoga Wagons that had been stowed away behind the livery.

Now he kept his eyes peeled for some branches or small downed trees he could use for support poles, and prayed that God would give him time to set up the shelter. As he led the horses, he kept one eye on Eli, who was half conscious in the saddle. At least he was staying upright.

Steven spied a small log, not much more than a stick. It was about ten feet long and three inches in diameter. He tied a rope from the mule to the pole and let it drag behind. Under the darkening clouds he found three more similar pieces of wood. With the four poles, he arrived at the spot he had scoped out.

Eli was hanging on, but the ride had been hard on him. Steven helped him down as gently as he could and laid him down on his bed roll under the rocky outcrop. He quickly hobbled the horse and mule and then grabbed the poles.

He leaned them against the outcrop and climbed to the top with the canvas tarp. He rolled it out and grabbed a bunch of large rocks to pin down the upper edge of the canvas. Once he had the top secured down, he rolled the tarp down the poles.

The wind was starting to pick up and the bottom edge began to flap around. Steven scrambled down as fast as he could and used some pieces of latigo to tie the corners of the tarps to the bottom of the poles. He gathered more small boulders and piled them around the base of the sticks to hold them into place.

Though the skies threatened a downpour, the rain still held off. He climbed back to the top and piled as many rocks as he could find along the top edge. He was confident none of the rocks would fall on them since the top of the out crop sloped away from the edge. If any of the rocks rolled away, they might lose their covering, but they would not be crushed.

He made sure Eli was beneath the tarp and comfortable. The first big drops of rain began to fall as Steven grabbed the supplies off the mule. It was coming down in sheets before he was all done, but the food and blankets were dry. Steven had chosen the spot well. They were on high enough ground so they were not in danger of flash floods. Instead, the rocks around them gave them shelter. Using the bundle of dry wood he had brought along, Steven started a fire.

His makeshift shelter let some water in, but the overhang gave them a dry area to rest. Steven knew the ride had been hard on Eli, but he also knew had they stayed where they were, he would have gotten soaking wet and in his friend's compromised condition, that could have been deadly. Steven was worried, but he also knew he had made the right choice to move their camp.

The rain and winds wailed and pounded against the canvas. In the midst of the storm, Eli slept from exhaustion and Steven gratefully tended the crackling fire.

When a gust of wind blew an upper corner of the tarp loose Steven ran out and re-pinned it, adding a couple of extra heavy rocks before sprinting back to cover. He was soaked to the skin and chilled to the bone, but the fix worked. Huddling close to the fire, he let its warmth slowly sink into his bones.

The storm lasted a little over an hour and as suddenly as it had started, it ended and the sun appeared as if nothing had happened.

Steven stepped from under the tarp to assess the damage, but thankfully there was hardly any to speak of. Their pots and pans and some of the canned goods were wet, but the stuff which mattered was mostly dry.

He laid out everything in the sun, then ventured out to gather up a bunch of wood from the surrounding area. The wood was wet so he arranged it in the sun to dry. He located a few pieces which had been sheltered and were not sopping wet. Those he put on the coals and the flames began to lick around them. It had been hours since breakfast, so he dug into the supplies and pulled out some smoked meat and a can of beans. He used his knife to open the beans and soon the smell of frying food filled the shelter.

Eli spoke up, "I can't even begin to tell you how much I appreciate what you have done and what you are doing for me. You are a true friend."

Steven was embarrassed at the words of praise. "Don't mention it," He tried to shrug it off.

But Eli was not going to let it go. "Steven, if you had not found me, I would be dead now. In the Bible, Jesus tells the story of the Good Shepherd who leaves the ninety nine sheep to go look for one lost sheep. Jesus is the Good Shepherd. But you, when you came looking for me, you followed in His footsteps without even knowing it. He found you and you found me. All in all, I think that everyone wins this one." He lifted himself cautiously onto one elbow. "You have proven yourself to be my true brother."

Steven reflected on it for a moment before replying, "Amen."

* * *

Early in the afternoon, Matt and the posse located the three men, they were boys really, after they'd lost a horse to a broken leg and had to double up. They were not savvy enough to hide their trail and they had worn their horses down too quickly at the beginning of their run. The youthful bandits never really had a chance to get away, as the posse stayed at a steady ground eating pace which strangely reminded Matt of the story of the Tortoise and the Hare. The boys who were just past the mid-teens in age, surrendered without any kind of a real fight. By the time the posse caught up with them, they had been unable to flee because their two horses had been used up.

The storm that had raged around Eli and Steven totally eluded the posse. They rode into town late that night, just past midnight--choosing to ride back to town instead of camping under the stars with three prisoners.

Matt led the three teens to the jail house and locked them up while the rest of the posse split up and went home, or went to the saloon to celebrate their capture and brag to each other about their adventure.

"Sheriff, what's going to happen to us now?" The fear was evident in the young man's eyes.

Matt answered, "The Judge is going to have to decide that, son."

"I ain't never done nothin' like this before." The boy was close to tears.

"I'm sure that will be taken into account when the time comes. In the meantime, y'all get some sleep." He threw a bedroll into the cell. "One of you'll have to sleep on the floor since we only have two beds. I'll be back in the morning to check on you and bring you breakfast."

One of the other boys responded, "I ain't hungry."

"Come morning, you will be."

"Hey, I need to use the outhouse." The third one finally spoke up.

Matt pointed toward the corner. "That's what the bucket there is for. Don't miss or you'll be mopping that cell in the morning. Good night boys." He double checked the lock on the cell and walked out to the other room. He made sure the chain was in place across the rifles in the rack and that the guns he had taken off the boys were locked in the cabinet. Once he was satisfied all was secure, he stepped outside and locked the door. He was hungry and Becky would be in bed, so he headed towards Sam's place.

Once there, he spied several of his posse drinking at the bar. Sam saw him and motioned him over to the end of the bar, away from the crowd. "I know you've been busy with robbers and what not, but have you heard anything on Eli, or Steven?"

"No, nothing yet," He sighed. "I had planned on going out there this morning, but duty called."

"I know. After that rain, there won't be any tracks to follow either." Sam slapped a hand onto the bar. "Now, Sheriff, what can I get you?"

"You have anything to eat around here?" Matt was ravenous.

"Got some bean stew on the stove and some cornbread in the cupboard. Will that do for you?"

"That sounds great. I'll have a beer as well."

Sam poured the beer, which Matt carried over to the nearest table. Sam dished up a large bowl of the thick savory stew. He grabbed a big piece of sweet cornbread, slapped a big slab of butter alongside on the plate before bringing them over and setting the meal down in front of Matt.

Matt took a bite of the stew and was pleasantly surprised. He looked up at Sam and said, his mouth full of the stuff, "Good grief. Where did you learn to cook? This is delicious!"

Sam laughed. "My mother didn't have daughters and I was the youngest of the boys, so my chores were things around the house, while my dad took my older brothers out to the field. My Ma taught me to cook when I was young and when she died, I took over all the household chores, including the cooking."

"You should be a chef at a fancy restaurant in 'Frisco, not tending a bar here in Scorpion Wells."

Sam beamed at the praise. "Yeah, but here I am my own boss."

"Sure, with long days and no time off," Matt joked.

"I 'spose, but I like it."

Matt grinned at him, "My guess is the town is the better off for it."

Sam moved away to help other customers and Matt dug into the food, polishing it off in short order. He had just about finished his beer when Sam returned with another plate holding a large piece of chocolate cake, "I had been saving the last piece for a midnight snack," he patted his rather large belly, "but I figure you can use this more than I."

Matt thanked him profusely, as he eagerly forked a piece of the luscious cake into his mouth. After he was finished he leaned back, full and content. He realized how important it was to tell people when they were doing a good job, but had never really thought of the return benefits of a compliment until now. He had been sincere in his appreciation of Sam's cooking and the payoff was delicious. He grinned. It had been a long time since he'd had cake.

It was high time he was moving, he thought to himself. Matt laid some coins down on the bar to pay for the food. Sam started to dig out his change, but Matt stopped him. "Sam, that piece of cake was worth way more than what I paid you. Thank you." He paused, then asked, "I have three prisoners to feed in the morning. Are you up for cooking breakfast for them?"

Sam grinned, "Sure as long as you don't need it too early."

Matt returned the smile, "its way better food than what they deserve," he said. "But it'll be worth the wait. See you in the morning."

He walked back to the jail house and bedded down on a cot in the outside room. No sooner did his head hit the pillow and he was fast asleep.

* * *

The sunlight was streaming through the window when screams from the jail cell awoke him. Matt bolted out of bed, grabbed his pistol from its holster and quickly unlocked the door leading back to the cell.

Two of the boys were cowering in the corner. The third was hanging from the jail door bars. The boy had looped his belt around one of the bars and over top of one of the horizontal supports, so that it was about five feet off the floor. He had buckled it into place and then put the loop around his neck. With his back against the bars, he had sagged down into the belt, cutting off his wind until he was dead.

'God help me.' Matt took one look at the blue face and bulging eyes and knew there was no helping the boy. His two friends crouched together in the corner, sobbing and whimpering.

Matt stepped out of the room to get help as one of the boys cried, "Don't leave us here." Ignoring his pleas, he hurriedly dressed and rushed to the home of the undertaker. He pounded on the door until it swung open. The man was fully dressed, but his messy hair gave away the fact that he had just gotten out of bed.

Matt quickly explained the situation and together they hurried back to the jail.

The Sheriff unlocked the cell and placed hand irons on the traumatized boys before he let the undertaker inside. The mortician lifted the body and Matt unbuckled the belt, keeping an eye on the other two prisoners, but there was no need. They were in too much shock over the death of their friend to try anything.

Once the body was removed and the cell locked up, Matt helped carry the body to the undertaker's office.

Still aware of the two prisoners he had to care for, Matt headed to Sam's place. He walked through the door to find Sam was already at the stove, cooking. He glanced up, with a cheerful, "Good morning Sheriff." He poured a cup of coffee and headed Matt's way, setting the steaming cup on the table.

He did a double take at the look on the sheriff's face and asked, "Matt, what's the matter?"

Matt felt unutterably weary as he answered, "One of my prisoners hung himself last night." He shook his head. "He was just a boy."

Sam's eyes opened wide in surprise. "How'd he get the rope?"

"He used his belt. Let his britches drop down around his knees and hung himself with his belt." Matt sighed. He really wanted to see Becky right now, talk to her, hug her and hold her close, but he had responsibilities. "What makes a kid like that hang himself?"

Matt felt Sam's hand on his shoulder. "You never know what demons a man is carrying with him. It's not your fault. Every man is responsible for his own actions and, according to Eli, each of us will have to answer to our Maker for our own decisions. You've got to stop eating yourself up over this."

"Thanks Sam, I appreciate the thought and I know you're right, but that boy was my responsibility. All I was worried about last night was making sure they didn't break out of the jail. Now I have a dead sixteen year old and, if I can find them, I have to answer to his parents for what he did."

Sam dished up two plates of food and Matt laid the money on the counter to pay for them. Sam stopped him. "Let me get you a plate too. You've had a rough night." Matt reached for another coin, but Sam held up his hand. "It's on me." Matt left with the three plates on a tray and carried it back to the Jail.

* * *

Steven woke to a sudden noise and as he reached for the rifle, Eli's voice stopped him. "It won't look good if you shoot me after you saved me."

"What are *you* doing up?" Steven protested, as he realized Eli was out of his bedroll, squatting down next to the fire.

"I can't just lay around forever," Eli explained. "I figured I would get up and move around, try to rebuild my strength." He placed another stick on the crackling fire, then stood up slowly, groaning with the effort.

"Well, just don't overdo it," Steven bossed, "cause if you get worse, we'll run out of food before I can get you back to town."

"How much food do we have?"

Steven pondered a moment. "I think we can last a week, if neither of us gets too piggy."

"Well then, I promise not to get too piggy," came the reply.

* * *

Matt went to the telegraph office and sent out a message to the town Marshall where the dead boy hailed from. He asked the Marshall to make the notification to the young man's parents.

Next he went to the head of the town Council and obtained authorization to hire a couple of deputies to guard the prisoners. He located a couple of men he knew from church, men he trusted to keep an eye on the boys--who would not torture them before their trial. The robbery had provided some excitement for most of the town folks, but some of them were still really sore about it. Matt wanted to make sure the prisoners got a fair trial.

Most of the morning was gone by the time he finished. He mounted up and headed home to his wife. She was a comfort to him—he loved the faint aroma of vanilla which seemed to follow her. With a cup of coffee that she gave to him, he filled her in on what had happened since he had last seen her.

"We need to pray about this," Becky said in her soft voice. They knelt down by their chair in reverence and together they lifted up the worries and concerns which were troubling Matt. They asked for God's protection for Eli, that Steven could be located and that he would not be in trouble--even though Matt was reasonably certain that he was. They prayed for comfort over the parents of the young boy whose body was laid out at the undertakers.

Matt stood up and realized he felt at peace.

Becky made him sit down as she prepared an early lunch. While he ate, she drew him a hot bath. Although the thought of a bath in the middle of the day seemed ludicrous, it provided some much needed rejuvenation, and as he relaxed in the tub, he marveled at the incredible woman God had given to him as his wife.

With a full stomach, a warm bath, a fresh set of clean clothes and spiritual refreshment, Matt knew he could face the remainder of the day.

Before he climbed onto his horse, he turned to his wife and took her in his arms. "Thank you. I'm sorry that work has interfered so much lately."

She drew back and gave him a big smile. "I hate it when you are away so much, but I love it when you are here. Just be safe and hurry back." She gave him another hug and in return he gave her a passionate kiss, lingering as long as he could.

She finally pushed him away, gently. "You keep that up and you are never going to get back to work."

He sighed and stepped back. "I love you so much. I will try my hardest to be back for dinner."

He rode to the telegraph office to see if there was a reply. The telegrapher handed him a slip of paper with a short message acknowledging the boy's parents had been notified. They were on their way to retrieve the boy's effects. The body would not last long in the heat, so the undertaker was already digging a grave.

As he left the telegraph office, he noticed Rob Handy riding out of town, heading east along the railroad tracks. Intrigued, Matt mounted his horse and watched him fade off into the distance. When he could no longer see the gunman, he turned toward the livery.

He got two horses from Adam then stopped at the jail and quickly threw together food and gear for a couple of days. Regretfully, he arranged for a message to be sent to his wife, then returned to the edge of town where he began to follow Rob's tracks. He wanted to see what the man was up to, and besides, he needed to get his saddle from the spot where he had cached it.

He retrieved the saddle in the early afternoon and put it on the spare horse, then resumed tracking the man ahead of him. He rounded an outcropping of rock only to hear the hammer cock on a pistol. He mentally cursed himself for getting careless, but carefully rested his hands on the pommel of the saddle, not wanting to give the man a reason to shoot.

"Why are you followin' me?" The voice was behind him and to the left.

Matt measured his words carefully. "I had to get my saddle I left behind the other day when my other horse went lame."

"I see you got your saddle, so why are you following me?" There was an edge to the gunman's voice.

"I've been out searching for a couple of missing men and you just happen to be going in the same direction as me." It was a partial truth and considering the circumstances, Matt felt he was justified in telling it that way. Rob Handy had no right to be holding a gun on him, but right or wrong, if he pulled the trigger Matt would be just as dead. He really wanted to stay alive.

Matt slowly turned the horse so he was looking down the barrel of the gun. Though he didn't feel that way, he nonchalantly rested his forearms on the pommel. He did not want to provoke the man into shooting. "Why are you riding out here?" he queried.

"That's none of your business."

"My riding along here was none of your business, but you've made it your business. I figure turnabout is fair play."

A smile suddenly danced across the gunman's face, still the muzzle of the gun never wavered. "I reckon you got a point there." There was a long pause, then Rob continued. "I was lookin' for a man myself."

"To help him, or to hurt him." Matt asked.

The smile disappeared and the gunman's eyes narrowed. "Don't go pushing your luck."

"Listen Rob," Matt replied, "I don't want to die here. You don't want the law to be chasing you for killing a sheriff. Why don't you holster your gun and we can talk. You know you're much faster on the draw than I am and you can also see the thong is still over the hammer of my gun, so I could never get it out in time. It makes me a bit nervous to have that thing pointed at me."

The gun remained pointed right at his chest.

Matt explained, "Eli disappeared a couple of days ago and I am trying to figure out where he went." He knew he was taking a risk, because if Rob had anything to do with Eli's disappearance he would probably shoot him out of the saddle. On the other hand, if he didn't have anything to do with it, he might relax. The tactic worked. Handy eased the hammer back down on the Colt and slid it into his holster but he left his hand resting on his thigh, only inches from the weapon.

"I've been wondering about him too."

The surprise must have shown on Matt's face.

He continued, "A couple of Sunday's ago, I went to his church. He stood up for me even though he knows about me. He could have snubbed me, but he didn't. A standup guy like that deserves ...." He left the sentence hanging.

Matt was startled to see the man cared.

"What makes you think he's out here?" Matt asked.

"There's talk about town. You ridin' this way a while back. I just put two and two together."

"Well, we are wasting time here. I'll make a deal with you, Rob. I give you my word I will not raise a hand, or a gun against you, if you will promise to do the same."

Once again, there was a long pause as the gunman considered the offer. Finally, he extended his hand. "Your word is good enough for me." Out west, where a handshake sealed many a deal, Matt knew Rob would be good for it. With that, the unlikely duo rode east, searching for tracks, or signs. Anything to tell them what had happened to the man they searched for.

When night fell they made camp. They ate without words and when everything had been cleaned up, they sat around the fire. Matt noticed Rob did not stare into the fire and neither did he. To do so would ruin his night vision. Such a mistake could cost a man his life out here.

"Why did you become a sheriff?" Matt was taken aback by Rob's question.

"I kind of fell into it. I was offered the job because I was a decent hand with a gun and the town council felt I had common sense. It turns out I'm pretty good at the job, although I have run into some opposition here, for not arresting you."

It was Rob's turn to be surprised by the candid response. "And why haven't you?"

"You're too good with a gun and no one is willing to risk their own skin to help. Besides, you haven't done anything in my jurisdiction, so as long as you stay out of trouble here, I can afford to turn a blind eye. That having been said, I hope you will not do anything to change that."

Matt could see the gleam of the fire on Rob's teeth as he smiled. "I'll do my best, so long as no one else gets stupid."

The conversation lulled and the fire died down. In short order, the men bedded down for the night.

Dawn found them riding out together, each of them casting about for signs of the missing man. Late in the morning, they came upon the small grove where Eli and Steven had camped. The heavy rains had washed away any tracks, but the charred wood told a story, making it clear someone had recently camped there, but there was no evidence of whom.

Matt got down and began to poke around the fire pit area, without any definitive results.

Rob watched from the saddle and when Matt stood up, Rob spoke up. "Anything that can help us?"

Matt scanned the country side before answering. "Nothing. This is a big country and I don't know this area that well." He looked around once more then spoke again, "How is your water holding out?"

Rob held up his canteen, judging the contents by its weight. "Today at most...if we don't find a watering hole."

"Do you know of any?" Matt asked.

"I'm too new to this country. I heard tell of some north of here, but those were just vague descriptions."

Matt nodded. He was encouraged by their find of the camp site, but the lack of leads dampened his enthusiasm. That, and their need for water. He was afraid for Eli, but like he'd already said aloud, it was a big country and without definite leads, it was a crapshoot.

Rob was the one who saw it.

"Look." He said, pointing into the sky.

Up above, the men saw vultures circling in the pale blue sky.

Matt threw his leg over his horse. "Let's check it out."

It was another hour before they located the cause for the circling birds. A mule lay on the desert sand, partially devoured by the coyotes. The birds were just waiting their turn.

Together the men checked out the animal and determined it was wild. Over the years, mules had been released or escaped from the silver miners and had banded together in the wilderness. They had grown into a formidable herd of animals out in the desert. This animal was not shod and there was no marks on its coat indicating it had ever carried a pack. This led them to the conclusion it was one of the wild animals.

Rob said what Matt was already thinking. "We need to head back, or we're going to end up like this mule...buzzard bait."

Matt nodded his agreement and they began the long journey back to town.

The next day, Matt faced the unpleasant task of talking to the dead boy's parents. They got off the morning train and came straight to the office. As soon as they walked through the door, Matt's heart went out to them. They appeared to be in their forties, with greying hair and their faces bore deep lines of a hard life, coupled with grief. The woman was plump, but her hands told a story of years of hard work. The man was bone thin, with calloused hands and a weathered face evidencing too much sun and long days of manual labor.

The boy's mother was sobbing while his father was trying his best to hold back his tears. In spite of his efforts, a tear would escape from his brimming eyes and trickle down his cheek as Matt explained the robbery, the arrest and then how he had found the boy hanging in his cell.

When he finished telling the story, being as gentle he could be in that circumstance, he opened one of his desk drawers and took out the boy's things: a folding knife, a couple of coins and a button which was missing from his shirt. Then he opened another drawer in his desk and removed the boy's pistol, which he handed over to the man.

He pointed them toward the grave site, a hill outside of town where strangers and the poor were buried.

Matt watched them as they walked together, toward their son's final resting place. His heart caught as he noted their sorrow and how they held onto one another.

He found himself wishing he could've had Eli there to help with the ordeal. Maybe the preacher would have had the right words to ease the pain of the parents. All Matt knew was he felt like he had done a poor job of dealing with them. He wiped his own tear away as he entered his office and closed the door.

* * *

Eli was true to his word. He didn't do anything stressful enough to re-injure the ribs, but he continued to get exercise so his healing progressed impressively. On the eighth day after the attack, Steven took stock of their supplies.

"We are going to have to head back soon." He informed his friend. "Our food is going to run out in the next day or so and I think I have chased off most the game close by." Steven had supplemented their food supply with a few rabbits, but they were getting scarce now. Even the coyotes seemed to know to stay out of rifle range, not that either of the men were anxious to eat coyote meat.

Eli nodded, "I anticipated that. I'm ready to ride back whenever you are."

Steven arranged the remaining gear so he could ride the mule and Eli could ride the horse. They could still get most of the gear back with them, stowing it behind their saddles. A few non-essential items they cached under the overhang to come back and get later.

It was mid-morning before they were on their way. They made it to the railroad tracks well before noon and got in another hour of riding before seeking a shady spot for lunch. They ate without much conversation and once everything was put away they made the decision to wait out the heat of the day before going any further. There would be moonlight tonight and much better travelling so now was the time to rest.

"What are you going to do when we get back?" Steven asked quizzically.

"What do you mean?"

"What are you going to do about those men, the ones who jumped you?"

Eli sighed. "I've been doing a lot of thinking... and praying on it. My human nature wants to hunt them down and make them pay for what they did. Yet God's word tells us to forgive. It took me a long time, but I finally came to the conclusion that I will leave them in the hands of the law. I'll talk to Sheriff Wheaton after we return and let him figure it out. Me? I'll go back to preaching God's word. There are still a lot of men and women who need to find Jesus and as long as there is breath left in me, I will be teaching about Him."

Steven nodded his understanding. "I know what you mean, I want to kill those guys myself, but after reading the Bible, I see how important it is to forgive folks who've hurt me or the people I care about."

Eli smiled. His face was almost healed but now it was covered with a decent growth of beard and he looked older than his years. "After all God has forgiven me for, you'd think forgiveness would be second nature. Yet here I am after all these years, struggling to forgive those who've wronged me. I guess it goes to show being a Christian is a growing process every day of life. Each day, I have to surrender my will to the Lord so he can work through me."

Steven looked up at him. "That's good to know. I feel like I am unworthy. How could God ever use a man like me?"

Eli looked at him, compassion warm in his eyes. "You are unworthy. Steven, I'm unworthy. There is none who are worthy and yet God chooses to use us. It is only the folks who recognize that, who are really usable. As soon as you start to think God chose you because of how great you are, you become worthless. My friend, it is only by God's grace we can be used by Him and I believe God is going to use you in a tremendous way!"

"I hope so," Steven replied, "I feel like so much of my life has been wasted. I want the rest of it to count for something."

Eli clasped a hand on Steven's shoulder. "As long as you are willing to be used by God, He will do so. Every day, my prayer is that God will open doors for me to share the Gospel--the good news, with folks. I ask that He will choose to use me every day. Much of the time, it seems He does just that." He grimaced as a jolt of pain shot through his ribs. "...Even these last few days, I've been all banged up and seemingly useless, yet He brought you to me and let me disciple you."

Steven nodded his agreement, "I am blessed I have had the opportunity to learn so much in such a short time." He had read through most of the New Testament during the previous week and even though there was much he still didn't understand, he had learned a mountain full. "I want to be baptized when we get back. I want people to know what Jesus has done for me."

"Steven, we will make sure that is one of the first things we do." Eli couldn't have wiped the smile off his face, even if he'd wanted to.

The men napped the afternoon away so they would be fresh for their ride later that night. As the cool of the evening set in, they mounted their steeds and began the long ride home.

CHAPTER SEVEN

"Sheriff, you got to see this." The man burst through the door of the sheriff's office, trying hard to catch his breath.

Matt grabbed his gun belt, slung it around his waist, buckled it into place and then grabbed his hat. He stopped at the doorway and glanced around before following the man who had run ahead.

There, riding past in the early morning light were two men. It only took a moment for it to register who they were. Steven, riding in the lead sat upright and confident. To his right and slightly behind him was Eli, slumped in the saddle, looking like he had definitely seen better days.

They rode past and slowly stopped in front of the doctor's office. Steven dismounted and tied the mule to the rail. Matt ran the block and a half, arriving just as Steven was pounding on the door.

The doctor's door swung open and the doctor was pulling a suspender up over his shoulder. "What do we have goin' on here," he demanded.

"I need you to look at my friend here." As Steven addressed the man, he gestured to where Eli slumped against the neck of his horse.

Doctor Mercer stared at Steven for several moments before turning his attention to Eli.

Matt was already helping his friend down off the horse. When his feet were on the ground, he slung one of Eli's arms around his shoulder. Eli winced, but uttered no sound.

"Careful," Steven called out, "His ribs are all banged up." He hurried to help Matt and together they maneuvered Eli into the doctor's office.

"He got beat up a while back." Steven explained. "He's been doing pretty well, but we had a long ride to get to town and it has taken its toll."

Doc Mercer looked at Steven while he was talking, as though he couldn't believe what was right before his eyes.

"I think he has some busted ribs. He had cuts and bruises, but most of those have healed up. He ain't had a fever for well over a week now." Steven kept talking as though he didn't notice the man's open mouthed expression.

"Let's get him over onto the cot there." The Doc suddenly regained his composure and turned his attention to his patient. He probed along

Eli's ribs and when Eli groaned, he undid the buttons of his shirt, opening it up. He looked over the bandages wrapped tightly around his torso and turned to Steven.

"Did you do this?" He asked.

Steven nodded.

"Well, you did exactly the right thing. There's not much more I can do for him. What he needs now is bed rest."

As it was, Eli was already snoring on the cot, exhausted after the night's ride.

Doc Mercer covered him with a blanket. "Well, as long as I don't have any other patients, I guess he can sleep here for now."

Steven nodded again. "Thanks Doc. I'll be back to check on him later."

Matt interjected at this juncture. "Steven, I need to see you in my office."

"Yes sir, I'll be right there as soon as I care for the animals."

Matt turned to the doctor. "Doc, can you send for me as soon as he is awake? I need to talk to him, clear some things up."

"Of course Sheriff, as soon as he is able," came the promise.

Matt hung around until Steven stepped outside and then spoke to Doc Mercer. He pointed to the sleeping figure on the cot. "How bad is he?"

"He looks to be in pretty good shape, just worn out from the trip. I don't know how far he had to ride, you'll have to ask Steven about that, but it appears he's been well cared for." He paused and then continued, "Setting that aside, I would really like to know what happened to Steven. I haven't seen him sober in years! You saw him! He's a changed man! I would really like to know what happened." He repeated, murmuring, almost as if he were talking to himself.

Matt shook his head. "I don't know, but you can be sure I'll find out. Mark my words. Thanks Doc." He turned and walked out the door and headed back to his office.

Matt checked on the two boys who were still waiting on the judge to show up and bring them to trial. He talked to them for a couple of minutes, trying to put them at ease. He recognized that being in jail was scary, especially since they were hardly grown. He didn't have any desire to make things worse for them by treating them harshly. When he returned to the front room, Steven was standing there, hat in hand.

Matt motioned to a chair and then sat down behind the desk.

"You know, you caused quite a commotion in this town," Matt began, "There've been people looking for the two of you for quite some time now. What happened?"

With Matt asking a pertinent question every once in a while to fill in any gaps, Steven filled him in on most of what had occurred. After Steven had given him the run down on the attack and what he knew, Matt changed the course of the questioning.

"Steven, I have to ask now, what's happened to you? Two weeks ago, you were the town drunk, yet here you sit in my office, stone cold sober."

"I'm afraid you wouldn't believe me." Steven replied.

"Try me." Came the response.

Steven paused, collecting his thoughts on how he wanted to tell the story. Finally he began.

"You know when Eli came to town, he made time to get to know me and to care for me. He would give me food and coffee. Every Sunday morning he took it upon himself to wake me, clean me up and feed me. Then he would practice his sermon out on me, even though half the time I was still so drunk or hung over, I could barely understand most of what he was telling me.

"Sheriff, that didn't matter to him, he just kept on trying to get through to me. He never looked at me with pity nor distain. He treated me like a real person, like I mattered." He paused then launched into the rest of his story. "One night, about two weeks ago, I heard two men come into the stable and they were talking about putting Eli on a train after they beat him up. I was so drunk I couldn't do anything about it that night. By the time I sobered up, I wasn't able to find anyone to help me, so I went out on my own."

Matt interrupted him, "I know you bought supplies, where did you get the money?"

Steven hesitated to tell the truth, because the truth was he'd stolen it. But after what God had done for him he could not bring himself to lie. "I took it from Eli's shed."

"I know you bought four bottles of whiskey. Did you use his money for that as well?"

This time Steven did not hesitate. "Yes... I had a half a bottle from the night before and it just didn't seem to be enough. Some cowboy felt sorry for me that night and bought me a bottle."

"Go on with your story," Matt urged.

"I bought the supplies, borrowed Eli's horse and mule and went out after him. I knew the railroad bull would throw him off the train when he was discovered and I figured I could help him. I made it part of the day without a drink, but I kept thinking about those bottles I had with me. I knew if I got drunk, I would never be able to help Eli. But the need to take a drink of that whiskey was overwhelming. I finally prayed God would take away my desire to drink. He didn't seem to hear my prayer, I still wanted that whiskey. I was dying to take a drink."

Fascinated, Matt leaned forward. "So what happened?"

"I got mad at God. I screamed at Him, claiming that He didn't care. I got the whiskey out of my saddle bag, and took a big swig. But then I got sick."

"You threw up?"

"Yeah, I threw it up. I tried again and I puked again. I haven't had a drink since."

"So you're saying it was a miracle." Matt sounded a bit dubious.

"Yes sir, a miracle. As much of a miracle as raising the dead. You see sheriff, in the last ten years, if I went without a drink for any length of time, I would get the shakes and I felt like I was going to die until I got another drink."

Steven continued, "I stopped drinking...Jesus saved me from drinking. In one moment I went from fierce craving and uncontrollable shaking to no desire and a steady hand. You ask Eli. My life has changed and it started with a bona fide miracle."

Matt shook his head. "Wow. That's an incredible story. I'm certainly happy for you. To tell you the truth, I never liked to see you the way you were."

"I never liked that man either," Steven confided. "I just never realized it until he was gone. I gave my life to Jesus that day and I don't ever plan on looking back."

"Welcome back to the land of the living." Matt grinned at him. "What are your plans now?"

"I don't know. I reckon I'll work at the stable for now until I figure that out."

"Well thanks for coming in and answering my questions. By the way, Adam has been looking for you. You might want to hunt him down. I think he was worried about you."

"Thanks sheriff." Steven stood up. "You know where to find me if you have any more questions."

Matt had been a skeptical about the story at first, but after thinking it over, he realized if Jesus could do miracles while He was on this earth, why should he be surprised to hear He had performed a miracle in the here and now. Besides, there simply was no other explanation for Steven being sober!

Most of the day had passed before a young boy entered the Sheriff's Office to tell Matt that Eli was awake. Once more, Matt made the trip to the doctor's office. He knocked on the door, then entered at the summons from within.

Eli was sitting in a chair, eating some soup. "Sheriff," he said in way of greeting.

"Well, you look a little better than you did this morning. How are you feeling?"

"All things considered, I'm feeling pretty good."

Matt was surprised, "Really? You looked like death warmed over this morning."

"I don't doubt that," came the reply, "but the truth is that I should be dead. If it wasn't for Steven, I would be."

Matt nodded, "Yeah, I got his side of the story and I wanted to hear what happened from your point of view."

Now it was Eli's turn to be surprised "Why? I mean, I have a crime to report, but I thought I was the one who would be making the effort to talk to you, not the other way around."

Matt flashed a quick grin. "For a newcomer, you've made quite a splash in this town. I had quite a few people coming to me, worried about you: Sam, Adam and the widow Franco to name a few. Everywhere I go, someone is asking about you. Your disappearance caused a bit of a commotion."

Eli set the bowl down and picked up a cup of coffee. He took a sip, then carefully shifted his position and leaned back in the chair. Every move still brought shooting pain to the ribs. He began the story of how he was lured into the alley by a woman and being hit over the head. He told of waking up and at the same time being mistaken as a drunkard and thrown off the train. He described how he had been beaten up, broken and nearly dead when Steven found him and saved his life.

Matt sat silently until he finished, then asked, "Do you know who the woman in the alley was? How about the person who clobbered you?"

"That's the thing, something about her was familiar, but I can't place her. I never did see who hit me in the head."

"What was the motive? Did they rob you?" Matt pushed.

"They took my gun and gun belt, but left behind the few coins I had on me."

"Have you made any new enemies since you moved into town, or have you seen any old enemies since you came here?" Matt desperately wanted to get to the bottom of this.

"I haven't seen any of my old enemies around," Eli replied, "but it seems in recent days Brother Smith has taken an intense dislike to me. I'm sure you've heard the Sunday before I was ambushed, he showed up at the Saloon on a soap box and held a rally trying to run me out of town. Apparently I have upset his sense of propriety."

Matt rubbed his chin, "Interesting." He recalled the meeting he'd witnessed between Smith and the two drifters. He related the event to Eli, then said, "I recall those drifters hung around for a day or two after that, but then they disappeared. I supposed they rode out, although I could not say for sure when." He described the two men the best he could from recollection. "Does that sound like your attacker?"

Eli shook his head, "I can't tell you. I didn't see the man who hit me and the other man was on the ground, laying in such a way that I couldn't get a look at his face. I couldn't even tell you how tall or how old. He was a white man I think...he did have a vest on, light brown or tan." He thought on it a bit more. "His hat was on the ground, near him and it was darker brown than the vest, high crowned, but not a ten gallon hat." He sighed. "It all happened so quick...I just wish I could remember where I have seen that woman."

Matt jotted some notes on a piece of paper. He had an excellent memory, but he did not want to forget anything. He looked up thoughtfully at Eli, "I'm sure it will come to you. Just let me know when you do remember. In the meanwhile, you get yourself some rest."

"I will," Eli said. "By the way, what day is it today?"

"Sunday" came the reply, "I had to sit through another one of Brother Smith's sermon's on how wicked evil I am. I tried to get out of it, but you weren't here to take me to the other side of the tracks." He switched topics. "That reminds me, there's a group of cowboys who are anxious for you to resume your Sunday meetings."

Eli seemed surprised, "Really? I was beginning to think they only came because I was a novelty, you know, church in a saloon."

"I believe you've really got those boys thinking about their futures and what tomorrow holds. Don't give up on 'em. Every one of them needs what you've been sharing with them. I would encourage you to keep pushing along, don't get discouraged. One day, you will break through. Remember, they are as stubborn a lot as you will find. But once they accept what the truth is, it will be an amazing thing."

"It won't be me who turns them around," Eli cautioned. "That will be up to the Holy Ghost. I'm am still just the messenger."

"Well honestly, I wish Brother Smith would let the Holy Ghost do His work in that other church!" Matt stood to leave, "If you think of anything else about the assault, let me know."

"I will." Eli replied.

The door had just shut behind the Sheriff, when Eli remembered something. He called out but Matt was already gone. Still too sore to get up and try to catch him, Eli cataloged it away for their next meeting.

CHAPTER EIGHT

Matt rode home for dinner that night and shared with Becky the news of Eli and Steven's return. As he ate his meal, he asked Becky how her day was. He looked up from his plate just in time to see her eyes welling up with tears. Puzzled, he stood up and walked around the table to her.

"Honey, what's wrong?" He knelt down beside her chair and tenderly put his arm around her shoulders. With that gesture, her tears burst forth and he held his wife as she sobbed on his shoulder. When the tears slowed, Becky tried to explain her sorrow, but her hiccups interrupted every other word.

Matt helped her out of the chair and supported her as he walked with her to the front porch. There was a porch swing for them to sit together on. He wrapped her in the blanket kept there for chilly nights and sat there with her, comforting her.

He held Becky and through her sobs she told him of being pregnant and carrying their baby for close to seven weeks. She told him she how she had wanted to keep it secret until she was sure and how she had lost the baby that very morning. She had not intended on burdening him with the loss but the pain was too deep, the sorrow too intense.

When she tried to apologize, he hushed her and stroked her hair as she cried on his chest. He held her until she fell asleep and then he continued to hold her in his arms until the night chill crept in. When it was too cold on the porch to remain, he gently picked her up and carried her inside. He laid her on their bed, kissed her forehead and left the room.

Out in the living room, he knelt down and prayed.

* * *

Eli had just awakened from another nap when Doc Mercer brought him a cup of coffee. He got up off the cot and sat down in the arm chair.

Doc Mercer sat comfortably in another chair. An end table stood between them. The chairs were angled so they could easily converse, but not such that they stared straight at each other across the table. Eli took a sip of the steaming brew then sighed, enjoying the simple pleasure of a cup of coffee. Doc on the other hand was sipping from a small glass of amber liquid, whiskey Eli assumed.

"You certainly have stirred up a fuss in this here town." Doc finally ventured.

"Everyone keeps saying that," came the reply, "Yet I really have done nothing."

"Perhaps, you have just upset the status quo?"

Eli smiled and took another sip of coffee before answering. "How do you figure?"

"Well, around here folks figure a saloon is for drinking and sinning. Church is for confessing all the sinning and drinking."

"Isn't that selling the church short?"

It was Doc's turn this time, "How do *you* figure?"

"The purpose of the church goes far beyond confessing sins. It is there to build people up in their faith, teach them how to live a life which puts Jesus at the center. That way the need to confess sins becomes less and less. That's because as people learn to live that way they become more and more like Jesus."

Doc looked thoughtful, "I've never heard it put quite like that."

"Let me give you an example," Eli continued. "When a man is conscripted into the Army, they don't just hand him a pistol, a rifle and a saber and tell him to go out and fight the enemy. They train him to drill, to shoot, to fight, and then, after his basic training, they continue to hone his skills with continued drilling, training and fighting."

"Okay, but what's your point?"

"When a person accepts Jesus as their Savior, they are forgiven their sins – past, present and future. A person who lives for God becomes a new man and is conscripted into God's Army. But there are two battles going on when that happens. One is against the old sinful man, who wants to take over again and the other is against Satan, the devil. These are both spiritual battles, but they are fought on two different battlefields."

The doctor was curious. "What does this have to do with church?"

"I'm getting to that. When a person becomes a Christian, the only thing most people really understand is that they are saved from their sins and they are going to heaven. That is like the recruit joining the army. The next step in one's new found faith is to be taught about what that faith entails. The disciples were a group of men and women who followed Jesus..."

Doc Mercer broke in, "Women?"

"Yup. Some of Jesus' followers were women. A disciple would follow in the footsteps of their master, and the goal was to become just like the master. It is like the basic training a soldier receives. Going to church every week is the ongoing training, such as a soldier would need. Let me ask you this, where do you stand?"

"Stand on what? On you holding a church in a Saloon?"

"No. Where do you stand with Jesus?"

"Well, I was baptized when I was a young boy. I go to Brother Smith's church now and again, when my clientele don't keep me away." He winked at Eli.

Eli smiled at him, but kept pursuing it. "When you got baptized, did you make a decision to live for Christ, or did you do it because it was expected of you?"

"Actually, there was a travelling preacher come to our town and did a week of tent meetings. On the final night, he gave an invitation. My older brother got up and started down the aisle and, well, I just got up and followed him."

"How would you describe your decision today as you look back on it?" Eli asked.

"I don't know. I guess I would say it wasn't even my decision. I was just following my brother." Doc Mercer answered.

"Would you like to make that your decision now?"

"Right here," he held up his whiskey, "With this in my hand? I don't think so."

"Why not," Eli asked. "Is your life everything it should be or do you think that there could be more to life?"

Doc began to fidget uncomfortably. "I got me a good life."

"No doubt that you do, but do you have peace, and joy? Is your life fulfilling, or are you just living day to day until someday you die?"

"Well, I don't see you living any fulfilled life! Here you are in my office all banged up!" Doc was getting defensive. "You live in a shed out behind a saloon and you mop floors. How is that a 'fulfilled' life?"

Eli grinned, defusing the tension in the air. "You're right. Doc, from the outside, my life does not look fulfilling. But God never said living for Jesus was going to be easy and my life isn't easy. On the other hand, I get to speak into the lives of two dozen cowboys and saloon girls and I got to see a miracle happen in Steven's life. If I hadn't been beat up and thrown on that train, who knows if that miracle would have happened otherwise."

"Yeah," huffed the Doc. "Well time will tell if that miracle takes."

"I'll tell you what. Come to my church on Sunday, and I will buy you the first beer."

"Really!" He had the attention of the doctor now.

"Yes, really." Eli set the coffee cup down. "I would love to continue talking, but I need to use your out house."

"Out back," Doc Mercer directed.

Eli pushed the door shut on the outhouse after he finished, only to hear a voice greet him, "Welcome home." For the first time since returning, Eli wished he had his gun on his hip because the voice behind him was that of Rob Handy. He turned to face the gunman, unsure of what the man's mental state would be like today.

"Glad to see your back." Rob smiled, as though he genuinely meant what he was saying.

Eli was relieved and returned the smile. "Thank you, I'm glad to be back."

The gunman looked uncomfortable, like he wasn't sure what to say next. There was a long, awkward pause.

Eli was about to turn back toward Doc's Office, when Rob spoke. "Thank you."

Eli was puzzled, "For what."

"You stood up for me that one Sunday." Rob appeared extremely uncomfortable, but he pushed on. "You were ready to let one of them other men leave, just so I could stay. No one ever did anything like that for me before."

Eli took a step toward him. "Rob, I meant what I said that day. You are always welcome at my church. In fact, I would love to see you again. Come back on Sunday."

Rob held out his hand, "Thanks, I just might do that."

Eli shook his hand, "I need a couple days to get all my affairs lined up. If you come in on, say Friday morning, I'll cook you breakfast and we can talk, just you and me."

Rob nodded, "That sounds alright."

Eli smiled, "Eight o'clock?"

Rob nodded and then slipped away using great caution as he went between the buildings.

Eli studied on the turn of events as he walked back to the office. He settled his bill with Doc, which amounted to two bits for the use of the cot, a bowl of soup and a cup of coffee. He headed back to the Saloon to see if he still had a building to hold church in on Sunday.

Any doubts he had vanished the moment he saw Sam. His face lit up as Eli walked through the door. Sam rushed around the bar, giving Eli a big bear hug. Eli tried to protect his ribs without success. He groaned with pain and Sam quickly let him go.

"I'm so sorry! Are you alright?"

Eli moaned, "Well I was up until a half a second ago."

"I'm sorry." Sam repeated.

Eli chuckled cautiously, afraid to laugh out loud and cause himself more pain. "Don't worry about it. It's nice to know I was missed. How are you doing, my friend?"

Sam motioned to an empty table and Eli sat down slowly easing himself into the chair. Sam answered, "I'm good, but I did miss you. I didn't realize how much you've been doing around this place until after you were gone." He went to the stove and filled two cups with his fragrant coffee. He checked the other customers to make sure they had all they needed, then brought the steaming hot coffee to the table.

"What happened to you? I was worried about you. Matt told me you had come back, but Doc wouldn't let me in to see you. He said you were sleeping and he wasn't going to wake you up."

Eli grinned as he sipped his coffee, waiting for a moment to open up so he could tell his story. When Sam finally paused, he filled him in on what had happened. Sam listened to Eli's account and when he finished, Sam asked, "You have no idea who jumped you and threw you on that train?"

"Not the men, but that woman, I'm sure I've met her before. She was yelling for help--quick to run back into that alley way where it was dark. But I'm sure it will come to me. I just wish I could remember."

"Maybe you're just trying so hard to remember that you keep pushing it back into the depth of your mind. Try not to think about it and maybe it will come to you."

Eli nodded, "That's really good advice. I'll try to do that. In fact, what I need right now is a nice hot bath and a shave."

Sam stood up. "Stay right here, I'll be back."

He walked back behind the bar and opened the cash box, returning with a few bills in his hand. "I was going to give you this, but you went and got yourself shanghaied before I could. Business has been so good since I started serving meals that I may need to put on another hand here soon."

Eli thanked him. Then an idea occurred to him. "You know, I might know someone who would do a good job for you here."

"Who?" Sam was puzzled, wondering who he had in mind after being gone for close to two weeks.

"Steven."

"The town drunk?" Sam was incredulous.

"Not anymore." Eli explained what had happened to Steven on the trail and when he finished, Sam sat there shaking his head in disbelief.

"I don't know, even if he is a former town drunk, I don't believe working in a saloon would be the best fit for him."

"I know, but I think if he was back in the kitchen with you teaching him to cook like you do, he wouldn't be tempted to drink and he could learn a new trade. Let's face it, he's getting to old to be breaking horses for a living again. Just think on it. That's all I ask."

Sam nodded, "Okay, since you have such faith in him, I'll think about it." He stopped and pondered the notion for a moment, "We'll see."

Eli finished his coffee and stood up. "Are my things still back in the shed?"

"They are." Sam explained that he had gone through Eli's things with Matt and it would be a little messy because of it.

Eli brushed it off. He wasn't too worried about a little mess. He thanked Sam and went back to the shed. He located some clean clothes and slowly walked to the bathhouse down the street. With the help of the proprietor, he got the bandages unwrapped from his ribs, then eased himself down into the hot bath. As the heat worked its way into his sore muscles, he began to relax and let the tension and pain of the past couple of weeks slide away.

The next day, Eli took his dirty clothes to be laundered because he had been wearing them for way too long. Then he walked the short distance to the barber. When his beard had been removed and his hair cut, he felt like a new man, almost ready to face the world again.

He headed to the sheriff's office, but Matt was not in. Eli rubbed his freshly shaved chin as he pondered what his next move would be. He thought about going to the telegraph office and sending out his own messages, but he thought of Matt's earlier reaction when he took down the bank robbers and decided to leave the official business to his friend. Eli did not want to step on any toes.

Walking down the street, Eli smelled the delicious aroma of baked goods. He followed the scent and came upon a painted sign advertising a new bakery. He stepped through the door and was greeted by the fragrance of freshly baked cakes, pies and bread lining the shelves. It was then he spied something he had not seen in years, fried donuts. His mouth began to water as he moved up to the counter.

Elizabeth Franco came out of the back room to greet her customer. When she saw who it was her face lit up in a warm smile. "Mr. Exeter. It is so nice to see you."

Eli was taken aback, surprised she knew who he was, for she had been unconscious the last time he had seen her. He swept his hat off his head. "Ma'am, how are you doing?" The bullet wound on her face was healed, but the scar was going to be there for a long time. In spite of the scar, she was a lovely woman. It was evident to him that even though she could cook, she did not partake too much of her own goods, for she had maintained a trim, attractive figure.

She moved around the counter to place her hand on his forearm. "I owe you a debt of gratitude," she began. "Thank you so much."

Eli felt a bit embarrassed. "Ma'am, you don't owe me anything."

"Mr. Exeter, I was told the town had decided to give that reward money to me, but I know for certain it was you who should have received it. It wasn't the town's money to give away. I am in your debt and I know it. Without that money, I could never have started this bakery." She moved back around the counter and asked, "What can I get for you? It's on the house."

Eli smiled at her, the laugh lines deepening around his eyes. "One of those donuts would be wonderful."

She placed a donut on a dainty plate and poured him a cup of coffee. Motioning to a small table by the window she said, "Please have a seat." He placed his hat on a rack by the door and after he sat down, she asked, "May I join you?"

Eli stood up again, "By all means, Ma'am." He pulled the chair out for her and after she was seated he sat down as well. "You have made yourself a nice little shop here." There were lace curtains in the window and gingham coverings on all the tables. *All those nice touches a woman puts on a place. She had made the small shop into a lovely boutique.*

As he ate the donut she told him how, when the men of the town discovered she was going to start a bakery, they'd all pitched in to help clean and repair the building, so she could open her business in record time. She described how Becky Wheaton had helped her decorate the interior, so the place had a homey feeling.

"All that does not surprise me one bit," Eli offered. "I'm sure some of these single men have not seen a cake or cookie in a long time. I know this is the first donut I've had in years. How has business been since you opened up?"

"It has been extraordinary," she replied. "You just missed the morning rush and there will be another around noon time. These shelves will be empty by tonight, you mark my words." She was beaming as she talked. Eli was struck by the fact she used the phrase "you mark my words." It was one he liked to use. For some reason he was happy she liked to use it as well. Eli was also pleased she was making a go of the bakery.

When he tried to pay for his pastry, she quickly turned his money away.

"You keep your money." She said firmly. "As far as I am concerned, you're part owner of this business. You fronted the startup money. You come in anytime and get what you want. I won't ever charge you."

"Careful with an offer like that," countered Eli, "I might just eat up all of your profits. That was delicious."

She placed her petite hand on his arm and Eli felt a tingle, as he encountered a feeling he hadn't felt in a long time. "You come back anytime," she repeated with a shy smile.

Eli eased himself out of the chair, fetched his hat from the rack and said his goodbyes. He was excited and pleased to see her succeeding in the venture. He hoped she would continue to flourish.

He returned to the sheriff's office to find Matt seated behind the desk. "Eli, sit down. How are you feeling?"

Eli seated himself in the chair across the desk, "Well, let's see, I feel like I was brutally beaten a couple of weeks ago, but other than that, I am doing well."

That brought a smile to the sheriff's face. "So, what brings you in this morning?"

"Yesterday, after you left, I remembered something."

"What's that?" came the query.

"You were asking me about any enemies here in town and it came to mind that when I had my run in with 'Brother Smith.' I questioned if that was his real name. It just slipped out at the time, but he reacted badly to my comment."

"What do you mean, 'He reacted badly to it?" Matt asked.

"It's hard to explain. All I can tell you is that after all of my years of dealing with outlaws, thieves and rustlers, I've learned to read body language and unspoken queues. I don't just listen to their words, I watch their reaction as a whole. My comment hit a nerve with him."

Matt nodded his understanding as Eli continued. "Maybe it was a flinch, or a twitch, but I saw that he did not like that comment. That's what got me to wondering. What do you know about the man's background?"

"Nothing really," Matt explained. "He came into town a couple years back and started preaching in the church that was vacated some time ago. Until you arrived, he was the only preacher in town."

"Do you know where he came from?"

Matt thought about it for a minute, "Not really, but then I try to find any excuse I can to get out of going to his church, so I don't know much about the man. On the other hand, Becky never misses a Sunday. I'll ask her if she has heard anything about his background. It might be an interesting thing to follow up on."

Matt was tracking with Eli's line of reasoning. "I'll ask her at lunch today."

"Good. I was thinking a few well-placed telegraph messages might yield some fruit."

Matt laughed, "I'm way ahead of you there."

CHAPTER NINE

Brother Smith was in a panic. He had just learned Eli Exeter had returned to town, a bit the worse for wear, but still alive. He took several deep breaths to calm his shattered nerves. As his panic receded, he began to go into a rage. *This should never have happened.* He let out a string of profanities. *Those imbeciles! They were supposed to have gotten rid of Exeter and here he was, back in town.*

Smith paced the front room of the parsonage, trying to think. Trying to come up with a plan. When no immediate scheme came to mind, he went to the bedroom, pulled a valise from under the bed and opened it. It was full of clothing, he always kept it ready for a quick getaway. He muttered to himself, "You never know when town folks might turn ugly." If it came down to that, it would not be the only time he had been run out of town.

The first incident had been back east in Philadelphia. The city of brotherly love! Well, they held no love for *him* there.

He had learned the ways of a con man from an early age, starting out by selling snake oil and running shell games. Over the years he began to target churches. He had become aware of how trusting church people were and how much they wanted to help the down and out. He used that to his advantage, letting them try to convert him while he took whatever he could until they wearied of him and the funds dried up. When that was not lucrative enough he hatched a plan. He had watched the way in which the congregation treated their minister and figured if he was in that position, he could con more people in less time. His mother had dragged him to church as a child and made him sit through so many sermons but now he found that he could convincingly pass himself off as a "man of God". He specialized in the Hell Fire and Brimstone style which allowed him to keep a moderate knowledge base and still convince the people that he was the real deal. That was until the head deacon of the church where he was "ministering" had found him in a very compromising position with the man's seventeen year old daughter.

Soon, seducing women became almost more fun than conning them of money. In Philadelphia he had slipped out of town, barely ahead of the angry father, with only the clothes he grabbed up off the floor.

After that, he got smart and always kept a getaway package ready, complete with clothes and money which could be grabbed at the first sign of trouble. He also learned to keep his indiscretions hidden. That first time, he got caught because of the folly of the young girl he'd taken advantage of. She had pursued him but after that affair, he planned better and he became the aggressor.

Still, in spite of the precautions, he had never lasted more than a year or two before some nosey busy body would raise havoc and he would have to run again. Sometimes it was money missing from the church treasury, but most often it was a woman. He was amazed how some women would throw themselves at their "spiritual leader." Who was he to deny them?

Usually, but not always, it started out with a married woman coming for marital advise. She would cry on his shoulder about a husband who was busy with everyday life and didn't pay enough attention to his lonely wife. It would only take a few sessions of listening to her and commiserating about how much she had been wronged, before she would succumb to his wiles and let him have his way with her.

Once the deed was done, those women felt too much guilt to admit to their husbands what had happened. He honestly did not know how many children he had likely fathered.

Often times, woman would seek him out, thinking they were going to defile the preacher! Fools! He would string those ones along, acting as if he would never give in to their evil ways. Then when the time was right, he would use them and cast them aside as if they were trash. In his eyes, women become tools to satisfy his own need, then to be discarded when no longer useful.

He grinned to himself. The truth was that the law did not want him for his trifling's with women. Oh no, that was not what he was wanted for.

In Missouri, he left under the cloak of night with the building fund of nearly five hundred dollars. In Kansas it was a wealthy woman's jewelry which netted him over a thousand dollars, and in Colorado it was the church's savings of one hundred and twenty five dollars. It wasn't a king's ransom by any stretch of the imagination, but still, better than a cowboy's pay of thirty dollars a month. Not to mention the lack of hard physical labor and the perks. How many cowboys had women throw themselves at them?

Then there was the body in Utah. As far as he knew, no one was aware he had killed that woman. He'd believed that he had left the area before anyone was the wiser. That fool woman had not followed the path of the others before her. She actually wanted to save her marriage and tried to stand up to him. When he forced himself upon her, she tried to scream, but he shut her up. He shut her up permanently!

The thought of her even now did not cause any guilt whatsoever. No, instead he felt a surge of excitement as he recalled that long ago afternoon.

He looked down at the valise and rummaged through it. Inside was seven hundred dollars he had siphoned from the church's coffers over the last two and a half years. The church treasurer was an elderly, trusting woman which made it easy to slip money off the table as she chattered away taking her time counting the offerings. A little misdirection was simple and she was none the wiser.

There was a false bottom in the valise where the money was stashed. Two fresh suits of clothes were folded over that. On top was a Bible, but when you opened the book, there was a cut out which held a snub nosed .38 revolver. The back cover opened, exposing enough of the gun so it could be cocked and fired while still in the book.

He chuckled to himself, *you never know when you might need the extra insurance that this set up offered.*

When he was satisfied everything was in order, he repacked the case and slid it under the bed. Next, he went out to the church's small shed where he housed his horse. He checked on the animal and gave it some oats. He kept his horse grain fed, because he was never sure when he might need a fast animal with staying power for a getaway. He contemplated saddling up, but decided he was being premature. There was no reason for anyone to believe he was behind the kidnap plot.

As he brushed the horse, his mind returned to his earlier ponderings. So far in this town, he had not seduced any women. His focus was on acquiring money and he did not want a dalliance to interrupt his plan. With the return of Exeter, he might not have a choice of whether he should leave or not.

He did not want to leave, but with the thought that it might be imminent, he decided on one last conquest. There was a beautiful young woman in the congregation who would be the perfect final hurrah before he left the scene. She was one of those ignored wives who should be easy to conquer. That fool husband of hers was always off working long hours while his wife stayed at home, pining for his attention. She was a beautiful wench and she would be an easy mark!

* * *

Matt had been making a point to come home for lunch every day after Becky lost their little one. He took extra time to comfort her, pray with her and just sit and listen. He knew how badly she wanted a baby, he did too, but for her, it was a longing that was so deep it touched all aspects of her heart. At night, he would hold her and tell her how much he loved her and how much he needed her. Time and time again he assured her that baby, or no baby, he would always love her.

The job pulled him in another direction, but this time he had made Becky his priority. He realized how important she was in his life and so he made a conscious decision to nurture her, to nurture their relationship in every way he could.

When Matt walked into the house for lunch, he placed his hat on the peg by the door. The smell of meat and biscuits in the oven made his mouth water. When Becky came out of the kitchen, wiping her hands on her apron, Matt swept her up in his arms and passionately kissed her.

She finally pushed him away and smiled. "My, what was that for?" she asked teasingly. Her eyes twinkling up at him.

Matt smiled right back. "That? That was because I love you. You know, you are so beautiful. I just love to look at you."

Becky blushed at the compliment. "Oh stop it. You just want one thing. I know you."

Matt grinned, "Okay, I'll grant you that, but I also love to look at your pretty face."

She stood up on her tippy toes and kissed the end of his nose. "You wash up, I will bring out your meal."

Matt poured water from the pitcher into the basin and scrubbed his hands and forearms well using the bar of lye soap she'd placed there for that purpose. He rinsed his arms off with more water from the pitcher then dried them on the towel that was hung on the wall. He sat down at the table as Becky brought out two plates, each with a slab of beef, some green beans and biscuits. He fondly noted that her serving was somewhat smaller than the one she gave him. He took her hand and together they bowed their heads as Matt prayed over the food.

As they ate, Becky told Matt about her day so far and when she had filled him in, she asked him about his day.

"I had a visit from Eli this morning."

Becky glanced up from her plate, "How is he doing?"

Matt nodded as he answered, "He's much better than when Steven brought him back. A good day's rest did him wonders. He asked me a question though. I did not have the answer, but I thought you might."

"Me?" Becky asked in surprise. "What is it?"

"Do you have any idea where Brother Smith came from? Has he ever mentioned anything about his past that you remember?"

Becky pondered for a moment. "Once in a sermon, he mentioned Utah. Why do you ask?"

Matt dodged the question, "Did he mention a town in Utah?"

"Let's see...It was Park something, or something Park. Why?"

Matt cut up some of the meat on his plate. "Eli is operating on a hunch. The Sunday before he was attacked, Brother Smith came over to the Saloon and tried to run him out of town."

"Yes," Becky interrupted, her sweet face bore an unaccustomed frown. "I remember hearing about that whole episode I was against it from the very beginning."

Matt looked at her seriously, "I'm glad. I don't hold with that kind of behavior. Anyway, Eli told me he made a comment about Smith's name and Smith reacted to it negatively. He asked me to follow up on it."

"Park Valley." Beck suddenly exclaimed. "It was Park Valley, Utah."

"Bless you dear." Matt finished off the meat on his plate and popped the last of the biscuit into his mouth, then wiped his lips with his napkin. He set the napkin on the table, stood up and came around to Becky's chair. He leaned down over the back of her chair and kissed her cheek. "That was delicious. I'll try to be on time for supper. "

Becky reached up and messed up his hair. "You better be," she teased.

Matt rode straight to the telegraph office, tied his horse to the wooden rail outside and walked in.

"Hi sheriff. What can I do for you?"

"Hi, Bert. I need you to send a telegraph for me."

"That's what I'm here for." Bert laughed as though he had just told a very funny joke.

Matt rolled his eyes and shook his head, just the reaction the man was looking for. The Sheriff wrote out his message and handed it to telegrapher.

Bert read it, then looked up in surprise. "Are you serious?"

"Very serious." Matt replied, "And don't you breathe a word of this to anyone, or I'll come back and throw you into jail. Am I making myself clear?"

Bert suddenly lost his jovial demeanor. "I understand."

"And as soon as you hear anything back, I need to know pronto. You got that?"

Bert nodded.

Matt paid for the message and gave Bert an extra coin to make sure the message got delivered promptly. Bert was a good man and had a good heart, but he could be a bit of a gossip, which is probably why he became a telegraph operator in the first place, although Matt did not know this for a fact. He felt that his threatening warning was warranted though and hoped that Bert would take it to heart.

* * *

Eli did his chores that morning, but he was moving slowly and did not finish until it was almost time to open. By then, he was worn out and amazed how quickly he'd become winded. He realized he needed to resume his evening walks right away so as to build up his stamina again.

Instead of laying down though, he walked to the stable, where he found Steven, who had also finished his morning's chores. Together, they made their way to the Widow Franco's bakery, toting Eli's Bible along. Over cups of coffee and sticky sweet pastries, they talked about what Steven had been reading during the time Eli had been recuperating in the desert. Eli took the time to explain different points and clarified some things Steven was unclear on. When it came time to pay, Steven suddenly looked uncomfortable, as Eli laid some money on the table.

"Sooner or later, I need to find me a job," he ventured. "I just don't know where, or how to go about it. Everyone in town thinks of me as the town drunk. I'm mighty afraid they'll laugh me out of town, if I ask. I can't be having you pay my way all the time. That just ain't right."

"I talked to Sam about having you cooking for him." Eli offered.

"I don't know about working in a Saloon. Not yet anyhow. I need to stay away from liquor...away from that temptation. I know God performed a miracle in me, but Satan would do anything to take it away."

Eli nodded. He, of all people knew the devil would try to find a person's Achilles heel and capitalize upon it. He wanted to see Steven not only succeed in his recovery, but to abound in his new life and new walk.

Elizabeth stepped in from the back room, wiping her hands on a towel. "Excuse me gentlemen. I did not mean to listen in on your conversation, but I could not help but overhear." She turned her attention directly to Steven. "Mr. Bosco, I could use some part time help here, lifting the heavy things, cleaning up and odd jobs."

"Ma'am, that's very kind of you but," he hesitated a moment averting his eyes, "I don't want to be a charity case."

"You look at me," Elizabeth said firmly, "This is not charity. This bakery is doing well, and I have every reason to believe things are going to continue to get better. If I'm going to expand, which I hope to do soon, I will need some experienced help. Who knows, it may turn into a full time position. What do you say?"

"Thank you Ma'am. I'm grateful. But before I start, you need to know some things about me."

Elizabeth smiled, "You used to be the town drunk. I've heard the stories, but I've also heard you came back from the desert sober. This is not a large town, Mr. Bosco and the stories get around. I believe God is a God of second chances and if He can give second chances...I can too."

Steven looked as if a great weight had just been lifted. "What time would you like me to be here?"

They worked out the schedule so Steven would come in the afternoon. He would start by cleaning up and doing the shopping for Mrs. Franco down at the Mercantile.

As Eli and Steven walked down the street, Steven turned to his friend. "God is so good. I was afraid to even start asking and He provided for me before I even had a chance to ask."

"Yes, that is the way God is." Eli thought of how one good deed could certainly have a ripple effect, like tossing a pebble into a pond. He had turned the reward for the robbers over to the Widow Franco and she in turn started the bakery, which now provided his friend with the job he needed. God was indeed very good. "Walk over to my place with me."

When they arrived at the shed, Eli threw back the blanket to let some light in. He removed the planks which made up his bed and opened one of the trunks. Taking a Bible out, he gave it to Steven. "This is for you." He held up his hand to stop the protests. "I brought these with me specifically for the purpose of giving them to the new believers. I'm going to give all of these away." He gestured toward the trunk. "I am more than proud to give the first one to you."

"Thank You." Steven held the Bible in his hands as though it was a treasure. Eli could see that his friend was having difficulty speaking.

"You're welcome. Now, we need to get you some clean clothes to wear to work. It won't do to smell like a stable hand when you show up to work in a bakery now, will it?" Again he stopped the protests. "This is a loan, you can pay me back when you get some money saved up."

This time, Steven nodded his acceptance.

Together, they walked to the Mercantile. Steven stopped at the door. "I've been kicked out of here for pan handling." He looked embarrassed. "I don't want to get kicked out again."

"Stay here."

Eli stepped through the door and let his eyes adjust from the bright sunlight. He walked over to the merchant behind the counter. "Hi Jerry, how's business?"

"Slower than molasses in the winter time. What can I do for you today?"

"Well, I have a customer for you, but he's afraid that if he comes in, you're going to kick him out."

"If he's planning on spending money here, I sure as hell ain't going to kick him out...Oh sorry 'bout that." He realized too late that he was talking to the preacher. Eli grinned. He knew the problem was that he didn't look like a preacher. He looked like any other cowboy that came in to buy supplies or tobacco. He figure the man was thinking it sure would be nice if he just looked the part.

"Don't worry about it. I'll go get your customer."

He moved through the doors and motioned to Steven. "Come on in, it's all clear."

Together they walked through the door and Jerry exploded. "I thought I told you never come back here...."

He stopped when Eli stepped between them. "Paying customer, remember." He waggled his finger in front of Jerry's nose. "From now on, if you want to keep my business, you treat Steven like you treat me. If he ever comes in here drunk again, you have every right to kick him out. Meanwhile, he is going to be working for Mrs. Franco and he will be coming in here to pick up supplies. Don't forget, there *is* another store in town."

Grudgingly, Jerry nodded. There was another grocer on the other side of town and Jerry knew it. Mrs. Franco was buying a lot of flour, sugar and her other baking supplies from him now that she opened her bakery and she was paying cash. Eli noted he helped Steven out like he was the president himself. He soon walked out with a new pair of trousers and a work shirt suitable for the bakery.

* * *

Matt checked with the telegrapher several times throughout the afternoon. On his third visit, Bert told him, "I was just informed Park Valley, Utah, is not even a town. It's more of a settlement or something. They don't have their own telegraph office, so I sent the message to the nearest big town which is Ogden. They will send it out on the next freight wagon, but it could take weeks."

Matt sighed. "Thanks Bert. By the way, did you ask the telegrapher in Ogden to give that description to the sheriff there? Who knows, maybe he might have some information too."

Bert shook his head. "I didn't but I can. I'll let you know if I get anything back."

"Thank you."

* * *

Friday morning arrived and Eli was up early. He was feeling much better, though each evening, he had Sam wrap his ribs up for him. He hustled as quickly as he could through his chores, cleaning the saloon and washing dishes. When eight o'clock rolled around, he had the coffee on and had sliced some ham. There were a couple eggs out on the side board, all ready for when his guest arrived. At five after eight, he was wondering if Rob was going to show up. Then he heard boots out on the board walk, boots without spurs. A moment later, the gunman came in through the front door.

Eli tossed the ham slices into a frying pan and almost immediately, the sizzling meat began filling the room with its aroma. He poured two cups of coffee and brought one to Handy and offered him a chair. "How do you like your eggs?" he asked.

Rob accepted the coffee and sat down in the offered chair with his back away from the door. Eli smiled because he himself did the same thing. In fact, he had picked the table where both of them could sit facing the door, albeit from different angles.

"Scrambled please."

Eli smiled at the man's politeness. The two were not friends but they both had great respect for one another based upon their respective reputations. He threw some lard into another pan and as it melted he cracked in four eggs out of the shell and added a pinch of salt and pepper into the bowl. Then he whipped the eggs with a fork until they were frothy and poured them into the pan. He flipped the ham and stirred the eggs, all the while sipping on his coffee. When the eggs were done and the ham was ready, he dished up two plates and expertly brought them over to the table in one hand, while he carried his coffee in the other.

Rob commented, "That's not really wise, is it, filling both of your hands like that."

Eli nodded. "You're right, but I don't have a gun anymore, so I am just going to have to trust the good Lord to keep me safe."

"What happened to your gun? That was a rather ancient piece of history. Not many people carry Dragoons these days."

"Ah, so you noticed. It was stolen when I was robbed a couple of weeks ago. It was unique, I inherited it from my father so I'll never be able to replace it."

"I'm sorry. A man should never be without a gun, not in this county."

They dug into the food, and since eating was serious business, the talking ceased until the food had been devoured. Rob leaned back in his chair and held his coffee cup in his left hand. "That was really good. You're not a bad cook. Seems you do it all; cooking, lawman, and preacher. Is there anything you don't do?"

"Probably wouldn't make a good lawyer." That brought a smirk to Rob's face.

Eli got up and brought the coffee pot to the table. He had been praying about this moment for a long time and now that it was here, he was dependent upon the Holy Ghost to give him the words to say. He poured the coffee, then sat down.

"Rob, because I was a lawman, I know about your past. I've seen the posters and I know some of the things you have done. Only you and God know *all* the things you have done."

Rob looked him in the eye without wavering. "You're going to have a tough time bringing me in on those posters...you without a gun."

Eli returned the stare. "I have no intention of bringing you in. My goal here is to save your soul. At least to give Jesus the opportunity to save your soul."

Rob snorted in distain. "Jesus can't save my soul now. All He can do is send it to Hell."

"Why? Do you think you're so bad you can't be saved? I've got news for you. As long as there is breath left in your body, as long as your heart is still beating, there is the chance to be saved." Eli was intense. "The Bible tells us there is one unforgivable sin and only one. It's not murder, it's not robbery or any other crime that you can be charged with. It is blaspheme of the Holy Ghost."

"Swearing?"

"No, not cursing or using God's name in vain. Blaspheme of the Holy Ghost is rejecting the salvation message I am trying to tell you about. You see, no one really seeks after God, but God seeks us. That inner voice which draws you to God; that is the Holy Ghost. Unfortunately, as people get older they tend to ignore that voice more and more. Each time they ignore it, each time they reject it, it's like putting another brick in a wall we build up between us and God. One day, we put that final brick in place and there's no going back. I personally believe that only happens when you die. I don't want to see that happen to you."

"You're trying to tell me that it's not too late for me to find Jesus?" Rob was incredulous.

"That's right. If you will listen to that voice of the Holy Ghost. If you confess to God your sins. If you ask Jesus to forgive you and come into your heart, you can be saved." Eli leaned forward and earnestly entreated Rob. "This is a matter of life and death. Eternal life in the presence of God or eternal death in Hell."

"I don't know..."

"Don't know what?" Steven's voice came from the back door.

Rob knocked over his chair, spinning around into a crouch, a gun in his hand where none had been a split second before.

Steven held his hands up, shoulder high. "Sorry, I didn't know I was interrupting anything."

Rob slid the gun back into the holster. "No, No, I'm just a little jumpy is all." He reached down and picked up the chair.

Steven dropped his hands. "That's alright. I'll just come back later."

Eli stopped him, "Wait. I'd like you to join us," he turned to Rob, "if you don't mind."

Rob shrugged, "I guess it's alright."

Eli got another cup and poured Steven some coffee. When they were all seated, Eli turned to Steven. "Rob doesn't think God can forgive him for the things that he had done. I was wondering if you might have any thoughts on that."

Eli watched as the gunman received Steven with interest. He had obviously seen Steven staggering around town, drunk and a mess and now here he was; sober, clean, freshly shaved and his hair was cut. He looked like an upstanding citizen, not the town drunk, and Rob wanted to hear the story....even if meant hearing more about God, which is what he suspected was coming.

Steven started from the beginning. He told his story of being a horse wrangler and weekend partier to becoming the town drunk. He told of Eli being the only person who showed an interest in him, actual concern for his well-being. Rob seemed to connect with that part of the story. Eli knew he was the only person who didn't give the gunman a wide berth because of his reputation, and in the lonely world of outlaws, Rob found that refreshing.

Steven told of waking up from a drunken stupor, hearing the two men talk of their exploits and finding out the next day that it was not some sort of a dream. He described his attempts to ride out and find Eli, only to battle the desire of the bottle. He spoke of praying and God's answer to that prayer and the miracles that followed.

"I tried to take a drink of that whiskey. I needed it so bad, but no sooner did it hit my gut and it came spewing out. The second time when I threw it up, that was when I knew God was real. I had asked and He answered. But the miracles don't stop there. I found Eli that night. It was pure dark outside, no moon and I just "happened" to make camp where Eli had been thrown off the train. That was no accident. It was the hand of God and nobody will ever be able to convince me otherwise!"

Steven finished up. "I can't tell you all the things that Eli can, as far as what is in the Bible, but I can tell you *my story*. I know what God has done for me and He can do the same for you. All you have to do is believe, confess your sins and accept Jesus as your Savior."

Rob nodded. "I've seen what happened to you. Both of you have given me something to think about, and I will. I'm just not convinced that it is for me."

"Rob, don't put it off." Eli wanted to make him see the light. "You never know when your life might end. Someday you might run into that young gunfighter who's looking to make a reputation. Maybe he's not as fast as you are, but he still gets a lucky bullet into you. Right now, if that happens, your soul will spend eternity in hell. I don't want to see that happen. Surely you don't want to see that happen!"

Sudden tears stung his eyes as he silently prayed. *"Jesus, please let him know how much You love him!"*

Rob was silent, thinking on the story he'd just heard.

"I reckon you're right, but I have to think on it." Rob wasn't offended by the truth because he knew it better than Eli and if anything, Rob was pragmatic. He knew his life was not one to brag over. He just wished he'd heard this message a long, long time ago, before he started down his path. Maybe it would have made a difference back then. He just wasn't sure he could change now.

"Thank you for breakfast and the coffee." Rob drained the last cold swallow out of his cup and set it down.

As Rob walked toward the door, Eli spoke up, "Rob, see you in church on Sunday?"

Rob spoke over his shoulder, "We'll see."

CHAPTER TEN

As Rob stepped out the door, the loud blast of a shotgun jolted Eli from his chair. He sprinted to the door with Steven just a few steps behind.

Rob was down on the sidewalk, his right gun in his hand, unfired. Eighteen .33 caliber rounds from both barrels of a shotgun had peppered his chest and stomach with .00 Buckshot and he laid in an ever widening pool of blood. Eli knelt down and cradled his head.

With his life flowing out of him, Rob tried to speak, but the words could not get past the blood that welled up inside of his mouth, evidence of his shattered lungs. Rob died in Eli's arms, the words unspoken.

Eli looked up and was shocked to see the killer. A boy, no more than thirteen or fourteen years old, stood in the street. He was tall for his age, thinner than a rail, but holding a man sized 12 gauge shotgun, with smoke still wafting out of the end of both barrels.

"Why?" Eli still couldn't believe Rob was dead.

The boy looked at him without remorse. "He killed my Pa."

Matt ran up, taking in the scene as he came. He holstered his pistol and removed the empty shotgun from the boy. He quickly ran his other hand over the boy's waistline to make sure there were no other firearms on him. Then he took the boy by the arm and sat him on the boardwalk, broke open the breach of the shotgun and ejected the empty shells from it.

"Eli, what happened here?"

Eli stood up and shook his head. Blood stained the front of his clothes. "Rob had breakfast and coffee with me. Steven and I had just shared the gospel with him and when he walked out the door, I heard the gun. I didn't see what happened, you'll have to talk to that young man there." He motioned toward the boy seated on the board walk.

By now, the reality of what he had done seemed to be sinking in for the boy. The lifeless body of the outlaw lay on the boardwalk in a pool of blood. There was blood spattered all over the wall behind where Rob had been standing, and the crowd of people that had gathered was starting to grow. The boy struggled to fight back tears.

Matt recognized the turmoil in the boy's face and put his hand on his shoulder. "Why don't you walk along with me?"

Frightened, the boy looked up. "Am I-I-I going to jail?" he stammered.

"No son, I just need to find out what happened here." He turned to one of the men. "Scott, would you find the undertaker and deal with this?" He gestured with his hand to include the body and the bloody mess. Scott nodded and trotted off toward the undertaker's place while Matt and the boy moved toward the Sheriff's Office

Matt sat the boy down in a chair and took his place behind the desk. "Alright son, let's start with your name."

"Joshua, sir." Came the answer.

"Tell me what happened out there." Matt was gentle and low key as he dealt with the boy.

"I was standing behind one of the poles and when he came out I shot him." At least the boy was direct and to the point. Obviously, he was not going to provide any more information than the question asked for.

"Joshua, why did you shoot that man? Do you know who he is?"

"Yes sir, he's Rob Handy." Joshua answered the second question first. Then the flood gates opened and the words came pouring out. "He shot and killed my pa when I was eight years old!" He cried. "Last year, my mama...mother died and they were going to put me into a county home." A solitary tear rolled down the boy's cheek as he struggled to hold back the ones that wanted to follow.

Matt pulled a clean handkerchief out of his hip pocket and handed it to the boy. "And then?"

"I fetched my pa's scatter gun and our old horse and loaded up as much goods as we could carry, then I lit a shuck out of there on my own. I've been looking for Rob Handy since the day I left home." His face crumbled. He clutched the handkerchief tight and balled his fingers into fists as he fought against the tears that threaten to flood down his face. "Yesterday I saw him. I recognized him from a picture on a poster I'd seen. I'd been watching for my chance. I saw him go into that Saloon and so I got me my scatter gun and I waited."

"Nobody asked you what you were doing out in front of the saloon holding a shot gun?"

Joshua replied defensively. "Nobody pays no never mind to a boy out in the street and I weren't advertisin' I was holding a scatter gun. I kinda kept it hid behind my leg, next to the horse. I waited 'til I heard footsteps coming out of the saloon and then I rared that gun up and..."

He stopped his recitation and hung his head. He was remembering the blast of the gun, the acrid smell of gun smoke in the air, the spray of the blood against the wall and the man falling at his feet, dying in his presence. His mind returned to the scene, seeing the ever widening pool of blood under the dying man and that other man holding him as he died.

Joshua had hunted and killed any number of animals, normal for a boy growing up in this day and age, but he had discovered that killing a man had its own different feeling and he found he did not like it much. He felt as if he had a lead weight sitting in the pit of his stomach and a wave of depression washed over him. He thought he would feel relief at the death of his father's killer, that revenge would be sweet. Now he was discovering that he felt just the opposite.

For a brief moment, Matt closed his eyes, almost as if he was reading Joshua's thoughts. Then he stood up and walked around the desk where he sat on the edge placing his hand on Joshua's shoulder. "Would you like to come home with me? I have a wife who's a great cook and loves to feed people."

"Thank you sir. I aint et in nearly two days." Obviously, though the boy's command of English was deplorable, he had been raised to be polite and respect his elders. Matt could definitely appreciate that.

It was very early for lunch, but Matt knew the boy couldn't wait. He put his hat on his head and motioned the boy toward the door. "Come on, times a'wasting. Where do you keep your horse?"

"Tied up down the street in front of the..." His voice trailed off.

The Sheriff just nodded. They walked out together and Matt untied his horse from the rail. As they moved toward the boy's horse, he called over one of his temporary deputies. "Keep an eye on those two fellas in the jail, will you?" The deputy nodded and Matt continued, "The Judge should be here tomorrow or the next day, then we can get them tried and out of here." The deputy headed toward the jail while they fetched Joshua's horse.

* * *

It didn't take long for Matt and young Joshua to arrive at Matt's home. Right away Matt spotted Becky's face looking out from behind the gingham window curtain. He saw her curious face break into a big smile and with a wave, she disappeared. He knew she had gone to stoke the fire in the cooking stove. Already it looked like there would be an extra plate at the table.

Matt and Joshua tied the horses to the post out front under the shade of the tree. "Go wash up in the basin there on the porch while I let my wife know we are here. Make sure you wash that dirt off your face and comb that hair, you hear?" Joshua nodded and obediently headed toward the basin and pitcher set out for that purpose.

Matt headed inside and quickly filled his wife in, being vague with the details of the shooting. "I need to figure out what to do with him. If we try to take him to the county orphanage, it might not go well."

Becky nodded. "First, let's get him fed and we'll think on the other later."

* * *

Eli was still in shock. He had seen men killed and had even killed men himself, but this was different. He had just been talking to Rob. He had thought Rob was going to turn around, accept Jesus, but now... He wondered what Rob had tried to say in those last moments. In his last moments, was Rob confessing his sins? Did he have time to accept Christ into his heart? Eli would never know, at least not until he himself was in the presence of the Lord. In the meanwhile, he was left to wonder.

Feeling as if he was in a fog, he got a shovel from the shed out back and placed sand on the boardwalk to cover and soak up the gunman's blood. He waited for it to saturate the sandy dirt and shoveled it into a bucket. He placed more of the sand onto boardwalk and left it there to cover the stained wood. Later, in the cool of the morning, he would have to come out and see about getting rid of the stain. *'It may take replacing the boards'* he thought to himself.

He finished the chore and sat down to finish preparing for his Sunday sermon. But his heart was heavy over Rob' death. He felt that Rob was starting to become his friend and he found that he cared deeply about what had happened.

He began to question himself. Maybe if he had been more aggressive in telling Rob about Jesus? But even as he second guessed himself and explored the "what ifs," he felt that small voice inside of him, speaking peace to his soul.

Slowly it dawned upon him that he would never know what Rob's final choice was. It hadn't been his place to convince Rob to give his life to God. He had given Rob the truth and it was the job of the Holy Ghost to convict the man, turn him around and save him. He began to feel peace and as that peace ebbed through his body and soul, he allowed himself to rest in it.

This time when he opened up his Bible, it was with renewed vigor that he put together the message he was going to give on Sunday. Suddenly he knew exactly what he needed to say. When his study was complete, he went back to the lean-to and grabbed up some of the extra boards.

With a pry bar, a saw and hammer in hand, he began tearing up the stained boardwalk. He worked slowly because his ribs were still tender and the sun was hot, but regardless, he was a man on a mission. It took him several hours, but when the job was finished, he yarded the blood stained boards back to the shed. He worked back there for another half an hour before he was done.

He cleaned up, took a sponge bath and dressed in clean clothes. With his Bible in hand, he walked to the undertaker's office. The pine board box was just being completed and the undertaker's assistants had finished digging a hole in the cemetery outside of town. In this heat, the body was already starting to decay and stink, so no time was wasted. Eli accompanied the body of his friend out of town and together with Steven, the undertaker and his two assistants, he prepared to do the funeral. Just as he was about to begin, he noticed a small caravan of men coming from the saloon. He waited until they were gathered to begin talking.

"Men, I thank you for coming out to pay last respects to Rob Handy. I'm sure many of you are probably glad that he is gone, as we all know his reputation. You may think you know all you need to about Rob, but I want to tell you about another side of him." He looked around at the faces of his audience.

"When I was injured and lost out in the desert just last week, it was Rob Handy who joined up with the sheriff to look for me. Why? He told the sheriff it was because I had been kind to him. He obviously felt one small kindness deserved spending a couple of days looking for me." Eli paused a moment.

"Rob's life was taken away from him in a way I'm sure he expected. A man who lives by the gun is more than likely to die by the gun." Eli let his gaze scan the crowd. Several of the men avoided his eye and looked at the ground instead.

"I had the opportunity to spend the last couple of hours on earth with him. We had breakfast together and I shared with him how Jesus loved him and offered forgiveness to him for all the wrong he had done. I know he wanted to believe it was so, but he told me he wasn't ready to take that leap of faith. Rob walked out the door into two barrels of buckshot." Eli paused to let the imagery sink in.

"Men I tell you this because that same forgiveness is available to you. If Rob could speak to you now, I know he would tell you to not wait another minute. You never know when your life is going to end.

"We all know men who have died. There is old age and sickness and there are people who think that they will wait to make that decision then. But there are also shootings, drownings, stampedes, accidents, illnesses--you name it and it can happen. We all know men who have gone like that."

He noticed some of the men nodding their heads in agreement. "It can happen to anyone of you at any time and if you have not made the decision to accept the forgiveness for sin that Jesus offers, if you have not asked Him to be your Savior, if you have not repented of your sins, you will go to hell."

"Men, I don't know about Rob. He tried to tell me something before he died, I just don't know what it was." His voice choked for a moment. "This has created in me an urgency to make sure you men all have the chance to come to know Jesus. I don't ever want to stand over another pine box in another graveyard, wondering if the soul who left that body is in heaven or hell." He spoke softly. "Those are the only two choices.

"'Jesus said, "I am the way the truth and the life. No one comes to the Father except through me." It is that simple. I am going to ask that you not walk away from here without making that decision for yourself."

He removed his hat and bowed his head and the men around the gravesite followed his example. He said a short and simple prayer over the body and then walked over to the exit gate. He shook hands with each man and asked each of them if they would like to pray to accept Christ. Most of the men just looked uncomfortable and shook their heads, all them in fact, except for Andy, a local carpenter and handy man. He stepped aside and held back until all the others left.

"It's time that I…that I accept Jesus."

Eli, Steven and Andy walked over to the shade of a lone tree. Eli turned to Andy and asked, "What is your story, Andy? How much do you understand about the Gospel?"

Andy gave him a lopsided grin. "I went to church as a yonker, and mostly pulled the girls pigtails and made a pest of myself. I'm sure the preacher was glad when I stopped going." He suddenly became serious. "The thing is, I know my momma prayed for me every day. When I was old enough to start out on my own, doing my own thing, I would come home all liquored up, and I'd find my Ma on her knees in the front room, praying for my soul. I always figured, kind of like you were talking about today, that I would take care of it in my own time. What you said over there," he motioned toward the gravesite where two helpers were shoveling dirt onto the casket, "hit me kind of hard. You're right. I've had my fair share of close calls and it's time for me to make amends with my maker and turn to Jesus."

Eli reached out his hand and placed it on Andy's shoulder. "I couldn't be happier. I only asked because I wanted to see what your understanding of salvation was."

Andy shook his head. "Not real clear, I wasn't a very good listener as a young boy. I guess I know some but I couldn't really tell you what."

Eli nodded, leaning against the tree to ease the ache in his ribcage, "Let's just start at the beginning. When God created the earth, He created Adam and Eve to have a relationship with Him and that relationship was perfect. When Adam and Eve sinned, it caused the destruction of that perfect relationship with a perfect God.

"That destruction led to spiritual death which required an unblemished and perfect blood sacrifice to save us from spiritual death. God sent His Son, Jesus to be that perfect blood sacrifice. He died on the cross in our place. He took our punishment so we could have salvation and a restored relationship with God.

But Jesus did not stay dead. Oh no, he was raised on the third day. All we have to do to make things right with God, is to accept the forgiveness that Jesus offers. All God asks in return is that we love Him with all our heart, soul and mind. Does that help to clear things up for you?"

Andy nodded, "Yes, Sir. I've never heard before that God wants to get to know me. That's absolutely incredible to think about."

Eli smiled, "Yes it is. To think that the Creator of this world wants to know us. That He cares about us in spite of the fact He knows everything we've ever done. With all of that, He still loves us."

"How do I accept Jesus," Andy inquired.

"That, my friend, is the simple part. In the Bible, Romans says, 'if you confess with your mouths Jesus as Lord, and believe in your heart that God raised Him from the dead, you will be saved.' Do you believe Jesus raised was from the dead?" Andy nodded his agreement.

"That means a simple prayer, confessing that you are a sinner, asking God to forgive those sins and asking Jesus to be your Lord is how you get started."

Together, under the shade of a tree next to the cemetery, the three men bowed their heads and Eli led Andy in a prayer of salvation. Andy finished praying and looked up, "That's it. I'm forgiven." It was a statement, not a question and his face was transformed with joy.

Eli nodded, a smile upon his face. "The word Lord, means Master. We are to confess with our mouths that we have willingly given our lives to Him. Once a person gives their life to the Lord, He becomes the master. Not like a slave, because a slave is a defeated foe who has been taken into captivity. A slave has no choice. But you do. You have chosen to surrender your own desires to follow the will of God."

"Absolutely. I want to follow Jesus. I want to do the things He wants me to," he said thoughtfully

Eli was all grins. "Good. Next you need to be willing to share your choice to follow God with your family and friends."

"I will. I want them all to have what I now have!"

Eli felt both sadness and joy. The death of his friend had dealt a blow—but knowing the death of Rob resulted in a transformed life for Andy, meant Rob had not died in vain.

Together they walked down to Eli's shed, where he gave out a second Bible to Andy. The three of them agreed to meet once a week so Eli could teach them how to live as followers of Jesus. Eli marveled over this great change.

* * *

Matt watched the boy eat. He was obviously famished, but even at that, he had not forgotten his manners. He treated Becky with respect, even waiting for her to sit down before plowing in. They did forgo saying grace to keep from embarrassing the boy. After Joshua polished off his plate, Becky brought out what was left of an apple pie from the previous evening's supper and served a piece to the boy. She added another piece to Matt's plate before plopping another on her own.

Before she could sit down, Joshua had all but devoured his. She glanced at Matt, who divined what she was thinking and just nodded. She reached over and placed the last piece of pie on his plate. Joshua's eyes sparkled as he mumbled his thanks through a bite of pie.

When they had finished, Matt leaned back in his chair so the two front legs were off the ground, a bad habit he had that Becky was constantly getting after him for. "Well son, are you feeling better now."

Joshua nodded enthusiastically, "Yes sir." He smiled at Becky. "Ma'am, thank you very much. That was delicious." There was a pause before he shyly continued, "'specially the pie."

Becky smiled widely at the praise. "You are very welcome." She turned to Matt, "Now we have to address the issue of where this young man is going to sleep."

Matt raised a surprised eyebrow.

Becky continued, "Well, if he's going to stay with us, he can't be sleeping on the floor, now, can he?"

Joshua watched the exchange between the two without saying anything.

Matt looked thoughtfully at his wife, and turned to Joshua. "Son, do you mind going out and checking on the horses for me? Maybe take them out to the barn and give them a little hay?"

Joshua nodded, "Yes sir."

After the boy left, Matt turned to his wife. "Absolutely not!" He began emphatically. "That boy just killed a man. Don't you think for one minute that I am going to leave him in my house with my wife?!!" He kept the volume down to keep his voice from carrying to the boy but the urgency of his message was clear.

Equally clear was the resolve of the woman in front of him. "Matthew Shawn Wheaton! Just what do you plan to do with the boy? Take him back to town and turn him out on his own? He's just a boy!" The set of her jaw let Matt know he was in for a fight.

He softened his tone. "I am going to take him to the county boy's home. Maybe now that he's no longer bent on revenge, he'll willingly go. That's what I am going to do with him."

A tinge of sarcasm entered into Becky's voice, "Right. And how did that work out last time?" She asked.

Matt just shrugged.

The discussion raged on, albeit in hushed tones, until Matt finally capitulated. He always knew that his wife had a backbone of iron but sometimes he forgot because of that beautiful, feminine exterior. She was relentless and he just ran out of responses to her arguments.

Matt finally pushed his chair back and walked out the door. He located Joshua in the barn currying his horse, although the saddle was still on the animal's back.

"Would you like to stay with us for a while?" Matt asked.

"You don't want me here, do you?" The boy was perceptive and direct.

Matt pondered his answer for a moment before replying. "Joshua, I think that you're probably a decent young man with a good heart, but I am responsible for the safety and wellbeing of my wife. Son, you just killed a man this morning and I need to know that she is going to be alright here with you."

Joshua had been looking at the ground as Matt spoke, but now he looked the older man right in the eye. "You have my word, sir. I would never harm a woman. *Never*!" He spoke emphatically.

Matt looked the boy up and down, sizing him up then nodded. "I don't believe you would." He paused then added, "You are welcome here, if you want to stay."

"Thank you sir. I'd like that." His young face grew determined. "I'd like that, but I earn my keep. I ain't no free loader."

Becky had been standing outside the barn door, listening. Now she stepped inside. "Joshua, if you are going to stay with us, you'll go to school. We have a really nice teacher here in town." With her hands on her hips, she added, "And yes, you will have chores to do, but school first."

Matt hid a smile as he and the boy exchanged glances.

"Well, Ma'am," he bashfully repeated himself. "I think I'd like to stay."

Becky's smile grew wider. She ruffled the hair on top of Joshua's head. "There's some work to do, if you're going to have a place to sleep. You two had better get started on fixing it."

Matt and Joshua spent the afternoon turning the back room into a bedroom for Joshua. Matt carefully folded away the baby's things into wooden chest, which he carefully stored in his and Becky's room. Then they fashioned a bed out of some old wooden crates with the determination to build something more permanent in the near future.

At first, when Matt assured him they would fix up a bed, Joshua shook his head. "This is all I need. I've been sleeping on the ground so long, I wouldn't know what to do with a real bed."

Matt chuckled, "Trust me son, you'll get used to a bed real quick. There'll be plenty of time to sleep on the ground in the future. We're getting low on meat, so at some point, we'll have to do some hunting. You ever done much hunting, Joshua?"

"Yes sir, I kept meat on the table after my Pa was kilt."

Matt wasn't surprised. It was a story played out all the time--children forced to grow up before their time because they'd lost a parent. *"In this country,"* he mused to himself. *"You have a choice. You either take on responsibility or you die."*

Leaving the boy with Becky, he mounted his horse and rode back into town. He was a pretty good judge of character and he firmly believed that in spite of the shooting this morning, the boy was harmless to his wife. Besides, he'd seen something good happen—a change in her which he couldn't quite put his finger on.

He believed Joshua had a strong sense of right and wrong. Unfortunately, the boy also had a strong sense of revenge which had led to the shooting of Rob Handy. But regardless, from what he'd observed, Joshua was a good boy. Of that, Matt had no doubts.

Once he was in town, Matt stopped by the telegrapher's office. Bert shook his head. No news yet.

His next stop was the jail to check on the two prisoners. The boys had been fed and were bored with sitting in the jail.

Matt moved on to the saloon, where he checked in on Eli. He found him around back, sitting on a bench, his open Bible next to him as he leaned against the wall, his eyes closed. Matt cleared his throat, not wanting to startle him, but Eli did not bother to open his eyes.

"I heard you coming. How is the young man?"

"He's staying out at my place for now. Becky is fussing over him." He laughed, "That poor boy doesn't have a chance."

Eli opened his eyes. "How do you feel about that?"

"Well, I believe he is really a good kid. However, he has an over-developed sense of revenge. With the correct guidance, I think he will grow up to be a fine man someday."

Eli grimaced. "You know he is in danger from here on out. He'll be known as the boy who killed the gunman Rob Handy. Some snot-nosed kid looking to make himself a name will come gunning for him. At this point, he'd be better off going back East to a boarding school where no one knows him."

Matt changed the subject. "So, how are you doing, my friend?" The sheriff recognized Eli had been putting himself out there for these men and he was afraid the hard work was taking its toll.

"It has been a trying day. But not all bad. This afternoon, after Rob's funeral, Andy accepted Jesus as his Savior."

Matt was pleased. "Andy? That's wonderful." He shook his head, "Eli, I know you must have been frustrated over how long it has taken for people to respond. But the truth is, you have done an incredible work with those cowboys. It is starting to payoff. First Steven, with his deliverance from drunkenness and now Andy. I believe you are going to have lasting impact in the lives of these men. They look up to you now."

Eli smiled. "I'm grateful God is using me here. I believe I was led to this town by Him for His purpose. I just hope I get to see this through."

Matt sat down on the bench next to Eli and enjoyed the comfortable silence for a moment. Finally, he turned to his friend. "I have to go over to the boarding house and check through Rob's things to see if he had any next of kin." He paused. "I was kind of hoping you would go over with me."

Eli stood slowly and carefully stretched, always mindful of his ribs. He sighed, "I might as well. I'm not getting a lot done sitting here with my eyes closed."

"Thanks," Matt said.

They walked the short distance to the boarding house. Matt knocked on the door, and when he had explained their mission, the elderly widow who ran the place let them into Rob's room.

The room was extremely neat. *Too neat,* Matt thought. *With everything in its place.* The bed was made, the drawers were shut, and the braided rug was set exactly in line with the edge of the bed--perfectly half way between the head of the bed and the foot of the bed. There were shirts, cleaned and neatly pressed, hanging in the wardrobe. His perfectly creased pants were folded into the dresser drawer. In another drawer there was an even row of clean socks and a neat pile of underwear in another. Everything was ridiculously neat and set in its place.

Matt turned to Eli. "I would have to say he was obsessed."

Eli nodded. "Definitely. I have never seen a place so perfect. It's like something you would expect to see in a museum back East."

Carefully, Matt and Eli began removing items from the wardrobe and dresser drawers and placing them on the bed. The widow who ran the place stood in the doorway to make sure nothing that belonged to her ended up in the pile.

Matt opened the bottom drawer of the dresser, and began removing the clothes. Underneath the clothing was a hidden leather wallet. As he opened it, his eyes widened and he let out a whistle. Eli moved closer to see what had caused such a reaction. Matt pulled out a wad of one hundred dollar bills which had been wrapped into a piece of paper.

"I'm pretty sure this was not legally gained." He commented.

Eli remained silent.

Matt carefully counted out the money onto the top of the night stand while the widow and Eli watched. "Two thousand three hundred," he counted as he placed the last bill on the stack. He picked up the money and squared it up, tamping it on the long edge to even out all the bills. He placed the stack into the wallet, set it down and picked up the paper to see what the gunman had written there. As he read, the expression on his face registered surprise. He glanced up at Eli. "You've certainly left your mark, Preacher." Matt handed the paper to him.

Eli began to read the letter. "If you are reading this, I am dead. This is my last will and testament. I have no relatives to speak of, so everything I have, I leave to Elijah Exeter." The writing started to blur and Eli had to blink rapidly to get the letter back into focus.

He continued to read. "Eli is the only person who ever cared about what happened to me." It was signed, "Robert John Handy" and dated two days prior to the man's death.

Eli's voice was husky with emotion. "I only talked to him a couple of times. I can't believe this."

"You may have only talked to him a little, but obviously, it meant a lot to him. As for leaving a will, look at how," he searched for the right word, "fastidious he was. Everything had to be in perfect order, including his last wishes. It's almost as if he knew the end was near."

"If only he had not walked away..." Eli's voice trailed off.

Matt stood there silently. There was nothing more to be said.

They finished packing up the room in silence. Matt placed the wallet with the letter into his inside vest pocket. They carried the stack of goods from the room and headed to the sheriff's office. Once inside they set it all on Matt's desk.

Eli opened the conversation. "You said it back there. That money was not lawfully gained, therefore it belongs to the victims."

Matt nodded his agreement. "I was thinking the same thing. In fact, I have an idea about that." He did not elaborate, so Eli left it that way. "I really don't have use for these clothes either." He decided. "I don't care to dress so flashy."

Matt nodded, "What do you want to do with them?"

Eli shook his head, "I don't know. Does the city have a donation closet for needy folks?"

Matt smiled, "I almost hate to mention this, but Brother Smith's church does."

For the first time today, Eli laughed out loud. "I hardly see that as an option."

"Maybe your church should start one." Matt countered.

"Yeah, I would love to. The only thing is, I have an issue with room; I don't have any." Eli was thinking of his shed and how tight it was in there.

"Maybe the sheriff's office can work in conjunction with the church and be a team. There's a storage closet back there which has enough room for something like this."

"Thank you Matt."

"There's one more thing." Matt stopped Eli before he could leave. He walked over to the desk drawer and unlocked it. He removed Rob's dual rig with the two Colt .45's. He handed the rig to Eli and said, "These won't replace your missing gun," He motioned toward the guns, "but they could be of good use to you. There is also a matter of a big black horse he kept in the livery."

"Yes, I'm sure they will come in handy." Eli was serious and the pun totally escaped him.

Matt looked at him earnestly. "Make sure you go out into the desert and practice with those Colt's. They handle quite a bit differently than that gun you used to have."

Eli nodded. "I will. Thank you for your concern. You've been a good friend....I'm glad I have you to talk to."

"Anytime."

* * *

Becky stuck her head out the front door. When Matt left, Joshua went out to take care of his horse. He removed the saddle, finished rubbing the animal down and made sure it had water and hay. Becky was pleased to see he did not neglect the animal. It spoke highly of the boy's upbringing so far. She lifted her head and smiled at Joshua, who was just coming out of the barn.

"Joshua, honey, would you bring in two buckets of water for me?"

"Yes ma'am." He changed course and headed to the well. He filled the two buckets and with one in either hand, hobbled across the yard to the front door, sloshing water onto the side of his pants legs. Becky let him in and directed him to the stove where there was a large pot over the fire. Together they poured the water into the pot, one bucket at a time and Becky asked him for two more buckets.

Becky smiled to herself. It was obvious Joshua was puzzled, but he did not complain, he just went out and got two more buckets. *"Like he'd told them, the boy was going to earn his keep."*

This time, Becky had him set the buckets next to the tub she had hauled out into the middle of the room. Joshua looked at the tub warily.

"Oh yes, young man, you are going to take a bath." Becky had both hands on her hips and suddenly realized she was acting just like her mother. She grinned at the thought.

"I don't think that's funny." Joshua grumbled.

"What's not funny is the way you smell, young man. How long has it been since you took a bath?"

"I dunno. Ain't no water out in the desert." Joshua had a pouty look which made Becky's smile grow even bigger.

"That water is going to take some time to boil. Why don't we sit down at the table and talk for a bit." Becky tried to make up for her inappropriate smile.

Joshua still wore a sullen look, but obediently he plopped down in a chair, leaning on his elbows. Becky sat down across the table from him.

"What would you like to talk about?" She asked.

"I dunno."

"Why don't you tell me a little about yourself?"

"Not much to tell. My pa was kilt by Rob Handy and my ma...mother died a few months back."

"How old are you, Joshua." Her voice was soft.

"Twelve and a half, ma'am."

"You're very grown up for twelve and a half. Don't you miss not having time to just be a kid?"

"I dunno."

Becky changed tact. "Joshua. It's a good, strong Biblical name. Were you named after Joshua in the Bible?"

"I dunno...I don't think so. My ma...mother, never was much for going to church, specially after pa died."

"Why is that?" Becky inquired.

"She said she didn't want to have anything to do with God if he was going to take pa away from us."

Becky mulled that over for a moment. "How do you feel about God?"

"I dunno. I guess I don't think much about Him."

"Would you like to hear a story about the Joshua in the Bible?" Becky asked.

Joshua shrugged his shoulders then nodded. As Becky started to talk, Joshua took the time to size her up. She was only about five foot two, a good six inches shorter than he was. Her auburn hair looked brown inside the house, but outside, the sun set off the reddish highlights. She was pretty and petite with pale skin and a quick smile. *I like her,* he thought. *I like how she made me feel welcome, even though she doesn't know me.*

"After God used Moses to lead the Israelites out of Egypt, Joshua was the leader of the Israelite army. He was a mighty warrior and trusted God with all things. God led the Israelites to the edge of land He'd promised them, and Moses sent in twelve spies to scout out the land. Ten of those spies came back full of fear and gave a negative report about the occupants of the land, saying they were too big and dangerous.

But Joshua and Caleb came back carrying the fruit of the land and argued that God would be true to his word. They encouraged Moses to go into the land and take it over, just like God had instructed them to."

He leaned forward eagerly. "What happened?" He was fascinated.

Becky continued, "The Israelites chose to follow the recommendation of the ten spies, so God did not allow them into the Promised Land. Instead, they wandered in the wilderness until all the men of fighting age had died off. All except Joshua and Caleb.

Joshua was into the story now. "Then what?"

"That is going to have to wait, because your bath water is ready." Becky got up from the table and proceeded to pour the boiling water into the bathtub. Next she picked up the cold water and poured it in, testing it until the temperature felt just right.

"Alright young man, I'm going to step out onto the porch. You take those dirty clothes off and hand them out the door to me." She handed him a bar of soap. "Oh, just a moment." She disappeared into the back room and returned with a towel and washrag, along with some of Matt's old clothes. "You can put these on when you're done. It is going to take a while for you to get all that dirt off. Don't think you're going to just jump in and right back out. You scrub yourself until you're completely clean, do you understand?"

Joshua's eyes grew large and he sighed. He understood alright. He nodded and Becky stepped outside.

* * *

A few minutes later, Joshua's hand appeared through a cracked door holding his dirty duds. Becky took them in her fingertips, and in a few minutes was scrubbing them on the washboard tub she kept outside. It was a good half hour before she finished and hung them on the clothes line. His clothing needed mending, but that could wait for now, at least until they dried.

A few minutes later, Joshua came out of the house wearing Matt's clothes. The shirt bagged way out and he had the pant cuffs rolled up. A belt finished the ensemble, cinched tight to keep the pants from falling down. Becky had to work hard not to laugh and to hide the smile that wanted to appear.

Joshua looked mighty self-conscious over the baggy clothing, but to his credit, he asked, "What do you want me to do now, ma'am?"

"Oh, I've tortured you enough for today, so why don't you just explore the ranch?" Becky went on to point out some crude boundaries for him and finished by saying, "Just be back here by supper time, you hear?"

"Yes ma'am." With enthusiasm the boy hustled over to the barn to saddle his horse.

Becky felt satisfied and happy. It was obviously one of the first times since his pa died that the boy had a whole afternoon just to play. No chores, no trying to figure out where his next meal was coming from. Just goofing around.

CHAPTER ELEVEN

Matt was at the station when the stage rolled into town in the late afternoon. The first person off was Judge Middleton.

"Good afternoon sir, how was your trip?" Matt asked.

"Hot and sweaty son. But you wouldn't expect any less now would you?" The Judge had a wide grin which seemed incongruous for his esteemed position. Looking at him, you would never guess he was a Judge. He dressed in newer jeans, a plain tan shirt, black leather vest, black polished boots and a cowboy hat which did not show sweat stains around the brim. There was no frocked coat, broadcloth suit or any of the other trappings you would expect from a circuit Judge.

Off the bench, he was known to be a jovial, gregarious man who did not hold himself above those around him because of his position. The only evidence of his importance was in his bearing. He was slim and stood ramrod straight, appearing even taller than his six foot frame.

"It's been hot and sweaty for all of us," Matt said. "I assume you are staying at the hotel?"

"I am. It's been long time since I've been in this town though. Are there any good places to eat? Frankly, I'm famished." Came the reply

"Sam is a wonderful cook, as long as you don't mind eating in a saloon."

The judge rubbed his hands together in anticipation. "I'm not proud, as long as the cooking is good."

Matt grinned. "I'll tell you; Sam could have been a chef in one of those fancy San Francisco restaurants you hear about. He stays here because he likes being his own boss. Trust me, you won't be sorry."

"Thank you. I'll give it a try as soon as I get rid of this bag. Would you like to join me?

"I think I would," Matt responded, "I have a small matter I'd like to discuss with you, If you don't mind talking business over your meal."

A short while later, the men were seated at a table in The Saloon. A heaping plate of delicious food was placed in front of the judge, while Matt sat nursing a cold beer.

"Are you sure you won't join me for dinner?" the Judge asked.

"Thank you, but my wife will have mine waiting for me. I don't want to disappoint her."

"You're a smart man. You need to treasure your wife if you want to keep her happy." He changed the subject. "What did you need to talk to me about?"

"We had a shooting in town this morning." Matt began, but the Judge interrupted him.

"Wait a minute. If this is about a case that's going to be prosecuted, I can't discuss it with you."

"No sir, it's not."

The Judge nodded. "Alright sheriff, I'm sorry to interrupt you."

Matt replied, "No, no, it's not a problem." He continued with his story, "Rob Handy, the gunfighter, was shot and killed by a twelve year old boy."

"WHAT!" The Judge stopped eating and dropped his fork with a clatter.

Matt told the story to him and wrapped it up with his explanation. "The boy is currently at my house and I am looking for legal guidance on what to do with him."

"Off the top of my head, he is an orphan and likely needs to be taken to the County Orphanage. I can look into it for you if you would like?"

"No sir, that's alright," Matt responded. "The problem is that my wife seems to have taken a shine to the boy. When I left the house this afternoon, she was already making plans for him to attend school and whatnot. I guess I'm asking for your opinion on what I should do."

"Are you thinking of adopting the boy?" The Judge asked.

Matt sighed, a frown furrowing his brow. "I honestly don't know. This all has happened so fast, I don't know what I think, or what I want. I just know a part of my wife suddenly seems to have come to life, like she has found new purpose."

Matt felt the freedom to confide to the Judge what he had told no one else, about Becky losing the baby and her heart break. "I don't know if having this boy around is good or bad, I just know that for the time being it seems important to my wife, so it is important to me."

The Judge nodded and thought for a few moments while he resumed eating. Then he put his fork down. "I don't want to play with this boy's life like he is a pawn in a chess game, but on the other hand, I don't see how sending him to an orphanage would be the best thing for him. I propose we leave him in your custody and see how things work out. If it is a good fit for both you and the boy, if that's what you want, we can see about making it legal when I come through next time."

"Thank you Judge. I'd like to see that boy have a chance in life."

The Judge changed the subject. "Wasn't there a reward out on Rob Handy?"

"Yes sir, quite a substantial amount."

"What are you going to do with that?" the Judge queried.

"I sent off a telegraph claiming it for the boy," he glanced around the room to make sure no one could hear what he was saying. "It's $5,000. That's a heck of a lot of money for a twelve year old. I need your advice on that as well."

"I would say that you go to the bank and open up a trust for him. Have it drawn up so he can't access the money until he is eighteen. The money will draw interest and by the time he has grown up, hopefully, he will know how to properly handle that amount of money."

Matt nodded. "Thank you." He changed the subject. "There is also the matter of the money that was found in Rob Handy's effects." He grimaced. "It was obviously obtained illicitly. The boy was a victim—Handy killed his father. At Rob's hand he lost everything. I was thinking maybe that money should be added to the reward."

"That's a great idea, Sheriff. I'll draw up the paperwork tomorrow to make it legal and you can add it to the trust."

Matt sighed. He felt lighter, as though a great weight had been lifted from his shoulders.

They were engaged in casual conversation when Eli walked in. He saw Matt and started toward the table, then changed his direction. It was obvious he didn't want to interrupt the sheriff, since he was talking to a stranger. But Matt caught Eli's attention and called him over.

"Eli, this is Judge Middleton. Judge, this is Eli Exeter."

The Judge stood and shook Eli's hand. "Eli Exeter from down Utah way?" He asked.

"Yes sir," Eli responded.

"You've made quite a reputation for yourself down there. Please, have a seat." The Judge motioned to one of the empty chairs.

"Thank you." Eli pulled out a chair as Sam brought him a cup of coffee. "Thank you, Sam." He smiled noting the sheriff sat the same as he did, where they could both keep an eye on the door.

Judge Middleton turned to Eli, "So what brings you to Nevada? Are you still a lawman?"

"No sir, I've hung up the badge. I'm now a preacher."

For the second time that day the Judge's face showed his surprise. "A preacher? Why a preacher? From what I've heard, you were a mighty good lawman!"

Eli shared his experiences with the Judge. After he finished his explanation, the Judge asked, "So what brings a preacher into a saloon in the middle of the day?"

"Sam makes one of the best cups of coffee in town. Besides, you're sitting in the middle of my church sanctuary."

The Judge stared at him in disbelief.

Eli grinned at the reaction. "You got to hold church somewhere."

The Judge shook his head and grinned. "Go to the sinner, don't make the sinner come to you?"

Eli returned his smile and nodded, "Yeah, something like that. I figure these cowboys and saloon girls are the forgotten folks and I want to reach out to them. If I am able get those folks to turn to Jesus instead of a life of crime, I've done far more for the person and the community than I ever could do as a lawman."

The Judge nodded his agreement. "You're absolutely right. These people need a heart change much more than they need jail time. I thoroughly understand your issue with criminals who constantly move in and out of our jails. Maybe we just need more churches and not so many jails."

"No." Eli disagreed. "We need more of God's people to care about those around them." He shook his head. "Judge, we all need to care that people are going to hell. We should be willing and able to reach out to them—to give them a chance at real, abundant life in Christ. Folks have got to stop depending upon the preacher to save all heathens. It's too big of a job for just preachers. Everyone needs to get involved." He spoke with the passion of his conviction.

The Judge nodded his head, "I've never heard it put quite like that, but I see your point."

They conversed for a while longer, until finally Eli pushed his chair back. He laid a coin on the table. "Judge, our church service here starts at eleven o'clock Sunday morning," he invited. "I'd be right proud to have you come."

The Judge smiled broadly, "I don't think I'd miss it for the world. I'll see you at the saloon on Sunday morning.

Matt returned home, riding straight to the barn to care for his horse. He had a few hours until the night rounds began and he didn't want to leave the saddle on the animal all that time.

As he walked to the house, Becky greeted him on the porch. "Food will be on in a few minutes. Why don't you wash up?"

He walked over and gave his wife a passionate kiss. She returned the kiss, but pushed him away, "Be good. We have company."

Matt smiled, "Being good never gets me anywhere."

"Oh you." Becky's cheeks were starting to show some color. "You just wash up." She wrinkled her nose at him.

The dinner smelled delicious. Matt realized he was famished and hurried to wash up. When he came into the house, the first thing he noticed was Joshua setting the table. The next thing he took note of was how clean the boy was, both his clothes, hands and his face. Even the boy's hair was combed and Matt realized Joshua was a nice looking kid.

After praying over the meal, everyone dug in. There was not much conversation as they ate, but when they had finished Matt pushed his chair back from the table and stretched out his legs, leaning back in the chair.

As he sipped on his coffee, he listened first to Becky, then to Joshua as they told him about their afternoon. As he did, he could not help but think of what a good life he had.

It was his turn to tell them of his own day—so he regaled them with his conversation at lunch with Eli and the Judge. They all laughed when he told them the Judge's reaction to Eli being a preacher in a saloon. The hours quickly passed, as he enjoyed being home. But too soon, it was time to head back into town and he found himself wondering where the time went.

The town was unusually quiet that night, so Matt made it back home relatively early. He climbed into bed next to Becky and together they whispered to each other as they held on to one another in the darkness. Finally they both drifted off to sleep.

* * *

It was in the pitch dark of night that Matt's eyes flew open and he grabbed for his pistol as Becky leaped out of bed, threw on her robe and bolted from the room. Matt sat up, rubbing the sleep from his eyes, endeavoring to identify what he was hearing. He suddenly realized the strange noise that had awakened him was sobs from the young boy in the next room. Becky had simply been much quicker in recognizing the source. Matt re-holstered the gun, got up, slid into his pants and threw on a shirt before going to the room.

Becky had lit a lantern in the room and he could see her as she sat on the edge of the bed hugging the boy. Tears coursed down his young face as he cried on her shoulder. Through his sobs, he told her of his anguish over killing a man. Matt watched in admiration and tenderness as he once again realized what a special woman she was. Her compassion was strong and she had the gentle touch of a mother as her soothing voice quickly calmed the boy.

As the sobs subsided, Becky made Joshua lay back down in the bed, then she stroked his forehead and hair, until he fell into a peaceful sleep. She motioned to Matt to bring her rocking chair into the room and to blow out the lantern. Matt brought her an extra blanket and wrapped it around her as she sat by the boy's bed. He then returned to his own bed and soon fell into a sound sleep.

* * *

Sunday rolled around, a beautifully sunny day. Eli and Steven had resumed their morning breakfast, and once again, Eli previewed his sermon with Steven. When he had finished, Steven nodded in approval. "You are spot on, Eli. Let's pray for these men and women now."

Together, the men got down on their knees and spent time praying for each man and woman by name. Then they prayed for those who might show up for the first time. They asked the Holy Ghost to make His presence known in the building and to work in the hearts of the men and women. When they had finished and gotten back to their feet, Eli turned to Steven.

"Can you help me with one more thing before you take off?" He asked.

"Of course."

Together they went out back and carried in the blood-stained boards Eli had pulled up from the porch and set them against the wall.

True to his word, the Judge showed up for the church service. He was the first one there. He gazed at Steven long and hard. Finally he must have realized he was staring, "I'm sorry. I thought I recognized you, but I can't place you. Please forgive me for staring."

Steven smiled and replied, "Don't think nothing of it. I don't expect you would remember who I am. My name is Steven Bosco."

"Steven? You used to..." He stopped himself.

Steven nodded, "Yes, I am that Steven."

"What happened to you? You look great." Amazement showed on the Judge's face.

"I found God and salvation through His Son, Jesus. He cured me from my drinking."

"Praise the Lord! Hallelujah!" Came the judge's reply

Steven nodded in agreement. "Amen to that."

It was nearly time for the service to start as Steven said his goodbyes and quietly slipped out the back door.

It wasn't but a few minutes later the next person arrived. News of Eli's return had spread like wild fire through the cowboy community, and every one of his former parishioners returned. There were even a couple of new faces in the crowd. The first thing everyone seemed to notice were three wooden crosses, covered with the reddish brown stain of blood, leaning against the wall.

Eli turned to the Judge, "Sir, can I get you anything to drink?"

"Coffee would be fine, thank you."

Eli handed him a steaming mug and then proceeded to serve everyone as they came to the bar. When everyone had their choice of drink, off came the apron and Eli picked up his Bible, but instead of opening it, he simply looked at the crowd.

Back in the corner were Susan and Mary. As he scanned the crowd he saw Slim and his riding partner. Adam was there, as well as Bert and Jerry. Matt Wheaton walked in at the last moment and took a chair in the back where he could watch the door. Somewhere outside, he knew Steven Bosco was on his knees praying for the souls of these men and women.

"How many of you fought in the army?" Eli asked. He was not surprised to see over half of the hands go up. Men of the west were patriotic and to serve their country was almost a given. "And how many of you have fought against the Indians?" All of the same hands were raised, as well as a number of added hands. "The Indian nations have all but been defeated. The white man have come in as conquerors and taken the land and we are flourishing. Isn't that true?" All of the heads were nodding, "Yet when is the last time you heard about an Indian attack?"

From the center of the room, came an answer from one of the men. "Three weeks ago, there was a raid on a ranch east of here. They got several head of horses, but no one was killed."

"Right, they come in and hit a place and run off some stock, but for all intents and purposes, the war is said to be over, right? Well, my friends, that's the same strategy Satan uses."

Eli continued. "The Bible tells us in the beginning God created the Heavens and the earth. God had existed for eternity past and He will exist for eternity future. Satan on the other hand, is a created being. God created him to be the head of all of the angels. But Satan grew prideful. He wanted to be greater than God himself. The created needed the Creator to *worship him.* As a result, Satan was kicked out of heaven, he and all of the angels who had aligned themselves with him. You might say the only thing Satan created was sin itself."

Most of the faces of the listening men and women were intent.

"Satan, or the devil--they are one and the same, tempted Adam and Eve, another of God's perfect creations and the two succumbed to temptation and sinned against God. With that, the perfect world God created became a broken world and all of creation suffered."

Eli had their full attention now. He ruffled the pages of his Bible as he emphasized, "Throughout the Old Testament, there is example after example of God seeking after mankind, seeking a relationship with men who often turned their backs on God. "

"Nearly nineteen hundred years ago, God sent His own Son, Jesus, to us. Jesus walked the earth; healing the sick and raising the dead. He taught folks about His Father God in heaven. The religious leaders of the day did not accept Jesus for who He was--the Savior of the world. Instead, they killed Him. The Son of God was nailed to a cross between two thieves."

He pointed to the three blood stained crosses leaning against the wall. "The devil thought he had won the war. He had deceived the religious leaders the way he had deceived Adam and Eve. They had killed the Son of God. He was crucified and buried on a Friday. But on the following Sunday He arose from the dead. In reality, Satan had won the battle, but Jesus won the war."

"I see it like this." Eli paced the floor. Then he paused. "Satan, just like the Indians has been defeated, but he still conducts raids. He strikes here and there, deceiving people, trying to get them to reject God. He is called the father of lies and he'll try to get you to believe God couldn't love you. He will try to make you think there's something better out there.

"Men and women, God created a hunger for Him within each of us. " Eli spoke softly. "Sometimes we try to fill that God-shaped, empty space with things that do not satisfy; money, prestige, women." He gestured toward the two woman seated in the back, "or men, liquor and all kinds of other things Satan tries to tell us will satisfy, yet those vices do nothing to quench our real hunger for God."

"When Jesus was on this earth, He met a woman at a well in the country of Samaria. His disciples had gone into town for supplies, leaving him alone there. The woman came to draw water in the mid-afternoon and He started talking to her about water. He described Himself as living water and that whoever drank of the water He gave would never thirst again. He described for the woman all the bad she had ever done, and she believed in Jesus because she knew then that He was a great prophet. She even brought the whole town back to meet Him."

"I believe there is a double meaning in this story. First, our spiritual thirst is quenched; and second, we can find fulfillment and purpose in life when we accept Jesus into our hearts and turn our will over to Him."

Eli continued. "Jesus also told the story of Lazarus, who was a beggar, and of the rich man whose front gate Lazarus begged at. Both men died and Lazarus went to Abraham's bosom and the rich man ended up in hell."

"Uh, what's Abraham's bosom?" One of the men interrupted.

Eli couldn't help but smile. "Abraham's bosom, or Paradise, was where the souls of those who were faithful to God went before Jesus' resurrection."

Eli patiently explained, "Before Jesus was resurrected, they waited in that place for the Messiah, God's Son-- for Jesus. Scripture says when Jesus rose from the grave, He took those waiting souls back to heaven with Him."

The man nodded and remarked. "Well, that makes better sense."

Eli returned to his sermon. "Then the rich man died. But he ended up in the fire on the other side of Paradise. He saw Lazarus and cried out to Abraham, asking for Lazarus to dip his fingers in water and to touch his lips because he was in such torment from the flames of hell."

Eli let his gaze scan the crowd before he suggested, "I have not spoken to you about hell before, because so many preachers seem to have made it their goal to scare people into heaven by focusing on hell fire and damnation.

But friends, I would be remiss in not mentioning that hell is a very real place in which souls will be tormented for eternity. When Jesus spoke of never thirsting again, I believe he was saying that folks who believe in Him will not face eternal torment---that unquenchable thirst which will torment those who spend eternity in hell.

You have a choice," he offered. "Heaven or Hell, but the choice is yours and yours alone."

Eli finished his message, realizing he'd gone longer than he'd intended. But his desire to get the good news of Salvation had trumped his desire to end on time. As he looked out at the men and women who made up his little congregation, the compassion he felt overwhelmed him.

He continued speaking a moment longer. "'For God so loved the world that He sent His only begotten Son, That whosoever believes in Him will not perish but have eternal life. For God did not send the Son into the world to condemn the world, but that the world would be saved through Him,' that's from John three, sixteen and seventeen.

I don't want to see any of you die and go to hell and neither does God. He sent His own Son to die on the cross, to pay for our sins so that we can have a relationship with God here on earth and spend eternity with Him in Heaven."

He gravely continued. "I want to see each and every one of you accept the forgiveness that He offers. If you want to receive the gift of Salvation, I am going to ask you to come forward. I have never pushed any of you to accept Jesus, but I am pushing you now."

Tears began to well up in Eli's eyes. "Two days ago, a man died in my arms and it broke my heart. I have no idea where he is spending eternity. I don't want to ever again be in a situation where I am left to wonder if I had done enough..." He left the thought hanging in the air.

Judge Middleton must have felt the Spirit's nudge, for he stood and addressed the small crowd, "I myself made that decision over twenty years ago and I can honestly say it is the best decision I ever made. My choice to follow Jesus set me on a course that changed my life, changed it for the better. Please don't fight it. If you know God is speaking to you now, don't ignore it. You just don't know, this could be your last chance."

As the Judge spoke, Eli began to offer up an earnest silent prayer.

No sooner did the Judge finish his entreaty, Mary stood up. "I want to be forgiven. I am so tired of my life, of who I am." She walked forward and Susan stood up and followed behind, tears streaming down her face. Across the room, Slim stood up as well, hat in hand and began the trek to the front of the room. Another and then still another stood to walk forward. It was as if a dam had broken and the flow of water could not be stopped. Soon more than half of the room was standing up front with Eli.

"Does anyone else wish to come to Jesus now?" He asked. But the remainder of the group remained seated, most of them holding their hats in their laps. Some didn't seem quite ready to take that first step. Others, as in Adam's case, had already trusted in Jesus.

Eli turned his attention to the gathering at the front of the room. "Welcome to God's kingdom," he exclaimed. "Why don't you bow your heads and repeat after me as I pray."

He led the group in a prayer of confession and salvation. When they finished, he looked up to find the room was empty except for Matt, the Judge, and those who had prayed to receive Christ.

"I am grateful that as of this minute, you are my brothers and sisters in Christ. Welcome." He turned to Matt, "Would you help me?"

"Please be seated." Eli asked the men and women to wait, as he and Matt went back to his shed where he retrieved Bibles for all of them. Each new believer received their own Bible. As they reverently opened the leather bound books—Eli could tell the gift meant a great deal.

As they left, Eli shook hands with each of the men. In no time, everyone was gone, except for Susan and Mary, who seemed to have purposely waited for the room to empty.

Mary spoke first. "For the first time that I can remember, I feel clean inside," the smile on her face seemed to have no end. "I want to know what I should do from here."

Susan was beaming as well, "Yes, I don't ever want this feeling of joy to go away."

"What you have now, can never be taken from you," Eli observed. "You have been sealed by the Holy Ghost, which is kind of like saying God has taken ownership of your soul. No one is powerful enough to rip you out of His hand."

Eli pointed to the Bibles in their hands and said, "This is God's love letter to you. Read what He has to say. The book tells you of His love for you and teaches how a child of God is expected to behave. Not because you can earn anything with your good behavior, but because you love Him and want to please Him. Finally, just like Jesus once instructed a woman who had been justly condemned for her sin of adultery, to 'go and sin no more,' I give you the same advice."

The two women, once prostitutes, but now daughters of the King, exchanged worried glances. "We are going to have to quit our jobs today. Hank is not going to like it."

Eli watched their faces wrinkle with worry and volunteered, "Would you like me to go with you while you talk to him?" But that seemed to raise the anxiety level in both women.

"No," Susan replied, "This is something we have to do ourselves."

"Let's pray together before you go." Eli took each of them by the hand, forming a small circle. They bowed their heads as Eli prayed for strength and protection over the women, claiming the promises of God over them. When he finished, he was moved by the great peace suffusing the faces in front of him.

"We can do this in God's strength and power." Susan pronounced.

"Yes, we can." Chimed in Mary

Eli smiled. "Amen."

* * *

Susan and Mary walked together up to the River Saloon. Hank met them at the door and sneered angrily, "Where have you been?" The women tried to engage him in conversation, but Hank interrupted them. "Get your things and clear out." He was yelling as loud as he could. "You're fired. I'm not having any of my girls goin' ta church. Get out of here and don't you ever come back!"

The women exchanged glances, then nearly skipped past Hank in their happiness and scurried up the stairs.

They were throwing their belongings into their carpet bags when the other saloon girls came rushing in. The self-appointed spokeswoman piped up. "We heard what Hank did. We are so sorry. What will you do now?"

Susan and Mary stopped their packing. "Don't be sorry. We were coming in to quit." They described how they had accepted Jesus that morning and the difference He had made in their hearts, of the joy and complete freedom they'd felt since.

They told of the pastor who had prayed with them because they were afraid of Hank's reaction once he caught wind of their decision. Then they shared the gospel message with the women, repeating to the brightly clad ladies of the night the hope they had learned and embraced.

When they finished, they invited the ladies to come to church. One of the girls stepped back in concern. "I can't lose my job. What would happen to me?" Mary turned to her, "God has promised to provide our needs. Susan and I, we're scared...we don't know what we are going to do, but we are also excited to see how God is going to provide. You just need to trust in Him."

They finished their packing and hugged the girls, quickly saying their goodbyes before leaving the brothel for the last time.

CHAPTER TWELVE

Becky and Joshua were leaving Brother Smith's church service. Joshua, seated next to Becky in the buckboard, was quiet. Finally, Becky broke the silence. "What did you think of church today?"

Joshua stared straight ahead and held his tongue for a moment before blurting out, "I don't like him."

Becky was about to chide him but instead asked, "Who, Brother Smith? Why not?"

"I don't like the way he looked at you."

"What do you mean?" Becky asked in consternation.

"I once'st saw a cowboy look at a whore like he was looking at you." Joshua suddenly realized what he had just said and began to blush furiously.

Becky felt the color rising in her neck as well, but wisely held her tongue. If she was going to get through to this boy, it would not do to keep correcting him when he misspoke. Besides, he had simply confirmed something which had been nagging at her in the back of her mind. Still, she felt she must defend the pastor.

"I'm sure it's nothing like that."

"Yes ma'am," he replied to Becky, but in his mind, Joshua was certain of what he knew.

* * *

Eli hurried downtown, looking for Matt. He did not find him at the Sheriff's Office, so he peeked in the door of the bakery and each of the restaurants in town without success. Asking around, he discovered Matt had met up with Becky and Joshua and was headed home for the afternoon.

He contemplated riding out to the house, but decided it wasn't that pressing. He went into the hotel to borrow some paper and a pen and jotted down a note. He blew on the ink to force it to dry quicker, then folded it and walked back to the Sheriff's office where he slid it under the door.

* * *

Peggy was the one woman who was not at the impromptu farewell party at the brothel for Susan and Mary. She waited in the shadows, out of sight, until everyone was gone. Then she walked in through the back door of the church, to find Brother Smith standing at the front of the church by the podium.

He turned to greet her as she entered through the back door, "Yes, my young lamb, how may I assist you?"

Peggy stared him in the eye. "I know all about you."

His lips tightened and he had to wait for his heart to start beating again before responding. "What do you mean, my dear?"

"You hired two men to kidnap and beat Eli Exeter almost to death."

His heart stopped again. *How did she know?* Inside, he suddenly seethed, *"those inept fools! How could they have been so careless as to leave a witness behind? How did she KNOW?"* He calmed himself down before replying. "I have no idea what you are talking about my dear."

Peggy's gaze never wavered. "Of course you do. I don't think Mr. Exeter would be happy if he were to find out you were responsible for his cracked ribs. Of course he does not have to find out, but it's going to cost you."

Brother Smith tried to continue to run his bluff, "You must have the wrong person..."

Peggy cut him off. Her no nonsense tone was harsh, "Cut the crap Preacher. The more you talk the higher the price will be. Right now all you owe me is $500. But if you keep on lying I can raise the price a hundred dollars a word." She spoke in a menacing tone, "I would be very careful before I opened my mouth if I were you. How do you want to proceed?"

Smith was taken aback by her bluntness but he had sense enough to shut his mouth. The silence was heavy for the next several seconds. Smith was contemplating how many steps it would take to reach her. Would anyone hear her yell? He could snap the woman's scrawny neck.

"Well?" All thoughts of killing her left his mind as he stared down the barrel of the revolver she had produced from her purse. The gun was rock steady as she pointed the muzzle straight at his chest. What decided him was when she thumbed back the hammer and her familiarity with the weapon was evident.

"It's going to take me some time to get that much money together. I don't have that kind of money just sitting around."

"How long do you need?"

Smith's mind raced, he needed to buy some time. "It'll take me at least a week."

"It will cost you a thousand then. If you want to keep it down to $500, you'll have it for me by tomorrow afternoon before my shift starts." Before he could answer, she de-cocked the gun, stowed it in her purse and quietly slipped out the door.

When she was gone, Smith cursed out loud, swearing vehemently before he calmed down. He had to think. He had a good thing going here, the people were trusting fools and he was skimming money from the church coffers without restriction. He had many of those idiots believing they could *buy* their salvation and he had profited greatly because of it.

Now it was all starting to unravel. He had to either kill this girl, or get out of town. Killing her would not be as easy as the others he had killed, for obviously this one was a woman of the world. She was neither innocent nor easy. His mind was racing as he headed back to the parsonage, still searching for a solution. It would have to be the solution from which he would profit from the most.

* * *

While Matt and Joshua stayed in the barn to care for the animals, Becky hurried into the house to prepare the noon time meal.

"How was church this morning?" Matt was simply making conversation to fill the void.

"I don't like him."

Matt was surprised at the intensity in the boy's voice. "What happened to make you feel that way?" he asked, surprised that the boy already felt the way he did after only one Sunday.

Joshua repeated his concerns, only this time he did not blush, as he shared with another man his observations.

Matt mentally kicked himself for not going to church more often with his wife. It was his job to protect her, not that of his young ward. "Joshua, I appreciate you sharing that with me. By the way, you're not the first one to bring up that concern about him. You have good instincts."

Joshua's face lit up at the praise. He was pleased Mr. Wheaton would treat him as an equal.

They finished caring for the animals and made their way to the house.

* * *

Dinner consisted of thick slices of ham and potatoes with some vegetables fresh from the garden. When they had eaten, Matt leaned back to enjoy his coffee.

Becky surprised him with a question. "How was the service at the saloon today?"

He had not advertised he had gone to Eli's church, nor had he tried to hide it. He had begun the day doing some work at the office, as he normally did, before heading on in.

By now he should recognize how intuitive Becky was.

"It was amazing," he confided. "Eli has put a lot of time and energy into those men and women and today it paid off in a big way." He spoke of the Judge's intervention and the flood of people who came forward to receive salvation in Jesus.

Becky, who was a woman of great faith, was animated with excitement. He watched the expression on Joshua's face, as the boy shifted from disinterest to being drawn into the story, even though he was trying to pretend not to care.

"Two of the local Saloon Girls were the first to come forward and receive Jesus today. God is working in a powerful way in this town. I can tell that there are going to be great things coming."

The three of them discussed the events of the day until Joshua became bored with it. He went out to play and Matt and Becky spent time together, enjoying one another's company until it was time for Matt to head back into town to make his evening rounds.

Matt saw the note under the door immediately and read it. *"Please come and see me, I have information for you. ~ Eli."*

The Sheriff left the office and headed toward The Saloon, where he found Eli helping Sam behind the bar. Eli took off his apron, grabbed two cups of coffee and pointed Matt to a corner table out of earshot of the rest of the room.

"What do you have for me?" Matt was right to the point.

"I finally remembered where I saw that woman."

"The woman who lured you into the alley?" Matt asked.

"Yes," Eli responded. "I met her at the river the first Sunday I was here. She was with Mary and Susan. If I recall correctly, I believe her name was Peggy. I didn't get a good look at her face that night, but her voice....I'm sure the woman was her."

Matt pondered that for a moment. "If you're sure, I will go question her."

"I'm certain." Eli answered with conviction.

"Okay," Matt replied, "I'll head on over to talk to her now."

Eli returned to work as Matt headed off to The River Saloon. He strode through the door and made a quick survey of the women in the room. Peggy was nowhere to be seen.

He made his way to the bar and waited for the bartender.

Slapping a white towel over one shoulder, the fat bartender asked, "What'll you have, a stiff whiskey I suppose?"

"I need to talk to Peggy." Matt brusquely answered.

"She's busy." The bartender was new in town and he eyed the badge on Matt's vest.

"I'll have a beer while I wait."

"I don't know how long she'll be." His tone was less than friendly.

Matt lowered his voice, forcing the bartender to lean forward to hear. "Let's get something straight here. I can be the nicest sheriff you will ever deal with, but if you want me to be a jerk, you keep on pushing. I want the beer and I want that young woman down here before the beer is done. Otherwise, you might want to find another town to tend bar in. Am I making myself clear?" His intense stare caused the man to avert his gaze.

The bartender moved in a hurry. The beer was placed in front of Matt, who put a coin on the bar and moved to a table out of the way and semi-private. His beer was less than two inches from the bottom of the mug when Peggy sashayed her way to his table.

"You wanted to talk to me? Or did you want to go upstairs?" She asked coyly.

Ignoring the second question, and focusing on the first, Matt motioned her into the chair across from him.

"Who were the two men you were working with when you lured Eli into the alley?"

His directness caught her off guard. She swallowed then stammered an answer before she had time to weigh it out, "I-I don't have a clue what you're talking about."

"I've got two bored young men in the jail, who would love to have you as their cellmate, Peggy. I want some answers and I want them now. Otherwise, you'll be standing in front of the judge tomorrow right along with those boys."

"I didn't do nothing," She was panicked.

"Stand up, you're going to jail." Matt pushed his chair back and abruptly stood, reaching for a bit of rawhide he'd looped at his waist. "Put your hands out, you're coming with me."

"Wait, wait," she pleaded. Matt just stood there, towering over the still-seated prostitute. She gave in quickly. "Alright, I'll tell you everything I know."

Matt sat back down, placing the rawhide on the table between them. "Go ahead. But don't start with the lying, or you'll go straight to jail."

"I was given ten dollars to wait for Eli to come down the street and to get him into the alley. I didn't know they were going to hurt him so badly, I thought they were just going to rough him up a bit, you know, scare him some. But then the man hit him over the head so hard, I thought he'd killed him. I ran and didn't look back."

"Who were the men?" Matt asked.

"I don't know, honest. They were a couple of drifters. They never did give me their names. I had figured it was an easy way to get ten bucks." She looked at Matt's face, which could have been chiseled out of stone. His unwavering stare unnerved her. "I swear to you, that's the truth."

"What did the men look like?" Matt's normally easy going demeanor disappeared. His eyes narrowed and he looked as though he might take a punch at her.

She quickly described the two men and Matt realized it was the two he'd seen talking to Brother Smith in the darkened street. "Who hired them?"

"I have no idea. I never asked and they never told. I swear to you." She repeated, tears of fright sliding down her face.

"If I find out you have lied to me, or withheld anything, I'll be back with a vengeance. The truth is, I should just haul you in now." Matt wanted to, but he realized logistically it was not feasible.

He swallowed the last of his beer then pushed away from the table. "Don't you dare leave town until I get to the bottom of this."

Peggy looked up at his face and he saw that her entire body was trembling. Matt realized she'd decided she did not want to make him anymore angry.

"I won't go anywhere," she whispered.

* * *

It was time for Matt to begin making his rounds in town. In spite of his watchful patrol, he missed Peggy as she slipped out through back door of the saloon. She tiptoed to the parsonage and tapped softly on the door. It opened after the first knock. Brother Smith looked down at the gun in her hand.

"There's been a change in plans," she informed him. "You better have that five hundred for me when the bank opens. I have the marshal hounding me and I'm not going to jail for you." She sneered, "Just remember, it would be in *your* best interests if I disappear from this town forever. I'll see you first thing in the morning." Before he had a chance to say anything she slipped away, into the darkness.

* * *

Matt woke up Monday to the realization that he had court this morning. He got out his best clothes, brushed any dust off them and put them on. He was adjusting his tie as he went out to breakfast, only to discover that not only was Becky up making breakfast, but Joshua had joined her in the kitchen.

Becky glanced up as he came in the room and then did a double take. "My goodness! Why are you dressed so nice today?"

Matt replied, "I've got court this morning on the two boys that are in jail. Remember the Judge came into town a couple days ago."

Becky sighed, "I forgot. I was going to ask you to take Joshua to school today."

Matt grinned at Joshua. "Looks like you lucked out son." He started to mess the boy's hair, but Joshua ducked out of his reach. "Tomorrow will be your day to start school, but today, I just can't take the time out to deal with it. I'm sorry."

Joshua smiled back, pleased he had gotten away. "Yes sir, I can wait one more day."

Still smiling, Matt pointed his finger at the boy who was now across the room. "Thanks buddy. We'll get you there." He quickly wolfed down his breakfast and coffee, as he still needed to saddle his horse. But when he went outside, he found Joshua had already done it for him--without being asked.

"Thank you." Matt told him, "You are a life saver buddy. I'll see you tonight." He mounted his buckskin and asked. "Would you look after Mrs. Wheaton for me while I'm gone?"

Joshua nodded. *I really like having that young man around. He's a good kid,* Matt thought, as he rode toward town. He was grateful for the few extra minutes he had to get there.

* * *

Brother Smith made up his mind up quickly after the second visit from Peggy. He grumbled to himself as he began packing, getting his suitcases ready for an emergency escape. It was a shame he had to leave, although this time, he was able to pack up the rest of his stuff as well. At least that tramp had given him forewarning. He'd be hanged if he was going to pay her any money. She could rot in jail, or in hell for all he cared, but he was not going down with her.

He opened the wardrobe and rummaged through the contents. He lifted out the gun in its holster which the two drifters had provided. He removed the gun and tossed the holster aside. He had no use for a left-handed draw holster. He sorted through the items he felt he could not do without and left behind those things which could easily be replaced. When the packing was done, he considered leaving during the night, but decided against it. There was some unfinished business he needed to attend to.

As the first light of day showed in the Eastern sky, Brother Smith was already well on his way out of town. Before dawn he'd saddled his horse and tied his packs to the spare animal. He took the back trails, skirting the town in the dark of the predawn.

He headed toward his final stop in Scorpion Wells, riding in a manner which kept him out of view of the general public. When he was within a mile of his intended destination, he led the horses off the road and secreted them in a grove of trees.

Then he hid behind some boulders, positioning himself so he could see anyone coming or going, without being seen himself. He did not have long to wait before he heard a rider cantering down the road toward town. He identified the rider as he rode by, and waited until the man was well out of sight before getting up from his hiding spot and walking back to his horses.

Brother Smith. *He had used that alias for so long now that it was how he thought of himself.* He mounted his horse and rode out from the grove of trees to the roadway. Instead of following the rider, he rode in the opposite direction. Within a few hundred yards of the house he sought, he dismounted and tied up the horses. The house was still out of sight. He had been out to visit before and knew the lay of the land. He crept the rest of the way. The closer he was to the house, the more cautious he became. If there were to be any surprises, he wanted to be the creator. When the building was within view he hid himself and watched the house. After he was satisfied with his surveillance, he continued his approach.

He reached the porch and tippy toed forward, walking on the balls of his feet. With great stealth, he moved across the wooden boards, testing each one for squeaks. It would not do to give himself away.

The outlaw stood to the side of one of the windows and peeked inside, scanning the interior until he spotted her.

Becky Wheaton was standing at the kitchen stove, pouring a cup of coffee. Smith felt his heart racing inside of him at the sight of her beauty. The excitement began building as he thought of what he was going to do to her in the next few moments. As the adrenaline coursed through his body, his hands began to shake and for a moment he felt light headed and giddy. But the feeling passed and he reached for the front door latch.

* * *

Matt rode straight to the jail where he and the deputy placed the two boys into shackles. They had been fed and had donned the suits of clothes their parents had brought for them. Matt walked them down the street to the building where court was to be held.

He sat them at the defendants table and let them talk to the attorney who was there to represent them. He stationed his deputy in the back corner of the room where he could cover the entire area--not that Matt anticipated any trouble. He just didn't want to take any chances. His second deputy arrived and was placed at the other corner. Matt himself would be seated at the prosecutor's table.

The building began to fill with people. All witnesses were seated in chairs behind the prosecution. The boys' parents were there, seated in the galley. Soon there was standing room only. This was a big event in a small town of this size, which definitely lacked adequate entertainment. Most businesses were closed and the proprietors were in court to watch the proceedings.

Matt surveyed the room and figured most everyone in town was there, then it struck him that Eli was not present in the crowd. As he thought about it though, he wasn't too surprised he would be absent. Eli had sat through any number of these trials in his career and he certainly didn't have a dog in this fight.

The judge entered and the Court was called to order. Once the room quieted, Judge Middleton began the proceedings. *'The lawyers, like most lawyers, loved to hear the sound of their own voices,'* Matt thought. *'With this large of an audience, they were going to take advantage.'*

There was bluster and shouting which would reach a high crescendo and then crash down to almost a whisper causing the crowd to lean forward in their chairs in order to hear. The barristers had an audience and like an actor on-stage, these men were going to play to the crowd, and they did it well. The town's folk were loving it.

Matt was called as the first witness. He testified of his arrival on scene, the forming of the posse and the subsequent chase. He spoke of finding the lame horse and quickly catching up to the boys who had doubled up on one horse. He told the court how they had arrested the trio.

When the prosecution finished, the defense asked the prerequisite questions: Did you see the boys commit the robbery? How do you know that it was the correct trail you followed and so on?

Matt dutifully answered, and to his relief, he was soon off the witness stand and back in his seat at the prosecution table. The next witness could now take his turn.

It was shortly after nine o'clock when Bert came into the courtroom. He pushed his way through the crowd and leaned down to whisper in Matt's ear. The Judge slammed his gavel and ordered silence as a murmur arose from the crowd. It took a moment before everyone quieted down.

Matt quickly read the sheet of paper that Bert handed him then lifted his face to address the Judge. "Your Honor, a very pressing matter has come up which needs my attention. I am requesting your permission to be excused from the rest of these proceedings?"

Judge Middleton addressed the two attorneys, "Is this witness needed any longer?" When both men assured the Judge the Sheriff's time on the witness stand was complete, Judge Middleton nodded, giving the sheriff permission to leave.

Together Bert and Matt pushed their way out of the crowded room. They parted ways on the sidewalk and Matt headed to the Sheriff's Office. He changed into his work clothes, and headed straight to The Saloon. When he walked in, Eli was there, just finishing up his morning chores.

"Good morning Sheriff. I expected you to be at the trial this morning." Eli walked to the stove and poured them both a cup of coffee.

"Morning. Oh, I was, but I got this message and didn't think it could wait." Matt pushed the paper across the table to Eli.

Eli picked it up and read as he sipped his coffee. "SMITH MATCHES DESCRIPTION OF JAMES JACKSON STOP WANTED FOR MURDER STOP USE CAUTION STOP"

Eli looked at Matt over top of the paper. "Are you going to arrest him?"

"I'd like you to come with me."

Eli gave him a wry grin, "I thought you didn't want me to interfere and try to take over your job?"

"I deserved that," Matt replied pensively, "But both my deputies are at the trial, as is the rest of the town for that matter. Besides, Eli, you have a stake in this. I thought you might want to trail along."

Eli responded, "That's the very reason I hesitate. I don't want to do anything out of spite or revenge. 'Vengeance is Mine, I will repay' says the LORD.'"

"I respect that, but I don't want to try to take him on my own, if he is as dangerous as this makes him out to be."

Eli nodded. "Alright, I'll ride with you. I'll be right back."

When he returned, Rob Handy's dual rig was strapped around his hips, turned so the butts were facing forward. He felt a bit self-conscious over the fancy rig, but he was grateful all the same that he had it.

"Give me time to saddle my horse." The church wasn't terribly distant, but it was far enough to justify them taking the horses.

* * *

Soon the men were on their way. They rode their horses into an alleyway two blocks from the church, just out of sight of the building. They tied the horses and silently drew their pistols. Together as a team, they continued on foot, using every bit of cover available as they approached the building. Eli appreciated the caution and good sense Matt used in his careful approach. For a young sheriff, he had good instincts and somewhere, somehow, he had gained good training from someone who knew how to stay alive.

The church doors were locked when they tried them and a quick glance through the window revealed nothing. They made a thorough search from outside on three sides of the building, looking into every window. No one was inside.

Next, they turned their attention to the parsonage. They were going to be out in the open, there was just no way around it. They sprinted across the yard to leave themselves vulnerable for the least amount of time possible. Again, they made quick glances in the windows, but many of the curtains were drawn and they could not see in. They had separated from one another to walk around different sides of the small building and met near the rear doorway.

Pistols in hand, the two men cautiously stood on either side of the door. Matt reached over and tried the latch. The door swung open. Matt entered first with Eli right on his heels. Not a word was needed between them. It was as though they'd worked together all of their lives, Matt entered the room at an angle and Eli button-hooked the other way. It only took a few moments to determine the building was vacant of bodies and a few more moments to figure out it had been vacated for good.

The men made a quick search of the place, looking for clues as to where Smith would have gone. That was when Eli found his gun belt, but the gun was missing.

They hurried outside to the stable and quickly found fresh tracks. The men retrieved their horses from the alley and were soon following the trail obviously left by Brother Smith.

The tracks led down a clandestine route to avoid any buildings. "He was trying to get away without being seen," Matt observed, "And judging by the tracks, he only left a few hours ago."

Eli nodded his agreement. "Do you know anything about this man, other than what was in the message?"

"No, I didn't take time back at the office to check for posters, so you know as much as I do."

The trail was easy to follow, as Smith made no attempts to hide it. They kicked their horses up to a trot until they reached the spot where he had hidden his horses and then followed his footsteps to where he had hidden himself. When he realized where Smith had hidden—and who he was watching for, Matt's face went white and his heart dropped into his stomach.

He turned to Eli and said in a strangled voice, *"Becky."* With that he sprinted back to the waiting animals, threw his leg over and spurred his horse into a gallop. Eli was only a step behind him.

* * *

Peggy watched the sheriff and Eli come out of the parsonage alone and she cursed to herself. Obviously that little worm had skipped out and left her high and dry. She was near panic! She was broke and had no way to escape town without that money. She cursed again and headed back to her room in the brothel.

* * *

Smith quietly swung the door open. Becky was humming to herself as she washed the dishes so her singing covered the sound of the opening door. The extra light let in through the door must have caught her attention, because she turned to see who was there. But it was too late to do anything. Smith crossed the few remaining feet and grabbed her as she cried out.

"It's not going to do you any good to scream," he said, "I watched your husband ride away this morning and he won't be back anytime soon with that trial going on in town. I figure I have at least six hours with you before I have to worry about anyone coming around here."

He held her upper arms and leaned in. He began to kiss her roughly. She struggled to get away, but to no avail. She jerked her head to the side, so his lips missed hers. Undeterred he mashed his face to her neck and pushed her toward the bedroom. Suddenly, stars blossomed in his vision and he could not focus on the woman in front of him because of the intense pain in the back of his head.

A tall boy stood there with the broom handle cocked back again, ready for another strike. "Get out!" He shouted.

Smith staggered back stunned, not entirely sure what was happening.

Becky took advantage of his disoriented state to push him away from her. In one swift movement she grabbed her coffee mug, and flung the contents of it into his face. The hot liquid scalded his skin and he cried out in pain, grabbing his face in his hands. Joshua took another swing with the broom and connected across the man's forearm, creating another painful howl.

Defeated, Smith ran for the door. Becky grabbed Joshua, giving him a big hug that restrained him from following the man outside.

"Are you alright?" She asked. She blinked hard to hold back tears.

"Yes ma'am," Joshua replied shakily, "Are you?"

"Yes. Thanks to you, I am fine. Thank you Joshua!" She sat down and suddenly burst into tears. Joshua stepped to the door. She could tell that the boy was extremely uncomfortable, and realized he more than likely did not know how to handle a crying woman.

Then they heard Smith's horses gallop away at full speed.

Joshua sprinted for the barn, quickly throwing a saddle and bridle onto his horse. The animal had been resting for a couple of days now and was ready to run. He led the horse to the front door where he ground hitched it and went inside.

When he walked inside, Becky was drying her tears. "I'm sorry, I didn't mean to be such a baby."

Joshua shook his head, "You ain't no baby. You done the right thing, throwing that hot coffee in his face. I just wish it had been the whole pot."

The boy walked to the cabinet where Matt had stored his shotgun and opened it. He removed the gun and picked up the burlap bag of shells in the bottom. He opened the breach and slid two of the shells into the chamber and snapped it shut then picked up the bag as well.

Becky stood up, wiping her tears away. "What do you think you're doing?"

He looked her straight in the eye. "Some animals need to be killed." With that, he stepped around Becky and went outside.

Becky followed him out. "Please Joshua, don't do this. Let Mr. Wheaton take care of it. He will be home soon. Please."

But Joshua mounted the horse without looking at her and rode off in the direction he'd heard the other horses go. Becky knew he was leaving his short boyhood behind, only to once again shoulder the burden of a man.

* * *

A half hour after Joshua left, Matt and Eli came galloping into the yard at a dead run. Matt threw himself from his horse, even as it skidded to a halt and ran into the house, gun in hand. Eli was still protecting his injured ribs but he was not far behind. They stopped short as they located Becky, now seated at the table with a worried look on her face.

"What happened? Are you okay?" Matt demanded.

"It was Smith. Joshua went after him." She said as worried tear began again.

"WHAT?" Matt exploded.

"I tried to stop him, but he wouldn't listen." Quickly, Becky filled him in on what happened and how Joshua had rescued her, only to leave in pursuit of the outlaw.

She handed the men a large package.

"What's this?" Matt asked.

"It's food for the trip. Please get Joshua before he does something that he'll have to live with for the rest of his life."

"I will." Matt replied.

Eli added, "*We* will."

They were right back on the trail after Matt shed his tie and jacket for his work coat. Again there was no attempt to hide the tracks. Their pursuit was swift. Although they wisely slowed each time they came to an area where an ambush might be possible. In spite of their carefulness, they made good time.

By four in the afternoon, the tracks were very fresh and at one point, Eli saw the edge of one of the tracks crumble in as they rode past. He warned Matt to keep his eyes peeled. They were getting close.

As they approached a large mass of rocks the men dismounted. They ground tied the horses and Matt removed his rifle from the scabbard. Stealthily they began to work their way around the jumble of boulders.

* * *

Joshua had ridden hard, but not so as to kill the horse. He was making good time. His horse was fresh and carrying a lighter load than either of Smith's horses. He reached a pile of massive boulders. But without the caution that comes with age, he rode right around them into the presence of the outlaw.

The preacher was standing well away from his horse. Instead of a gun the man held a Bible in his hands. Joshua had been riding with the shotgun across his lap for a reason. The boy dismounted putting his horse between him and the preacher. When he came out from behind the animal, his shotgun was pointed right at the man's belly.

"Yore a low down worthless skunk." He spoke as he thumbed back the hammer on both barrels of the shotgun.

"But you wouldn't shoot an unarmed man would you?" The outlaw asked almost too innocently.

Joshua made the mistake of talking instead of taking action. "You tried to have your way with her."

The end of the Bible in Jackson's hand suddenly blossomed in flame as he fired the pistol secreted inside of it. Joshua never felt a thing as the bullet struck him in the head, dropping him in his tracks.

* * *

Matt and Eli heard the shot and instantly recognized that it had not come from Joshua's shotgun. Caution was thrown to the wind and they rounded the pile of boulders at a run. They both knew that the boy had caught up to the outlaw before they did.

The first thing Matt saw was Joshua, crumpled down on the ground and then through an angry haze of red he saw the outlaw standing just beyond the boy's body. He skidded to a halt and was bringing the rifle up, when the preacher held a Bible out to him. Puzzled, Matt paused for a split second and the Bible exploded in front of him. He felt the wicked tug of a bullet against his ribs, causing his aim to go awry as his own rifle went off. Dimly, through his pain, he heard the blast of guns off to his left.

Eli was behind Matt, with his right-hand pistol out and ready, but when the Bible spit flame, he took a step to the side as he drew his left hand gun. Both weapons began to buck in his hands, as he ran full tilt toward the outlaw. He fired round after round even as he watched the astonishment on the face of Smith. The man folded in front of him even as the hammers began to fall on spent chambers. Eli stopped his advance, then moved carefully to the fallen man, kicking the Bible away from his hand. Blood was spreading across the front of his shirt and pooling under his body. Smith tried to say something, but blood prevented any confidences as it bubbled and flowed from his lips.

Eli squatted and patted around the exposed portion of Smith's waistband, then checked his sleeves for any other hidden guns. Satisfied the outlaw was harmless, he listened to the man's agonized breathing and realized there was nothing he could do.

He stood up and looked down at the outlaw, "May God have mercy upon your soul." With that he turned and walked away.

Eli reached his friend who had drawn himself into a seated position, holding his hand over his bloody left rib. Matt waved him off as he knelt down. "Please, go check on Joshua."

Rising, Eli turned his attention to the boy. Blood covered his face and matted into his hair, but Joshua's chest was still rising and falling with each breath. It took Eli quite a while to discover where the wound was, because of the volume of blood. Finally he located a long crease along the side of the boy's head, under the mop of hair. The bullet had knocked him out and split the skin, but Lord willing Joshua was going to be okay.

Eli carefully tended to the wounds of both the man and the boy. When that was accomplished and they were resting in the shade, he removed all Smith's effects from his clothing and buried the body of the outlaw in a shallow, sandy grave. He hunted around and soon had covered the grave with rocks he'd found nearby.

Just as he was beginning to wonder if he needed to set up camp like Steven had done for him, Joshua began to groan. Eli brought him a canteen and made him sip the cool water as he emerged from his trauma. The boy gingerly felt his forehead and complained of a terrible headache, but he left the bandage alone that Eli had put on.

Both Matt and Joshua were in great pain, so Eli decided to camp overnight and wait until the cool of the morning before making the decision to travel or not.

When they were set up for the night and Joshua had bedded down, the two older men quietly discussed the boy and his over-accomplished sense of vengeance. It was Eli who suggested Joshua could certainly benefit from a discipleship program which would teach him spiritual values. Matt agreed with him wholeheartedly.

It was early afternoon when the trio rode into the Wheaton's homestead. Becky came running out of the house and straight to Matt, when she saw the bloody shirt. She helped him off the horse while Eli dismounted to help Joshua. Slinging the boy's arm over his shoulder he half carried him into the house while Becky helped Matt inside.

Becky knelt down on the floor beside where they sat. "What happened," she pleaded. "Are you alright? Where is Smith?"

Together they told the story of what had happened, leaving out many of the gory details.

As she listened, Becky washed and re-bandaged the wounds of both of her men. She procured a clean shirt for Matt and gently helped him put it on. Their conversation continued as she worked to make them comfortable.

"What is going to happen to our church now?" Becky wondered out loud.

Eli set his coffee down and answered, "I'm sure there are plenty of legitimate preachers who would be willing to come out here and serve."

"You wouldn't be interested would you?" She asked hesitantly.

"Thank you, but no. I'm where God wants me to be right now." Eli responded.

The conversation steered away from the subject of the church and eventually Matt asked Eli to bring the packs in off Smith's horse. Matt sat at the kitchen table as Eli removed items from the pack. After a careful search, Eli found the false bottom in the case and all of the money Smith had stolen.

Matt carefully pulled another of the bags closer and began to go through it using the hand on his uninjured side. He was the one who located Eli's gun. "I think it is safe to say that we know who was behind the attack on you, even if he's not the one who actually slugged you over the head." Matt went on to tell Eli what he had gleaned from Peggy. "I surmise she probably knew about Smith and lied to me about that."

When Eli left, it was with the promise to send the doctor out as soon as he got back to town and to arrange for Matt's deputies to keep an eye on the town until he could return.

* * *

Sunday rolled around, a bright and sunny Nevada day. Eli met with Steven before the service, as was his habit. He explained to the younger man how the service was going to go and arranged a place for them to meet. He posted a sign on the door informing the small congregation that church was going to be held at the river and then he went down to wait. It wasn't long before Steven showed up, then Adam, followed by Mary and Susan. Soon each one of the people who had come forward and placed their trust in Jesus last Sunday were gathered at the river bank.

As a group, they stood and held hands, praying for the Holy Ghost to move in the hearts of anyone who might be nudged to come. When they had finished praying, they waited expectantly.

Even as Eli began to wonder if anyone else was going to come, the first few began to filter in. Soon the regular crowd had arrived, but to his surprise more people kept coming. Eli's grin was from ear to ear as the displaced congregants from the other church began to assemble. He saw faces he did not know. It was with joy he recognized his friends; Matt, Becky and Joshua as well as Elizabeth. But the biggest shock came when Peggy showed up. She stayed back at the very fringe of the crowd, but she was there nonetheless.

By the time the people stopped coming, it seemed the whole town was present. Eli turned to Steven, "Are you alright?"

Steven swallowed hard, but he nodded, "Yeah, I'll do my best."

Eli put his hand on his shoulder, "Remember, Steven, trust the Lord to give you the words you need to say. I will be praying for you the whole time."

Eli stood to address the huge crowd. "Jesus commanded us to go into all of the world and preach the gospel to all creation, baptizing them in the name of the Father, Son and the Holy Ghost. I came to this town to preach the gospel."

He gestured toward the collection of men and women standing close together off to the side. "These folks are those who have received the gospel, the good news, and allowed it to change their lives. They want to follow Jesus in baptism to publically proclaim their faith in Him. Before we start with the Baptism, I have asked Steven to share his story with you."

Steven stepped forward, but when he turned to face the crowd, his knees began to shake so hard he was afraid he would not be able to stand. The shaking coursed its way up through his body until his whole frame shuddered with fear.

Unable to speak, he closed his eyes and lifted his face toward the sky. He sent up a silent prayer and as he did a sudden calm washed over him. He opened his eyes once again and this time boldly looked out at the crowd. The words came with confidence.

"Y'all know me, because I used to be stumbling around this town, drunk. I remember not too many weeks back, I stumbled down to this very spot of the river," he remembered his audience and decided to leave out a few details, "I was soberin' up after a night of hard drinkin'. Most mornings I could not even remember the night before, or at least most of it."

He continued. "Not long ago, a man rode into town, who was here because he cared about people, about their souls, about their eternity. He cared about me," Steven pointed his finger at his own chest, "when no one else seemed to. Oh, many of you would occasionally spare me some food, and many of you bought me drinks I did not need. I was not a good man. I had nothing' to live for. But that man sought me out. He intentionally showed me he cared."

He turned toward Eli, "But this is not about Eli. It's not even about me. It's about Jesus, God, who came to earth as a man. He loved the world so much He took our punishment on Himself. He died on the cross so we could have eternal life with Him and an abundant life here on earth.

I put my faith in Jesus and He saved my soul. But He also saved me from the drink. Miraculously, He saved me from liquor."

He shared the story of his desperate prayer and God's immediate answer. Tears sprang into his eyes. "When I called out to God, He helped me and now I am going to live my life for Him. I am here to be baptized so everyone here knows that this is my pledge before God."

Eli, who had been praying just as he promised, looked out into the crowd. He was astonished to see both men and women with tears running down their faces.

He stepped to the front again. "Folks, we are going to move into the water now. "

They headed into waist deep river and Eli began with Steven. As he dipped him into the water, he recited, "I now baptize you in the name of the Father, Son and Holy Ghost." When he brought Steven up out of the water, someone started clapping. Soon the whole crowd joined in. For each person baptized, the roar of the crowd got louder. Mary and Susan were the final two and the sound was deafening as they rose up out of the water. Everyone in town knew them and what they had been.

Still standing waist deep in the water, Eli turned to the crowd and asked, "Is there anyone else who would like to follow in the footsteps of these men and women and accept Jesus as their Savior?" Once again the flood gate opened!

The first man cried out, "I do!" He kicked off his boots and ran into the river. Eli led him in a prayer of confession and then baptized him in the water. Man after man came down into the river. They prayed with Eli and then were baptized. Three women walked into the water to accept Jesus and be baptized. By the time they had finished, seventeen men and women had trusted their lives to Christ. As Eli waded out of the water, one of the women began singing, "Amazing Grace" and soon the entire group was singing along.

When the song ended, Eli addressed the crowd one last time. "God's grace is amazing. It is amazing to me that He would take my place upon that cross. It is now up to each and every one of you to uphold these men and women in prayer. We need to encourage them and be unified in one purpose with them--to live a life that glorifies our Maker." He led them in prayer before the crowd dispersed.

That night Eli fell into bed, exhausted, but it was the best kind of tired, because today he had watched God work in the most miraculous way. He knew without a doubt God had placed him in this town for a reason.

Eli rejoiced over the day. He rolled the events of the past few weeks over in his mind and was filled with joy. His work wasn't done here. God was on the march; He was using him to spread the Good News.

Monday morning dawned and Eli was still riding on the spiritual high from the day before. It was mid-morning when a young boy came running up to him with a letter. "Sir, are you Mr. Exeter?" he asked.

"I am. How can I help you this morning?" Eli responded.

"This jest came for you, sir." The boy held out the letter and Eli took it. He dug down into his pocket and handed the boy a penny. The young man thanked him and then went running off.

With a start of happiness, Eli recognized his son's handwriting on the envelope. He slit the envelope open with his knife and pulled out the letter.

Dear Father,

I received your letter and was immediately struck by the parallel of the situation you describe, to that of your namesake in the Bible. Where in 1 Kings 19, Elijah is running for his life and when God asks him why he is running, he cries out to God and tells him that everyone has turned their backs on God, except for him.

Please Dad, remember God's answer to Elijah. Elijah witnessed a strong wind, and then an earthquake, and there was fire, but God's voice was in none of those. Then he heard a still small voice-- God's voice, as a gentle whisper.

God said to him, "Yet I have left me seven thousand in Israel, all the knees which have not bowed unto Baal, and every mouth which hath not kissed him." Not that you are running from anything, Father. But I think you might be experiencing the same kind of discouragement Elijah faced.

Please do not be discouraged in your ministry. Go in the Grace of God, for I believe He is going to accomplish great things in the desert - through you.

The Nevada Badlands are going to bloom and produce a great harvest, for our God is a Great God and nothing is too big or too awful for Him. He is a God of miracles and so I encourage you to just trust Him for your strength.

Don't forget, it is the job of the Holy Ghost to perform a work in the hearts of the men and women to whom you minister. Don't try to carry a burden which does not belong to you. Allow God to work in you and He will accomplish that which He has called you to do.

With that having been said, Father, Naomi and I are doing quite well. My medical practice is flourishing, and we are happy. Very, very happy.

This is why. You see, Naomi has been putting on some weight over the last few months and now we feel the time is right to let you know. Sometime soon, within the next six months, you are going to be a grandfather! We are so blessed! We hope to see you soon.

With all of our love, your son, Benjamin.

Thank you for reading this book. I am thankful for each and every one of you, especially if you made it this far! If you liked this book I would love it if you would rate it on Amazon and would appreciate it if you would share it on Facebook. Thank you for helping me in getting the word out. I hope to have the next book in the series out before 2019.

I also want to thank those who had an integral part in this book. First and foremost my wife who read this story in its rawest form and still saw something in it. Then there is my daughter Dani, who was the next to read it and gave me great encouragement.

The editors, Beth Niquette, her mother Eva Gibson and Debbie Pettie all helped to polish this manuscript and make it shine.

Thank you as well to the "beta readers", those who read it before it was published and provided input. My parents, Tom and Mary Anderson, Ann Middleton, my mother in law, Mike and Mark Anderson, who are my two older brothers and my cousin Fred Prosser. Outside of my family there is Lori Jensen and Hope Gehrke who gave me valuable input and encouragement.

Finally, I owe a debt of gratitude to two men, strangers really, who were willing to help out a fellow author so they lent a hand. Jeremy Myers showed me how to format this text for publishing and gave me so many tips to make this happen. Howard Shifke gave me a lot of good advice. Both men are authors you can find on Amazon.com.

I am truly blessed to have all these people in my life!

It has been said that the West was won by Winchester and Colt. In truth, it was won by prayer warriors on bended knees. It has never been about conquering the land. It has always been about capturing the heart! The land will be traded away, turned over, or passed on, but the heart given to Jesus will live on for eternity.

ABOUT THE AUTHOR

Gary Jon Anderson is a thirty two year veteran of Law Enforcement and is currently working the road as a Patrol Officer in a small town in Oregon. He has chosen not to advance up the management ladder, preferring to remain as he calls it, "a grunt". Throughout the years he has been a K9 handler, a Motorcycle officer, a Firearms instructor, a Crash Reconstructionist, a Commercial Motor Vehicle Inspector and an Emergency Vehicle Operations instructor. Before joining the Police Force, he worked as a carpenter, a printer and a warehouseman. After the death of his father-in-law in 2006, he ran a walnut orchard for several years for his mother-in-law.

He is married to Lorie, his wife of thirty five years and has three grown children, one granddaughter, a step-granddaughter, a step-grandson and a step-great grandson.

Like the main character in this book, Eli Exeter, he recognizes the severe lack in our current criminal justice system as the Law seeks a physical solution to a spiritual problem. It was this issue that led him to begin writing this book.

"The Nevada Badlands" is actually the second book in a series that encompasses at least four book, although the other three have yet to be completed. The goal is to publish book Three next and then go back and publish book One. Book Four will round out the set, although there is a good possibility there will be more books in the series.

Besides work and church, Gary loves doing short term missions trips. He has travelled to both Mexico and Haiti to build houses, train Police Officers, and teach job skills. In addition, he loves to preach the good news of redemption through Jesus Christ.

Made in the USA
Columbia, SC
03 March 2019